"Someone tried to burn you alive. That means you've got a roommate until I get my hands on him."

"A roommate," she murmured, dropping her gaze.

With one finger, he nudged her chin up until her eyes met his. "I'll sleep on the couch, Sky. If, and when, that location changes, you'll be the one making the decision. I'm not doing this to pressure you. I'm doing this to make sure no one has a chance to hurt you again."

She took a deep breath. "Grant, about us sleeping together. It's something I want, I'm just…"

Afraid. She didn't have to say the word, he could see it in her eyes. He cupped her cheek. "You need to understand something, Milano. I don't want to sleep with you."

"Oh." With color flooding her cheeks, she began to lean away.

He slid his palm to the side of her throat, held her still. "I want to seduce you, very slowly, then make love with you."

Dear Reader,

It's time to go wild with Intimate Moments. First, welcome historical star Ruth Langan back to contemporary times as she begins her new family-oriented trilogy. *The Wildes of Wyoming—Chance* is a slam-bang beginning that will leave you eager for the rest of the books in the miniseries. Then look for *Wild Ways,* the latest in Naomi Horton's WILD HEARTS miniseries. The first book, *Wild Blood,* won a Romance Writers of America RITA Award for this talented author, and this book is every bit as terrific.

Stick around for the rest of our fabulous lineup, too. Merline Lovelace continues MEN OF THE BAR H with *Mistaken Identity,* full of suspense mixed with passion in that special recipe only Merline seems to know. Margaret Watson returns with *Family on the Run,* the story of a sham marriage that awakens surprisingly real emotions. Maggie Price's *On Dangerous Ground* is a MEN IN BLUE title, and this book has a twist that will leave you breathless. Finally, welcome new author Nina Bruhns, whose dream of becoming a writer comes true this month with the publication of her first book, *Catch Me If You Can.*

You won't want to miss a single page of excitement as only Intimate Moments can create it. And, of course, be sure to come back next month, when the passion and adventure continue in Silhouette Intimate Moments, where excitement and romance go hand in hand.

Enjoy!

Leslie J. Wainger
Executive Senior Editor

Please address questions and book requests to:
Silhouette Reader Service
U.S.: 3010 Walden Ave., P.O. Box 1325, Buffalo, NY 14269
Canadian: P.O. Box 609, Fort Erie, Ont. L2A 5X3

ON DANGEROUS GROUND

MAGGIE PRICE

Silhouette®

INTIMATE™ MOMENTS®

Published by Silhouette Books

America's Publisher of Contemporary Romance

This book is dedicated to my mom, Clarissa Neaves, who passed on her love of books; to my husband, Bill Price, who gives me the time to create my own books; and to my critique partners, Debbie Cowan and Merline Lovelace, who help give those books a firm foundation. I wish to acknowledge and thank Joyce Gilchrist of the Oklahoma City Police Department for her invaluable and generous assistance. All liberties taken in the name of fiction are my own.

 SILHOUETTE BOOKS

ISBN 0-373-07989-3

ON DANGEROUS GROUND

Copyright © 2000 by Margaret Price

Visit us at www.romance.net

Printed in U.S.A.

Books by Maggie Price

Silhouette Intimate Moments

Prime Suspect #816
The Man She Almost Married #838
Most Wanted #948
On Dangerous Ground #989

MAGGIE PRICE

turned to crime at the age of twenty-two. That's when she went to work at the Oklahoma City Police Department. As a civilian crime analyst, she evaluated suspects' methods of operation during the commission of robberies and sex crimes, and developed profiles on those suspects. During her tenure at OCPD, Maggie stood in lineups, snagged special assignments to homicide task forces, established procedures for evidence submittal, even posed as the wife of an undercover officer in the investigation of a fortune-teller.

While at OCPD, Maggie stored up enough tales of intrigue, murder and mayhem to keep her at the keyboard for years. The first of those tales won the Romance Writers of America's Golden Heart Award for Romantic Suspense.

Maggie invites her readers to contact her at 5208 W. Reno, Suite 350, Oklahoma City, OK 73127-6317.

IT'S OUR 20th ANNIVERSARY!
We'll be celebrating all year,
continuing with these fabulous titles,
on sale in February 2000.

Special Edition

#1303 Man...Mercenary... Monarch
Joan Elliott Pickart

#1304 Dr. Mom and the Millionaire
Christine Flynn

#1305 Who's That Baby?
Diana Whitney

#1306 Cattleman's Courtship
Lois Faye Dyer

#1307 The Marriage Basket
Sharon De Vita

#1308 Falling for an Older Man
Trisha Alexander

Intimate Moments

#985 The Wildes of Wyoming—Chance
Ruth Langan

#986 Wild Ways
Naomi Horton

#987 Mistaken Identity
Merline Lovelace

#988 Family on the Run
Margaret Watson

#989 On Dangerous Ground
Maggie Price

#990 Catch Me If You Can
Nina Bruhns

Romance

VIRGIN BRIDES

#1426 Waiting for the Wedding
Carla Cassidy

BREWSTER
BABY BOOM

#1427 Bringing Up Babies
Susan Meier

#1428 The Family Diamond
Moyra Tarling

The WEDDING AUCTION

#1429 Simon Says...Marry Me!
Myrna Mackenzie

#1430 The Double Heart Ranch
Leanna Wilson

#1431 If the Ring Fits...
Melissa McClone

Desire

MAN
OF THE
MONTH

#1273 A Bride for Jackson Powers
Dixie Browning

#1274 Sheikh's Temptation
Alexandra Sellers

#1275 The Daddy Salute
Maureen Child

#1276 Husband for Keeps
Kate Little

#1277 The Magnificent M.D.
Carol Grace

#1278 Jesse Hawk: Brave Father
Sheri WhiteFeather

Chapter 1

Three hours ago, Grant Pierce watched his partner's coffin lower into the sunbaked earth. He figured his day couldn't get much worse.

Tipping back in a chair that creaked beneath his weight, he raised his glass and downed the first shot of Scotch on the road to getting plastered. Senses jolted; air sucked in through his teeth while the sharp-as-glass whiskey ripped past his lungs, then boiled like molten lava in his gut.

"Damn!" The chair's front legs thudded against the floor. Blinking hard, he gave a rueful thought to how he'd sullenly told the flirting waitress to bring him the first bottle she grabbed from behind the bar. When he turned the bottle and checked the label, the unfamiliar brand had him raising an eyebrow. Not exactly the twenty-one-year-old blend he kept in his bar at home, but considering his present mood, this near-poison was preferable.

He didn't want fine-aged Scotch that would ease the pain of Sam's death into a vague throb. He wanted just what he had—whiskey that had the bite of a ticked-off K-9 and was guaranteed to deaden his misery.

Normally he didn't drink much, at least not for the sole purpose of getting loaded. But Sam Rogers's death had hit hard.

Grant forced his gaze to the chair at the other side of the small round table. *Sam's chair.* When Grant first arrived, he'd stripped off his black Armani suit coat and tossed it over the chair's back. He hoped to hell everybody got the message he didn't want company.

He had considered holding his impromptu wake for Sam at some place where no one knew him. But doing that hadn't seemed right. What felt right was settling in at the dimly lit bar at the Fraternal Order of Police Lodge. He and his partner had spent uncountable hours hunched over this very table talking through leads, analyzing suspects' motives, planning strategy. Grant figured the FOP club was the ideal place to toast the man who had taught him that solving a homicide was a lot like a mental chess game. The trick was to use people's predictability instead of playing pieces. Study someone's moves, Sam had said, and you could just about figure out where they'd been, and where they were going. Do that, and in no time you'd sniff out the do-wrongs.

Grant poured another shot, held his breath and tossed back the cheap Scotch. It hadn't been one of the hundreds of bad guys whom Sam had come face-to-face with that had ended his life. He'd gone fishing over the weekend, and keeled over in his bass boat in the middle of the lake.

"Dammit, Sam," Grant muttered, feeling the sharp blade of regret pierce through him. He knew his partner's preference for thick cigars, fast food and an abhorrence for exercise had put the older man on the fast track to a heart attack. Not to mention the stress that went arm in arm with working homicides.

Like the one case they had open now. The Peña rape/ murder. It was a real mystery, a stranger-to-stranger killing, the kind that almost never got solved. Grant refilled his glass while vowing to Sam that he would nail the vicious bastard who did it, and keep his partner's enviable clearance record intact.

A bark of laughter sounded from the other side of the club. Turning his head, Grant stared idly through the smoky air. The usual off-duty cops who appeared at the club almost every night were huddled on tall stools at one end of the bar. The mirror behind the bar reflected the bartender's scurrying movements as he shoveled ice into glasses, poured the beer on tap, made change. Few of the tables that bordered the dance floor were occupied, but it was only seven o'clock—still too early for a good crowd on a Thursday night. The sound of coins clattering down the slot of the jukebox registered in Grant's brain. Glancing over, he saw C. O. Jones, a curvy patrol cop, punching in a selection. Seconds later, a throaty-voiced singer chided her lover to don't be stupid.

Once the club started filling, Grant planned to move on. He had spent the past couple of days at the side of Sam's widow, listening to an unending stream of mourners lament her loss. Grant wasn't up to hearing any more gut-wrenching stories about the man he'd idolized. All he wanted was the bottle of demonic Scotch, and solitude.

With fatigue seeping through him, he tugged on the knot of his tie, flicked open his starched shirt's top button, then refilled his glass. He didn't care about the hangover he knew he would have to deal with the following morning. Didn't care if he had to leave his Porsche in the club's parking lot, stumble across the street and check in at the less-than-spectacular motel that had seen its share of drunk cops. Didn't care about much of anything at this point, except numbing the ache inside him.

Across the bar's dim expanse, the bubble light that had once done duty on the roof of a black-and-white, and now hung upside down from the ceiling, began its red rotating flash. That was the signal someone had opened the building's outer door, concealed from view by a small alcove. Right about now, that someone was standing in the alcove, face-to-face with a poster of Clint Eastwood doing his sternest Dirty Harry impersonation, Smith & Wesson .44 magnum clutched in his iron grip.

Seconds later, Sky Milano stepped into view, sending a fist of emotion slamming into Grant's chest. His already-rotten day had suddenly gotten a whole lot worse.

"Hell," he muttered, his gut tightening while he measured the graceful economy of motion that took her toward the bar. Her dark hair was pulled back in its usual tight bun at her nape. Sometime over the past months she'd replaced her tortoiseshell glasses with the trendy wire-rims that now perched high on her nose. As he studied her, his eyebrows knit. Except for the quick glimpse he'd caught of her earlier at the cemetery, it had been months since he'd seen her without the obscuring white lab coat she habitually wore over her clothes. Now he took in the trim black suit that belted at her waist. The suit's soft folds couldn't quite camouflage the weight she'd lost. Weight she hadn't needed to lose. Ten pounds, he figured. Maybe more. Feeling his mood darkening, Grant downed his drink and poured another.

He kept his gaze locked on her.

When Sky reached the bar, she smiled while exchanging a few words with a couple of the regulars. A scruffy vice cop with a ponytail and diamond ear stud moved in, settling his palm at the small of her back while he leaned and whispered in her ear. Grant tightened his fingers on his glass and waited. It took her only seconds to ease back just far enough to break the contact.

He looked away, trying to ignore the muscle in his jaw that worked double time. It had taken him twice, maybe three times to figure out that Sky Milano was gun-shy around a man's touch. It had taken him a little longer to realize she didn't want to be touched. Not the way he'd wanted to touch her.

Sipping his Scotch, he shifted his gaze back and studied the compelling curves and angles of her profile. Except for a few encounters in the hallway and one in a courtroom, he'd managed to avoid Oklahoma City PD's head forensic chemist since she ended their relationship before it ever really got started. After that, he hadn't wanted to see her. Hadn't wanted to think about how she'd turned down his offer of support after she'd told him about the nightmarish part of her past. He sure as hell didn't want to relive the pain that had accompanied her refusal to see him. It had taken time, but a headlong plunge into his work had muffled the hurt. No way did he intend to ever open *that* door again.

From the corner of his eye, he saw the vice cop point in his direction, then Sky turned and looked directly at him. Grant refilled his glass while her smooth stride brought her across the dance floor. Despite the fiery knots that had settled into his shoulders, his hand remained steady.

"I'm sorry about Sam."

He heard the hint of nerves in her voice. He'd heard that tone before—the night she told him goodbye.

He sipped his drink, studying her over the rim of his glass. "You come here just to tell me that?"

Her fingers played with the purse strap looped over her shoulder. "I wanted to tell you at the cemetery, but you left before I had a chance."

He'd seen her standing in a pool of sunlight a few feet from Sam's grave. In a moment of weakness he'd caught himself thinking about approaching her. Common sense stopped him, and he'd simply turned and walked away.

"Now you've told me," he said, his voice a level slide. "No offense, Milano, but I've had a tough couple of days, and this wake is private."

"I need to talk to you." Despite the dim light, he saw the smudges of fatigue beneath her eyes, the small lines of stress at the corners of her mouth. "Grant, it's important."

He stretched out his long legs and raised his glass. "Well, darlin', so is this," he drawled, then poured the Scotch down his throat. "If you want to talk, catch me at the office tomorrow." He squinted at his empty glass while he fuzzily calculated the number of shots he'd already poured into his empty stomach. "Better make that the day after."

Behind the lenses of her glasses, irritation flashed in the stunning blue eyes that had robbed him of uncountable hours of sleep. "This can't wait."

He angled his head. "How'd you find me?"

"Someone at the cemetery heard you mention coming here to toast Sam." She settled a palm on his black suit coat that lay across the top of the chair opposite him. "Mind if I sit while we talk?"

He studied her through hooded eyes. He wanted to curse the hard knot her presence had lodged in his throat. Didn't want to acknowledge the roiling in his stomach that had nothing to do with rotgut Scotch. He had cared about Sky Milano too much. He, who had always made it a point to avoid strings in his relationships with women, had stunned himself by wanting to create some with her. Too late, he learned she hadn't trusted him enough to let him be a part of her life.

The thought had him expelling a controlled breath. His surly mood wasn't going to run her off; he could see that by the upward tilt of her chin and the glint of determination that had settled in her eyes. No one had to tell him about the slender core of pure steel that ran through the woman. He had plowed headlong into it himself and knew it was unbendable. She would stand by the table all night if that was what it took to get him to hear her out.

He rubbed a hand over his gritty eyes. All right, he would listen to whatever she'd come to say. Then he would grab the bottle of Scotch, check into the motel across the street and get commode-hugging drunk in Sam's honor.

"Take a load off," he said, using a Gucci-shod foot to ease the empty chair back. The minute she sat, her tantalizing scent slid silkily across the table and into his lungs. He felt a quick, sharp pull of want, and instantly steeled his senses against the emotion. Dammit, why did she have to wear the same perfume after all these months?

She laid her practical black leather purse on top of the table, then wrapped one ringless hand around the other in a gesture that he recognized as all nerves. Now that she was closer, he saw pure exhaustion in her eyes.

"Nice glasses."

She blinked. "Thanks."

Just then, the waitress sauntered over and directed her kohl-lined eyes in Sky's direction. "Get you something?"

"Tonic water with a lemon twist," Grant said in reflex.

Sky looked at him, clearly startled that he'd remembered what she habitually ordered. "That's fine," she said to the waitress.

The woman shifted her attention to Grant, her red-glossed mouth curving as she settled her palm on his shoulder. "How's the Scotch, handsome?"

"It'll do."

When she leaned to check the level in the bottle, her breast brushed his arm. "You going to want more later?" she asked softly.

"Only if I decide it will be a good night to die."

She laughed, low and throaty. "I'm off at midnight. I'll be happy to have a drink, or whatever else, with you."

"I'll keep that in mind." He remained silent until the woman moved out of hearing range, then slid his gaze back to Sky. "I'm listening."

She wetted her lips. "I need to talk to you about the Benjamin case."

"Closed," Grant shot back, even as he felt the first pinging of an alarm in his head. Whatever was going on, it had to be serious for Sky to seek him out regarding a murder he and Sam had worked—and cleared—two years ago. "In case you've forgotten, Ellis Whitebear slit Mavis Benjamin's throat. He's sitting on death row. Your testimony helped put him there. End of story."

"Maybe not."

Deciding he didn't need to fog his brain further at the moment, Grant shoved the bottle aside and leaned in. "You want to tell me exactly what that means?"

"Two days ago, I got the results from the blood off the bandage we believe the suspect lost at the Peña scene."

"The *Peña* scene?" Grant narrowed his eyes at her mention of the brutal rape/murder that had stumped Sam and himself. "Did you just change the subject, or are we still talking about the Benjamin case?"

"Both cases…" Sky's voice trailed off, and she pulled her bottom lip between her teeth. "Grant, you're not going to like what I have to say."

"You're sending that message loud and clear."

The waitress returned with Sky's drink, an oversize lemon wedge hooked precariously on the rim of the glass.

Ignoring the woman's intimate wink, Grant waited until she turned her attention to four cops with empty beer mugs at a nearby table, then he shifted his gaze to Sky's hands. They were still wrapped one around the other, and her knuckles had turned as white as one of her lab coats.

"You've got my full attention," he said quietly.

"The blood found on Mavis Benjamin's clothing matches the suspect's blood from the Peña crime scene."

"You mean," Grant began carefully, "the suspects in homicides that occurred two years apart have the same weird blood type?"

"I mean they have the same DNA."

Grant felt sweat gather at his lower back. "Identical?"

"Yes."

A double-fisted punch to the gut would have been easier to take, he thought as he stared across the table. "Ellis Whitebear is sitting in a cell on death row at the state pen. I doubt they issued him a pass so he could go out and cut the Peña woman's throat, then rape her for good measure. That means he's got a hell of an alibi."

Sky kept her eyes locked with his. "I know."

"What else do you know?"

"That my test results are accurate."

"On which case?"

"Both."

Grant uttered a ripe curse. "How the hell could both be *right?* We've got two murders. There's no way the man who killed the first woman killed the second. So how could your tests show the same suspect DNA at both crime scenes?"

When Sky shifted in her chair, light from the nearby jukebox touched her sculpted cheek with gold. "The only way I know for two people to have the same DNA is if they're identical twins."

"You're sure about all of this?"

She arched an eyebrow. "About identical twins?"

"About the results from the Benjamin and Peña crime scenes."

"Yes. I couldn't believe it when the computer got a hit on both cases. I went to the evidence bay and pulled Benjamin's clothing. I did another DNA profile on the suspect's blood found on her dress. The latest result didn't vary from the first one. The DNA is Whitebear's. I did the same thing with the evidence from the Peña scene. I've spent the past three days…and nights double-checking my work. Grant, I'm positive. One man, or two with identical DNA, killed both women."

This time, Grant's curse brittled the air. The bartender glanced their way. A scathing look from Grant had the man quickly returning to his business. Grant tightened his jaw. He could almost picture Sam sitting across from him, one of his thick cigars clenched in the side of his mouth, thumbs under the suspenders he habitually wore, as he smiled and said, "Well, pretty boy, sounds like you've got one hell of a mess to clean up." Grant rubbed at the knot that had edged up his shoulders and settled in the back of his neck. Sam was gone, and *he* was the one who had to negotiate some damn mental chessboard.

He refilled his glass, nudged it across the table toward Sky. "Forget the tonic water. You could probably use this about now."

She glanced at the glass, then her glossed lips curved into a slight smile that only reminded him of how it had felt to kiss that warm, lush mouth.

"If I thought it would help, I'd drink the whole bottle."

"You might just have to fight me for it."

She massaged her right temple as if pain had lodged there. "I don't remember all the details of the Benjamin case, just the work I did. Was there ever any doubt in your mind that Whitebear did it?"

"No, though he kept claiming he was innocent." As he spoke, Grant felt the numbing effects of the Scotch, fought against it. "Most of the evidence against Whitebear was circumstantial, but compelling. The victim was the manager at the apartment complex where he did the maintenance and yard work in exchange for an apartment. It was well-known that the victim and suspect didn't get along—tenants often heard them yelling at each other. We had two credible witnesses who swore that, hours before the homicide, Mavis Benjamin threatened to fire Whitebear and toss him out on the street."

"She was killed in the communal laundry room right off her office at the complex," Sky said, adding the details with which she was most familiar. "Hundreds of hairs and fibers from people's dirty laundry contaminated the scene. The only evidence I found on the victim's person that linked to the suspect was one drop of his blood."

"Sam and I figured he'd been injured while they struggled—a nosebleed, or something like that," Grant said. "You took blood samples from all the male workers at the apartment complex and got a match to Whitebear's. That made the case." Grant settled a forearm on the table and leaned closer, forcing himself to ignore Sky's punch-in-the-gut scent. "You're sure it was Whitebear's blood on Mavis Benjamin's sleeve?"

"Yes." Her brow furrowed. "His, or his identical twin's, if he has one."

"*If?* Whitebear's in a cell, and I'm pretty sure he's not Houdini reincarnated. You think there's some way to explain the suspect blood from the Peña scene if Whitebear doesn't have a twin?"

"Not that I know of." She picked up her glass, then set it down without drinking. "If he is innocent, and there's a twin brother out there murdering people, why didn't Whitebear mention him?"

Grant raised a shoulder. "The guy's got a room-temperature IQ. He dropped out of grade school. To him, DNA is probably just three letters."

"His attorney, then. Surely Griffin found out about

Whitebear's family. He would have zeroed in on a twin if he knew his client had one.''

"Ellis Whitebear's DNA, or what we believe to be his, was found on the first victim—"

"It *is* his DNA," Sky said, the tiny lines around her mouth deepening. "I know what I'm doing in my lab, Pierce."

"Dammit, Milano, I'm not questioning your ability," Grant shot back, then set his jaw. It had been that same confidence and determination that had attracted him to her in the first place. Where her job was concerned, Sky had no equal. She didn't waver. She was in control. It was her personal life that had splintered into hundreds of pieces, and driven her from him.

If you care about me, you'll let me go.

The memory of the words she'd spoken that night six months ago assaulted him like sniper fire. She had taught him what it was like to want. To feel helpless. To hurt. He stabbed his fingers through his hair. He didn't need this. He *had* let her go. He was over her. Why the hell was he even allowing her presence to bother him?

"All right," he said, forcing his mind back to the problem at hand. "*Whitebear's* DNA was on Benjamin's dress. Because of that, I doubt Griffin thought his client's protests of innocence held any weight. But then, we'll never know since the esteemed public defender died in a car wreck a month after Whitebear got shipped to the pen."

Grant settled back in his chair and forced mental chess pieces to move in his Scotch-soaked brain. "There's another angle we haven't talked about," he said after a moment. "Ellis killed Mavis Benjamin. His twin killed Carmen Peña. It's a stretch, but anything's possible at this point."

Sky nodded slowly. "You're right."

Just then, a grizzled, retired detective with a gray beard

stopped by the table. He nodded, then spent a few minutes reminiscing about the time he and Sam cornered a do-wrong inside Uncle Willie's Donut Shop.

When the detective moved off, Grant felt the now-familiar drag of grief over his partner's death. "Dammit, Sam."

He wasn't aware he'd spoken the words until he saw Sky's eyes soften. "I'm sorry, Grant. I know you're upset about Sam. The last thing you need right now is a mess like this. But both of these cases were yours and Sam's...yours now. I couldn't put off coming to you any longer."

"Yeah." Because he was tempted to reach out and smooth his fingers across the strain at the corners of her eyes, Grant balled his hands on the table. She had drawn Whitebear's blood from the man's arm, performed tests, testified in court to her findings. Her word had helped put Whitebear on death row. It was now possible a different man should be in that cell, and Carmen Peña was dead because he wasn't.

If that was true, the press would have a field day with mistaken-identity stories. Not to mention make chopped liver out of both his and Sky's careers along the way. For his part, the idea of getting shipped to Larceny to investigate lawnmower thefts held little appeal.

Grant heard the clatter of more coins going down the jukebox's slot. A heartbeat later, a low, weepy love song drifted on the air and the dance floor filled.

As he watched couples glide together in the shadowed light, it hit him that the need to hold Sky in his arms was just as sharp now as it had been six months ago. His jaw locked when he realized he was actually sitting there, thinking about asking her to dance. Damning himself for being the biggest kind of idiot, he tightened his grip on control and shifted his thoughts squarely back to business.

"What's your next step on the blood?"

She met his gaze. "The first thing I need to do is have the suspect samples from both crime scenes checked at another lab," she said, her voice void of emotion. "I'll package them in the morning and take them to the OSBI," she said, referring to the Oklahoma State Bureau of Investigation.

"Do you have to tell them what's going on?"

"No. We always use code numbers on the evidence that refers to the case, not the suspect's name. All the OSBI chemist will know is that we need DNA profiles on both samples."

"How long will it take to get the results?"

"Three to four days. Five, max."

Grant looked at the Scotch bottle, acknowledging that his mind was too fogged to develop a game plan right now. With an inward sigh, he swept his gaze upward. "Sorry, Sam, the wake's over." He pulled his money clip out of his pocket, peeled off a couple of bills, then tossed them on the table.

"I need to sort this out," he said, meeting Sky's waiting gaze. "I'm going home to hot coffee and a cold shower." *And an empty bed.* Biting back a swell of frustration, he conceded that what he most needed was to get the hell away from *her.*

He shoved back his chair, rose and instantly felt the room spin. "Holy hell." He slapped a palm against the table to keep his balance and waved his other hand toward the bottle. "Stuff's as bad as swamp muck."

"Worse, I'd say," Sky countered. "I don't think swamp muck makes your eyes cross like that." Rising, she folded his suit coat over her arm while giving him an appraising inspection. "You're plowed, Pierce."

"That was my objective."

"And in no shape to drive."

He grinned. "Next thing you know, Milano, they'll be giving you an award for observation." Dragging in a deep breath, he waited until the room righted itself. It did...barely. "I'll call a cab."

"You don't need to. I can give you a lift."

He stared down at her, surprised she'd offered. They'd been at his house that last time they were together. Grant knew if he slid into a car beside her, the minute they pulled into the gated drive that led to his family's estate he would remember how her kisses tasted, how soft her cheek felt against his cupped hand. Remember, too, the panic that had shot into her eyes when his arms had tightened around her. The absolute paleness that had settled in her skin. The choked sound of her voice when she'd told him goodbye.

If you care about me, you'll let me go.

Dammit, he had done both.

Keeping his eyes locked with hers, he took a step forward. "Do you really think your taking me home is a good idea?"

"I don't know." She raised a hand as if to press her palm against his arm. He saw the hesitation in her eyes, then her fingers slowly curled and she lowered her arm. "Grant, I think we should at least try to be friends."

"We already made a stab at that," he said, frustration hardening his voice. She couldn't even bring herself to touch him. How the hell had he ever expected her to give herself to him? "It didn't work."

"We tried being more than friends."

Without thinking, he raised his hand, traced his fingertip along the soft curve of her jaw. Staring into the depths of those blue eyes, he found himself stupidly pleased when she didn't shrink from his touch.

"Sweetheart, there's not a chance I'll forget what we tried," he said softly. He saw the instant flush that rose in her cheeks, caught the jump of the pulse in her throat, felt his own pulse respond in kind. He damned himself for giving her the power to shoot such searing need into his system.

As he lifted his suit coat off her arm, he looked over his shoulder at the bartender. "Mind calling me a cab?"

"Sure thing."

Grant turned back. Sky's expression was now controlled, emotionless. Her chemist's face. "I'll call when I get the results from the OSBI," she said quietly.

"Fine."

He watched her turn, watched her sleek gait take her around the dance floor and into the alcove. Then she was gone.

Standing beneath the rotating red beacon of the overhead bubble light, Grant ruthlessly kept control in place to keep from going after her. She was the first woman he had thought about a future with, the first woman who had really *mattered*. The first to reject him. Pride was as strong as the hurt he'd endured when she walked away six months ago. Pride had kept him from seeking her out. Kept him from begging for whatever scraps of her life she would agree to give him.

He jerked on his suit coat, then shoved his fists into his pockets. Damn if he couldn't stop his hands from shaking.

Chapter 2

Hand unsteady, Sky rang the doorbell on the elegant Tudor brick house that sat bathed in silver moonlight. She was barely aware of the white roses that tumbled out of a massive planter near the door, paid no attention to their sweet scent that hung in the warm summer air. Two hours had passed since she'd walked out of the FOP club—away from Grant—and every nerve in her body was still scrambled.

So much for well-laid plans. Facing him had been hard. More difficult than she thought it could ever be. She had rehearsed everything in her mind before she walked into the club. Knew exactly what to say about the results of the DNA profiles. Had fought to keep her voice steady.

Nothing inside her had stayed steady, she conceded while she waited in the overlapping puddles of light from the carriage lamps bordering the house's massive front door. She closed her eyes, picturing again the sight of Grant nursing his drink in a dim corner of the club. His thick, sandy hair had been rumpled, his broad shoulders bent as if they carried the weight of the world. His chiseled features had been set, remote. Yet, when he'd raised his head to meet her gaze, his eyes had been full of the pain of his partner's death.

Just one look and he had shaken her off balance.

She thought she had grown stronger over the past six months. Maybe she had in other areas, but she still had few defenses where Grant Pierce was concerned. She needed those defenses. God, did she need them.

From somewhere behind her, a sharp, metallic click sounded on the still night air. Sky's scalp prickled, followed by a jolt of sheer terror. Years of self-defense training kicked in; she raised her arms and whirled. The screech that followed could have doubled for the tornado warning siren.

"Good grief, Sigmund!" Sky stared down at twelve pounds of gray, outraged tomcat whose fur and tail were standing straight on end. "Sorry I stepped on your tail," she muttered after her heart unfroze in her chest. How did you explain to a cat that she'd mistaken the metallic click of its tags with the snick of a switchblade shooting out of a hilt? The all-too-real memory of that sound echoed in her head, had her swallowing back bile.

Just then, the front door swung open and she jolted.

"Sky, what a pleasant surprise," Dr. Judith Mirren commented in a soft voice that carried the faintest hint of her native Louisiana. Her searching gaze swept past Sky's shoulder. "Please tell me it wasn't you who just howled like a banshee."

Sky pushed away the chilling memories that had surged from her past. "Sigmund snuck up on me and I stepped on his tail." She motioned toward the shadowy porch rail where the cat now sat staring with regal feline disdain, tail twitching as if it had electrodes attached.

"No harm done, I'm sure," Dr. Mirren said, pulling the door open wider. "Come in."

The woman's brown eyes were kind—and sharp. At sixty, she had settled comfortably into middle age, the lines on her face revealing a quiet intelligence that came only with experiencing life. Her hair was a mix of honey-brown and gray, scooped up in a loose topknot. She wore trim black slacks and a chic linen blouse the color of storm clouds.

Sky gave an apologetic smile. "I should have called first."

"Nonsense. This evening's group left about ten minutes ago," the doctor said as she stepped back to let Sky in. "I was considering making myself a latte, but Richard's out of town and I didn't want to drink one alone. Now I don't have to."

"I didn't plan on dropping by," Sky explained as she entered the large wood-paneled foyer with glossy pine floors. "I went for a drive and somehow wound up here."

Dr. Mirren arched an eyebrow. Wordlessly she shut the door and nodded toward a wide doorway. "Make yourself comfortable in the study. I'll be back with our lattes."

"Need some help?"

"Thank you, no. I'll just be a minute."

Sky walked across the entry and into the room where she had spent every Monday evening for the past six months. The study was warm and vibrant with thick rugs, polished brasses and solidly constructed furniture. Faint wisps of lavender haunted the air. Always before, the mood of the room soothed, but tonight Sky was as taut as a coiled spring and the feeling had nothing to do with her close encounter with Sigmund.

Her fingertips grazed the top of the inviting tobacco-brown rolled-arm sofa. She'd sat here and told people she barely knew about the terrifying event that had altered the course of her life. Related intimate details she could not share with Grant, not after the way she'd humiliated herself that last time they were together.

Getting involved with him had been wrong, so *unfair.* She had hurt him—not intentionally, but she'd hurt him all the same. Now he would rather take a cab than climb into a car with her. The knowledge made her want to weep.

"Here we are," Dr. Mirren said as she swept through the arched entrance, bringing with her two oversize cups and the heady scent of rich coffee.

"It smells wonderful," Sky said, accepting the cup the doctor offered.

"Let's hope it tastes that way. I've only had the espresso maker a week, so I'm still practicing." Smiling, she sat in a leather wing chair on the opposite side of the rug that spread a soft pattern along the wood floor. She blew across the rim of her cup, then sipped. "Not bad."

Sky settled on the sofa. "It's perfect," she said, savoring the creamy heat that slid down her throat.

"You mentioned you went for a drive and somehow wound up here." As usual, the psychiatrist took little time getting to the heart of a matter. "Did something happen tonight?"

"I saw Grant."

"A date?"

"Hardly. I had to tell him about the results of a comparison on DNA found at two of his homicide cases."

"Did you go to his home to tell him?"

"No." Although she'd made only a few vague references about her relationship with Grant to the Monday-night group, she had told Dr. Mirren all the details during their private sessions. "I wouldn't have the nerve to just show up and knock on the door. Grant's partner died of a heart attack, and the funeral was this afternoon. I knew he'd gone to the FOP club, so I went there." She lifted a shoulder. "A mistake."

"Why do you say that?"

"It's a social setting. We don't have that kind of relationship anymore. Never will have again."

"Could you have waited until tomorrow to tell him about the DNA results?" Dr. Mirren asked, her eyes meeting Sky's over the rim of her cup.

"I suppose. He needed to know, though."

"I'm sure," the doctor said agreeably, as if they were discussing the weather. "Could you have put this information in a memo?"

Sky tightened her grip on the cup's ceramic handle. "I have to do that, too."

"So, you chose to face this man."

"I don't know why. We've had no contact in six months." That hadn't stopped a greasy pool of jealousy from churning in her belly when the waitress at the FOP club put the moves on Grant. Sky chewed her lower lip. It had taken everything she had to sit there while the temptation to deck the woman passed.

She set her cup on the thick wood coffee table in front of the sofa. Too unsettled to stay put, she rose and walked to the leaded-glass windows that spanned one wall of the paneled study. Outside, an obviously recovered Sigmund scuttled full speed across the porch after a fluttering moth.

"I think I decided to tell Grant in person because of how he looked at Sam's funeral," Sky said after a moment. "So miserable. Alone."

She'd felt the same way, and it hadn't had anything to do with Sam's death. Seeing Grant at the cemetery had sent memories storming through her. Of the stolen lunches they'd managed in the midst of a grueling serial killer task force they'd both been assigned to. His nightly phone calls when his deep, husky voice slid like velvet across her senses. The department's Christmas dance when she'd first found the courage to step into his arms. The few tentative kisses that had sent need whipping through her. An intimate restaurant where violins stroked as soft as a lover's touch, then later at his house when he'd pulled her to him and the rich male taste of his mouth swept her teetering toward the edge of control. Seconds later, her stomach had knotted, her lungs refused to work and she'd almost hyperventilated from the feeling of being trapped, with no way out. No way to save herself—though there'd been nothing to save herself *from*. On the heels of that panicked terror had come the agonizing realization that, no matter how much she wanted to—*longed to*—give herself to him, she couldn't.

Now those memories gained strength, slamming into her so hard, so unexpectedly, that Sky found herself blinking back tears. She felt acid in her throat as humiliation pooled inside her.

"I wish…" She paused and steadied her voice. "I wish that night with Grant had never happened."

"Sky, listen to me." Dr. Mirren sat forward, her eyes sharp and knowing. "The rape you experienced in college was violent and sadistic, and it cut through the core of your existence. To make matters worse, the therapist the college sent you to was inept. If he hadn't eventually lost his license, I would personally hunt him down and make a professional eunuch of him."

Sky stared in silence, surprised by the woman's candor.

"Because of his incompetence," Dr. Mirren continued, "you never had a chance to properly deal with the attack. Certainly you healed physically from the knife wound. You became skilled in self-defense so you can now protect yourself if necessary.''

"Right. I can take down most any man," Sky shot back. "I just can't let one love me." She gave her head a frustrated shake. "My hormones were in full swing that night with Grant. I wanted. Oh, God, I wanted…" Her voice trailed off. "I just couldn't."

"Because you repressed your feelings about the rape, denied your emotions and blocked the experience so you could function and get on with your life. Everything boiled to the surface while you were with Grant and you reacted very strongly."

"I almost upchucked on his shoes," Sky said miserably. "How's that for impressing a man who wants to make love to you?"

"It makes you human. And memorable."

"I'll say." Sky tried a smile, but it didn't gel. "Grant mentioned tonight he won't ever forget that particular experience."

"Will you?"

"Not a chance."

"It appears it affected you both equally."

"Him worse. I hurt him." As if chilled, Sky wrapped her arms around her waist. "When the panic hit me, I could barely even get out the words to make Grant understand I'd been raped in college. I could hardly breathe, much less give him details about the attack. He asked me to stay with him, just stay with him so he could hold me. All he wanted was to be there for me." She closed her eyes. "I couldn't let him. Couldn't trust myself not to fall apart again. I still can't," she added softly.

"Don't be so sure." Dr. Mirren set her cup aside. "You've done admirably over the past months coming to grips with the trauma of the rape and its aftermath. Whether you realize it or not, you've begun to make some small changes in your life.''

''Changes?''

''Your glasses, for instance,'' Dr. Mirren said. ''Until a few weeks ago, you wore large glasses with tortoiseshell frames.''

Baffled, Sky nodded. She'd chosen the understated wire-rims on impulse during her last visit to the eye doctor. Even ordered a pair of contacts, which she now wore almost as often as her glasses. ''My vision changed and I needed a new prescription, that's all.''

''Instead of frames that conceal a large portion of your face—your looks—you chose an attractive pair that draw attention to you, not away. A man's attention, perhaps.''

Sky felt her spine stiffen. ''I don't want men to notice me.''

''For years you haven't. Now that you've begun dealing with the rape, your outer self is changing. Your clothes are different, too. You're wearing black today probably because you attended a funeral, but you wear more colorful clothes than you did when you first started therapy.''

''My wardrobe needed updating.'' Sky turned and stared out the window at the glowing ball of the full moon. A month or so ago, she had walked into her closet and found herself grimacing at all of the blacks, browns and grays. On a whim she'd taken a rare day off from the lab, gone to the mall and spent hundreds of dollars on a new, colorful wardrobe. She'd had no idea what prompted the trip, just that all that blandness had suddenly made her feel edgy and unsettled. Restless.

Just like she felt tonight.

She turned. Dr. Mirren had remained in the high-back leather chair, looking her usual calm and serene self. ''Okay, so maybe I'm no longer hiding behind big glasses and drab colors," Sky conceded. "There's some things I can't change. And one of those is my relationship with Grant."

"You faced him tonight." Eyes filled with ready understanding, Dr. Mirren folded her neat hands in her lap. "You could have sent him a memo about your DNA findings, or even phoned. Instead, you went to him."

"On business. I had to tell him about the DNA."

"You don't have to explain why, Sky. You just need to understand that for years your life has been focused on your work. Now you may be ready to also focus on a relationship. When, and if, you act on that is up to you."

Massaging her right temple, Sky paced the length of the built-in shelves where antique decoys nested amid leather volumes. The ache that had settled in her head while she'd been at the FOP club had transformed into a throb.

Before she met Grant Pierce, she had felt so in control. So content with her life. *So safe.*

Her hand slid slowly down her cheek; she pressed her palm against her jaw where his fingertips had skimmed. When he first walked into her life, everything about him—his sinfully handsome face, burnt-whiskey voice and roguish reputation—had tempted her to turn tail and run. Nevertheless, she'd stayed put. Told herself she'd healed completely. Refused to acknowledge the inner wariness that spiked inside her whenever Grant got too close. For the first time since the rape, she had wanted a man.

As much as he'd wanted her.

Too late she learned the monster from her past still had her in its grip.

Now, according to Dr. Mirren, that monster was breathing its last breath.

Sky dragged air into her lungs that should have cleansed, but didn't. She knew there was no way she could trust that she had truly closed the door on the past. No way to be sure the monster wouldn't spring back to life.

No way she could risk doing anything about the searing need for Grant that still burned inside her.

Leaning back, feet propped on his desk, Grant listened intently to the party on the other end of the telephone. It had taken him five days to track down this lead that could be a starting point at locating Ellis Whitebear's twin brother. Finally he was getting somewhere.

The next instant, Grant's eyes widened. "Are you sure about that?"

"Positive. Ellis Whitebear became a ward of the State of Texas at the age of two months when his mother gave him up for adoption."

"I need to take a look at those records."

"They're sealed. I suggest you direct any questions about his family history to Mr. Whitebear himself."

Grant muttered a few choice words under his breath. *Adopted. Sealed records. Mystery DNA.* How much better could this get?

"Did you say something, Sergeant Pierce?"

"Nothing you'd want to hear." Grant swung his feet onto the floor and started searching for the name he'd jotted on a yellow sticky note. "Look, Mrs...."

"Kanawa."

"Mrs. Kanawa, Ellis Whitebear is sitting on death row at the Oklahoma State Penitentiary. I helped put him there. He's not likely to schmooze with me about his relatives. Besides, the information he gave to the Department of Corrections doesn't mention anything about being adopted. Which means Whitebear may not even know about it, much less the details of his birth family."

"That's highly possible."

"More like probable," Grant added. "Mrs. Kanawa, I called you with what I thought was a routine request for information. I figured you could check Whitebear's birth certificate and read me his parents' names. Then I planned to ask if you could check for a birth certificate for his twin brother. Now you're talking about adoption and sealed files."

"Nothing wrong with your hearing, Sergeant."

The woman's steely tone told Grant he'd better crank out some charm if he was going to get anywhere.

"Look, I'm a civil servant, too." He added a soft chuckle for effect. "I know all about red tape. God knows we're drowning in it here in Oklahoma City. But you and I can get around all that. I'll skip asking you the names of Whitebear's parents, if you'll check his file and tell me what it says about any natural siblings. Specifically a twin brother. Yes, he exists. No, he doesn't. That's all the information I need from you."

"Sergeant, here in Texas, sealed means *sealed*. No one has access to that file. Not even me."

Grant scraped his fingers through his hair and held on to control. "What sort of paperwork does the great state of Texas require for me to get access?"

"You have to appear before the presiding judge in this county and show cause why the court should make that information available to you."

"I have to *appear?*"

"Yes. I can fax you the judge's information so you can contact his clerk."

"Great," Grant said, then rambled off his fax number before hanging up. He propped his elbows on his desk and rubbed at the knot of tension in his neck.

This late in the afternoon, the Homicide squad room was filled with detectives sitting behind ancient metal desks.

Several talked on the phone, one pounded thick fingers against a computer keyboard, still another leafed through a stack of crime scene photos from this morning's whodunit. Across the room, Jake Ford sat at his desk, taking information from a tall redhead wearing half a dress who'd walked in off the street claiming to have information about a homicide that occurred ten years ago. Thank God it wasn't one of Sam's cases, Grant thought as he idly watched the redhead sweep her hand through the air to make some point. If it had been, *he'd* be the one sitting there with his eyes crossed, instead of Ford.

Grant caught movement at the door, turned his head in time to see Julia Remington breeze in. She was slim, beautiful and had an enviable homicide clearance rate. The printout draped over her arm was thick enough for Grant to know he'd be working some heavy duty overtime. "You owe me big bucks for this, Pierce," she said, then plopped the printout onto the clutter in the center of his desk. "Pay up."

"*Pay up?* You're married to the CEO of Remington Aerospace, and you're trying to extort money from *me?*"

She smirked. "This coming from the guy who lives on his family's *estate,* wears Armani suits and Gucci."

Grant raised a shoulder. He was independently wealthy, having inherited a nice little enterprise called Pierce Oil, the company left to him and his older brother years ago when their parents died in a plane crash. The only thing Grant had ever wanted to be was a cop, so he gladly left the running of the company to his brother. But he didn't try to hide the fact that he lived beyond his city salary.

"Give me a break, Julia. I live in the guest house. I haven't bought a new suit in months, and the Gucci shoes are two years old." He gave her a caustic grin. "How come you're so prickly? You chip a nail when you went to Communications to pick up the printout for me?''

"Stuff it, Pierce.'' She slid a hip onto the edge of the desk and swept her hand toward the pages. ''The names are in alphabetical order. The only Whitebear that NCIC lists is your buddy Ellis.''

"Great.''

There *had* to be a missing twin, Grant thought. He'd hoped the ghost search he'd run through the National Crime Information Center for all Native American males with the same date of birth as Ellis Whitebear would bring up the man's brother. Maybe it had, Grant mused as he thumbed through the printout's pages. If a different family had adopted Ellis's twin, then he'd probably be using that family's surname. And maybe a different date of birth, if that date had been unclear when their mother handed her two-month-old sons over to the state of Texas. Or, maybe the twin hadn't ever been arrested, never did military service, had no mental health commitments or contracts with law enforcement. If so, he wouldn't show up in NCIC's database.

"Dammit, Sam and I closed this case. It's not supposed to jump up two years down the road and bite me on the rear.''

Julia skimmed her gaze to the desk that butted up to the front of Grant's. "Any idea how long it will be until they bring in someone new?''

"No.''

"Whoever it is will be your partner. The lieutenant will ask for your input.''

Grant kept his eyes off Sam's desk. The day before, he'd finally boxed up the photo of his partner's wife and kids and the Mickey Mantel-autographed baseball Sam had displayed on one corner of the desk. After adding the cache of cigars and personal papers he'd dug out of the drawers, Grant had taken the box to Sam's widow. He wondered how long just looking at the now-bare desk would put a knot in his gut. He couldn't even think about anyone else taking up residence there. "If Ryan asks, I'll tell him to take his time."

Julia nodded as she thumbed through a stack of messages she'd picked up from the secretary's desk on her way in. "Meanwhile, let me know if you need any help. Halliday and I just cleared our last open case."

"Lucky you."

She hesitated. "I almost forgot. Lonnie asked me to tell you Sky phoned while you were on your last call."

"Thanks." Grant set his jaw against the instant zing that shot through his blood. For six months, he and Sky had avoided each other. He knew she was probably calling to tell him she'd gotten the results from the blood samples she'd sent to the OSBI. Nothing between them had changed, he reminded himself. If it wasn't for work, they still wouldn't have anything to say to each other.

"Don't bother calling the lab," Julia said when he reached for his phone. "Lonnie said Sky is at the Training Center teaching recruit school this afternoon. She'll call you back when the session's over."

"Yo, Remington," one detective bellowed from across the room, the cord on his phone dangling from his fingers. "Your old man's on line three."

Sighing, Julia slid off the desk. "Sloan would love hearing himself called that."

After Julia moved off, Grant retrieved the printout she'd left, intending to start scanning the names. Ten minutes later, his forehead creased when he found himself still staring at the first page. His mind ought to be centered on the computer-generated names, not on Sky Milano's take-you-to-heaven blue eyes.

"Get a grip, Pierce." It annoyed him that he hadn't been able to completely forget her over the past six months—more, that he'd been unable to lock her out of his head since she'd walked into the FOP club five nights ago. One of his cases had turned to hell, and that was what he should be focused on. Only that. Instead, he felt himself being pulled by a woman who had made it clear she didn't trust him, and had forced him out of her life.

He was achingly aware that he wanted to *see* her, not talk to her on the phone.

Cursing himself for a fool, he rose, jerked his suit coat off the back of his chair and stalked toward the door.

The white-haired, bespectacled secretary glanced up from behind a desk piled high with files. "Where're you headed, Pierce?"

"Recruit school," he muttered.

Thirty minutes later, an OCPD academy instructor pointed Grant toward the gym. He went through the high double doors and froze. He blinked as if to clear his vision, but there was nothing wrong with his eyes. It was his heart that had stopped at the sight of Sky lying flat on her back, her dark hair tumbling over her shoulders as her hand rose silkily upward and slid around the neck of the man straddling her.

"What the hell?" A mix of anger and fang-infested jealousy consumed Grant. Then he saw red.

Fists clenched, he'd made it halfway across the gym's waxed floor when the man's head jerked up. A second later, the triumph in the bastard's eyes shot to wariness, then his body jerked and flew sideways. Air escaped his lungs with a muffled "Oof" when he landed hard on the padded mat that covered a section of the wood floor.

Grant skidded to a halt just as Sky bounded to her feet, clearly unaware of his presence. "Okay, recruit, you wanted to know how to get up when somebody has you down. That's how."

Face flushed, lungs heaving, the man looked up and shook his head. "Yes, ma'am."

"Stop saying *Yes, ma'am,* and get up!" Sky commanded. "If you stay down, Johansen, you're a target."

He got up…slowly.

"Fast. Get up fast. You're vulnerable when you're down."

"Yes, ma'am."

Through hooded eyes, Grant watched the recruit. He was young, tall and good-looking. His gray police academy T-shirt and gym shorts molded to the strong, toned body of an athlete.

"Rush me," Sky said. It didn't seem to matter that the top of her head came just to the hulk's shoulders.

Where her opponent had bulk and power, she had grace and speed. She sidestepped his rush, kicked his legs out from under him and had the sole of her tennis shoe against his throat the instant he hit the mat. "You're dead. I just crushed your windpipe."

"Yes, ma'am," the hulk croaked.

Grant felt a stiff tic of pride at how effortlessly she'd toppled the mountain.

She stepped back from her prey. "Don't stiffen when you fall. You have to be boneless, Johansen. *Boneless.* When you hit, roll and get back up on your feet in one fluid move. You might wind up dead if you don't."

"Yes, ma'am."

"Practice with the other recruits." Slicking the back of her hand across her forehead, Sky leaned and retrieved a hair clip off the edge of the mat. "If you need more help, you can reach me at the lab," she added, then turned and nearly collided with Grant.

"Having fun with the cavewoman routine, Milano?"

Her eyes widened and went dark. "Maybe."

Her glossy black hair was a gorgeous mess, her cheeks were flushed, her flesh slicked with sweat. Her breathing came fast and hard; her breasts moved rapidly up and down against the baggy T-shirt marked Academy Instructor that she'd tucked into a pair of loose-fitting gym shorts. The smell of woman and heat pulsed off her in little waves. Grant wanted to pummel the hulk into the mat just because he'd touched her.

"Get lost, recruit," Grant said, keeping his eyes locked with hers.

"Yes, sir." Johansen jogged across the gym, the rubber soles of his shoes squeaking against the shiny waxed floor.

"No need to be rude," Sky said as her student shoved through the swinging door that led to the locker rooms.

"You have to be rude to recruits. It's the law."

She arched an eyebrow. "That one must have gotten by me."

"I came in upstairs by the classrooms." The mugginess in the air had Grant slipping out of his suit coat and hooking it on a finger over one shoulder. "One of the instructors pointed me in this direction. I thought you were teaching recruit school this afternoon about the exciting world of the forensic lab."

"I teach that block of classes next month." She took a few steps and retrieved a white hand towel off a metal stand that held a row of basketballs. "When this academy started, I signed on to help teach self-defense to the female recruits. That's what I did this afternoon."

"*Female* recruits?" Grant gave her a cynical smile.

"Your most recent student was a few quarts over the legal testosterone level."

"Johansen asked for some extra help, so I stayed."

"The guy could bench-press the entire SWAT team. You really think he needs tips on self-defense?"

Her eyes narrowed. "Not if he stays on his feet." She blotted the towel across her forehead, then slowly down the seductive arch of her throat.

Grant felt heat streak straight to his loins.

"Johansen's big and strong, like an ox," Sky continued, apparently oblivious to what her ministrations were doing to him. "That's to his detriment if some scumbag manages to knock him off his feet. When he's down, Johansen lumbers around trying to get back up. Meanwhile he could get shot. Or stabbed." Her eyes closed briefly. "He recognizes his limits, and he asked for my help."

Grant knew there was sense in that, but at the moment he didn't want logic. He wanted to touch that tanned, moist flesh so bad he could taste it. Taste her.

Drawing in a slow breath, he took a casual step forward. "Want to go a few rounds with me, Milano?"

The hand gripping the towel froze against her throat. Her gaze skittered to his mouth, then to his eyes, then settled back to his mouth. She swallowed hard. "No."

"It's one thing to take on a goo-goo-eyed recruit who's afraid to toss the instructor—"

"I didn't give him the chance to toss me."

"Really?" The defensive thread in her voice had Grant fighting a smile. When they'd first met, he'd savored the verbal sparring they'd engaged in. Then their relationship got personal and everything changed. And ended. Somehow, after months of silence, they'd all of a sudden slid back into sparring mode. Standing there, in the expansive gym that smelled vaguely of hard workouts, Grant knew there was no way they'd wind up rolling around together on the mat. He knew Sky knew that, too. But, dammit, he was enjoying just being with her after so long and he wanted to prolong the pleasure of the moment.

"When I walked in here, Milano, your student had you flat on your back."

Her chin rose. "I *let* Johansen put me there. He wanted to know how to recover when someone knocked him down. I showed him."

"Hmm." Grant took another step forward and leaned in. The sweet, compelling scent of her hair drew him, and without thinking, he turned his head, inhaled. And savored. "He had you flat on your back," he whispered against her cheek.

She took a jerky step sideways. "I had control of the situation." Her fingers clenched and unclenched on the towel. "Total control."

"He had you pinned—"

"Not even close. I had full use of my legs. He hadn't even managed to restrain my arms. I could have disabled him with one palm strike to the nose."

"You could have killed him with a palm strike to the nose."

"My point, exactly."

From behind Grant, the echo of voices filled the air; he turned in time to see two brawny patrol officers clad in gym shorts and muscle shirts push through the door. They acknowledged his presence with a nod. The taller of the two men snared a basketball off the metal stand and lobbed it to his partner, then grabbed another ball and dribbled off toward the hoop.

Grant turned back, his eyes locking with Sky's. He had never seen her with her hair tumbled down around her shoulders. Never gazed into the stark blueness of her eyes without looking through the lenses of her glasses. Never glimpsed her in shorts with her bare legs long and tanned and soft. It hit him then, that if he could get his hands on that barrier she'd put between them months ago, he'd rip it apart.

He let out a slow breath against the realization. Barrier or no barrier, he wasn't ready to let her go—not yet.

"Come on, Milano. Some scumbag might knock me on my butt someday. Maybe if you gave me some pointers—"

"You're not a recruit. You're trained, and you've worked the street. You know how to move."

"True. But I might be rusty."

She shook her head. "You don't have a rusty move in your body, Pierce." She glanced in the direction of the clock bolted high on the wall, then looped the towel around her neck. "I've got two minutes to turn in my class-evaluation sheets before the office closes."

Lips pursed, Grant studied the graceful swing of her hips as she turned and walked away. When he heard an appreciative grunt, he shifted his gaze. Both patrol cops were dribbling their basketballs in place, their gazes plastered on Sky's trim bottom. The familiar tightness that settled deep inside Grant had him acknowledging that his desire for her was unchanged, as sharp as ever. Maybe sharper.

"Great," he muttered, shoving his fingers through his hair. Offhand, he could think of about six women who'd be happy to spend time in his company. What the hell kind of idiot was he, trying to steal a few extra minutes with a woman who had made it clear she wanted nothing to do with him? He turned to go, then remembered what had brought him to the Training Center in the first place: Sky's phone call.

She'd just cleared the opposite side of the mat when he

jogged up behind her. Reaching, he snagged her shoulder. "What did you call—"

Before he could even react, she'd jerked his arm almost out of the socket and flipped him. For a breathless second, Grant had the sensation of flying. Then he landed hard, flat on his back.

The catcalls and whistles from the two patrol cops echoed off the gym's cement block walls and high ceiling.

"Oh, God." Sky crouched, patting his cheek with her fingertips. "Grant, are you okay?"

He shoved up on his elbows and blinked away stars. "Damn, Milano."

"I'm sorry." She leaned closer, her eyes anxious as she peered at his face. Her dark hair swept forward, bringing her maddening soft scent into his lungs. "It was reflex, Grant. I just reacted to your touch, that's all."

He gave her a dark look. "Yeah. Thanks for saying that. I feel a whole lot better now."

Chapter 3

"I'm sorry I flipped you," Sky said again as she and Grant walked out of the gym into air that sat still and gauzy and full of early-evening humidity.

"Yeah."

As they walked along the sidewalk toward the Training Center's parking lot, she watched him out of the corner of her eye. He looked irritated, and he carried his suit coat gripped so tight in one fist that it would take a heavy steaming to get the wrinkles out. She knew his present mood wasn't a result of her having tossed him on his butt in front of the two patrol cops. What she'd said *after* she'd flipped him had been the thing that had turned his gray eyes the color of rolling storm clouds.

I just reacted to your touch, that's all.

Sky stifled a groan. How could she have been so insensitive? Beneath her baggy T-shirt, dampness pooled between her breasts; nerves had her switching her gym bag from one hand to the other. After Grant had regained his feet, he'd informed her in a voice void of emotion that he'd come there because *she'd* called him. They obviously had business to discuss. Would she please give him a few minutes so they could just get their damn business out of the way?

Business. No way did business have anything to do with the fact that his presence in the gym had unsettled her far more than she'd cared to admit. Or, that when he'd slid off his suit coat, the sight of his formidable shoulders and chest beneath his starched white shirt had stirred something dark and dangerous low in her belly. There had been no way— *no way*—she would have accepted his challenge of going one-on-one and possibly winding up rolling around with him on the padded mat, their legs and arms locked in an intimate tangle. The image of them doing just that rose up with erotic insistence, and for a moment she couldn't quite remember how to breathe.

Business, she reminded herself, forcing away the image. She had the DNA results from the OSBI, and she and Grant had business to discuss. That was what they'd do, then they'd both go back to their own lives, just as they had for the past six months.

The knot in her chest tightened at the thought. Fine, they'd go their separate ways, but first she had to make amends for tossing him to the ground. She had hurt much more than Grant's pride, and she needed to make him understand why.

His long strides took him around a corner of the building, and she had to double-step to keep up. Just ahead, their cars sat side by side; his sleek red Porsche with its convertible top down made her gray Blazer look like a hulking mammoth. It reminded her of the recruit Johansen.

"Grant, I want to tell you why I reacted—"

"Dammit, I *know* why."

Eyes blazing, he wheeled on her so fast, she collided into

his chest. For a split second she had the sensation of crashing against steel. Her gym bag slid from her hand, landed with a soft plop on the toe of her tennis shoe. "Some recruit off the street can touch you, but I can't." He made no move to steady her as she shook the gym bag off her foot and took an uneven backward step. "For you, my touch is poison."

"It had nothing to do with you." She knew he was talking about more than what had just happened in the gym. He was also addressing the night she'd literally fallen apart in his arms, but she didn't trust herself right now to discuss how she'd reacted then.

"Nothing to do with me?" He lobbed his suit coat into the Porsche's passenger seat. When he turned back, his expression had settled into cop mode, slightly remote, definitely cynical. "I didn't notice anybody else around, Milano."

"Not *you* specifically," she amended. "I'd have reacted the same with anyone who came up from behind me like that."

He jerked at his tie, flicked open the top button on his shirt. "You knew I was behind you."

"Not that close. I'd walked away. I didn't know you'd followed. The patrol cops were dribbling basketballs. I didn't hear you. Didn't know you'd gotten close enough to…" She closed her eyes. The heat seeping beneath her skin had nothing to do with the evening's thick humidity. "The night I was raped, that's how he got me. From behind."

"Damn," Grant said quietly as regret slid into his eyes. "Sky—"

"I didn't know any self-defense then," she hurried on, afraid if she stopped she'd be unable to get out what she needed to say. "He was tall and powerful and he had a knife. I couldn't…get away." Her voice wavered, and she dragged in steamy air that cloyed in her lungs. Her hands trembled and she jammed them into the pockets of her shorts. Six months ago—before she'd found the Monday night group and Dr. Mirren—telling Grant even that much had been impossible for her. Now it was just simple agony. "He came from behind and grabbed me. He...knew how to rape...."

"Sky." Eyes eloquent, Grant reached a hand toward her cheek, then stopped. His mouth tightened; she saw a muscle tic in his jaw. "I'm sorry," he said, and let his hand drop. "So sorry."

The thought of what she had just lost in that unfinished gesture tightened the fist around her heart. "No, Grant, I'm the one who's sorry. You had no way of knowing what happened to me. I overreacted. Big-time. You and I were in the *police* gym, for heaven's sake. A relatively safe place."

"Unless there's some jerk cop in your face, wanting to roll around on the floor with you."

Again, the image of their sweat-slicked bodies locked in an intimate clench flashed in her brain. She moistened her dry-as-dust lips and forced a smile. "There is that."

A breeze stirred, picking up the ends of her long hair that in all the turmoil she hadn't bothered to clip back. As if in reflex, Grant reached, caught a few strands and toyed with them. "I confess to being selfish," he said, his voice as soft as the breeze itself. "I wanted to spend some time with you. Just spend time."

He was standing close. Close enough that, even in the waning sunlight, she saw the individual crimson threads in his silk tie. The faint lines on either side of his mouth. The tiny specks of granite in the smoky gray eyes that gazed down into hers.

The breeze picked up. She smelled the salty tang of his skin mixed with the overtly male scent of expensive cologne. The heady mix made her knees weak. In another lifetime, she would have closed the distance between them and dissolved into a puddle right there in his arms. She held back a sigh. This wasn't another lifetime. It was the same one in which she'd proven she could melt into his arms, but *that* melting had nothing to do with desire, and everything to do with sheer panic followed by desperate humiliation. She would not—*could* not—do that again to Grant or herself.

When she stepped back, the strands of her hair slid through his fingers. His closed his eyes for the space of a heartbeat.

"I need to tell you about the report I got from the OSBI," she said, snagging her gym bag off the ground.

Grant looked toward the street where traffic hummed. The hand he'd had in her hair seconds ago curved slowly against his thigh. "And I need to bring you up-to-date on the search for Ellis Whitebear's twin brother," he said after a moment. Looking back, he unbuttoned his shirt cuffs and began rolling his sleeves up to reveal tanned, muscled forearms. "Look, I'm not feeling too fresh in all this heat." His gaze slid over her baggy T-shirt and loose-fitting shorts. "You probably aren't, either."

Sky raised an eyebrow. She'd taught two hours of strenuous self-defense to the academy's female recruits. Then worked up a sweat with Johansen. She'd put off taking a shower so she could talk to Grant before he left the Training Center. Now, her skin was moist from the heat. He was right—she definitely didn't feel fresh.

"We need to compare notes, I missed lunch and I'm hungry as hell," he stated, pulling a small ring of keys out of his pocket. "There's a hole-in-the-wall drive-in two blocks over that serves killer chili dogs, fries and shakes that come in giant gulp size." He swept his hand toward the Porsche. "They've got a couple of ceiling fans hanging from the metal awning. If we leave the top down, it'll be cool enough to eat in the car.''

Sky blew a slow breath between her lips. She had spent the past six months avoiding Grant Pierce. She knew she should turn down his dinner offer, climb inside her Blazer and drive home. She needed to take a shower. She had a briefcase bulging with lab reports to review. It made sense to ask Grant to call her later so they could compare notes over the phone. That would be the smart thing to do.

Her gaze took in the man who stood inches away, his thick, blond hair rustling in the breeze, his starched shirt stretched appealingly across his broad shoulders, his handsome face an alluring arrangement of planes and shadows. God help her, this was one instant she didn't want to be smart. She didn't want to avoid Grant; she wanted to be *with* him. They would go their separate ways soon enough.

She tilted her head. ''You're sure that hole-in-the-wall has *giant* gulp shakes?''

Amusement slid into his eyes. ''Positive.'' He bounced his key ring in his palm. ''If you talk nice, I'll spring for double chocolate.''

She narrowed her eyes. ''Does that lame line usually get women into your car, copper?''

The grin he shot her was pure male. ''Works every time, Milano.''

''So, the OSBI chemist confirmed your findings.'' Grant selected a French fry from the cardboard carrier wedged on the Porsche's console, then looked over at Sky. He fought a smile when he saw that her eyes were barely visible over the rim of the cup that held her double-chocolate giant gulp shake. Silently he calculated the calories in the chili dog, fries and shake, and figured they might help add back some weight to her too-thin frame.

''Right,'' she said, sliding her straw up and down in the

creamy drink. "The DNA from the suspect blood found at the Benjamin and Peña crime scenes is identical. You can take that to the bank."

"Since I checked and made sure Ellis Whitebear is still in his cell on death row, we can also take it to the bank that he has an identical twin brother."

Sky pursed her lips while gathering up napkins and unused salt packages. "Unless that was actually Ellis's blood on the bandage found under Carmen Peña's body," she mused as she dumped the trash into the paper sack the food had come in.

Grant set his shake aside. He'd thought of that angle, then discarded it for being too far-fetched. He had also worked Homicide long enough to know you never completely wrote off any scenario until you had cuffs on the suspect and a full confession. And sometimes even then you held your breath.

"You really think a man on death row would give a bandage with his blood on it to some *other* guy to leave at a crime scene?"

"If the man in prison wanted to make it look like he was innocent of the first murder. No way he could have killed the second woman while he was locked in his cell. So, logically, the cops might start to question if he'd actually committed the first crime."

"If that's the case, whoever planted the bloody bandage would have made sure the MO's on both murders matched. That'd give us more reason to think the same person killed both women, and that the real killer had been running around free the whole time. We don't have identical MO's. Benjamin died in the communal laundry room off her office at the apartment complex. The suspect stayed around just long enough to cut her throat. Carmen Peña's killer kidnapped her from her job at the convenience store. Took her to an abandoned house. He probably spent hours with her.

Granted, he cut her throat, but he raped her, too. Repeatedly. The only real thing that links the crimes is the identical suspect DNA.''

''That takes us back to the twin brother theory,'' Sky said, sliding her empty cup into the sack.

Grant nodded. ''I doubt the brother even knows he left the bloody bandage at the house where he took Peña, not when he was so careful about everything else,'' Grant continued. ''He didn't leave any prints. No semen, which means he either wore a condom or used a foreign object to rape her. You found no stray hairs on her body.''

''He probably wore a knit watch cap,'' Sky stated. ''Had it rolled down to cover his hair.''

''No footprints, no fibers from his clothing,'' Grant added. ''Nothing but the bloody bandage.'' He tapped his fingertips against the steering wheel. ''The guy was too careful. I put my money on the fact that the bandage was on his neck or face when he kidnapped Peña. The bandage is small, the size a man would use if he got a deep nick shaving. He put it on, and forgot about it. The defense wounds on the victim's hands and arms suggest she put up a fight. The bandage probably came off in the struggle and wound up under her body. I doubt the guy knows he lost it there.''

''Or maybe he didn't figure out until later what happened to the bandage.''

Grant thought for a moment. ''No,'' he said finally. ''The body wasn't discovered until at least two days after she died. He had plenty of time to return to the scene and look for the bandage.''

A car with a spitting muffler sped by on the dimly lit street. Grant flicked a look sideways, then let his gaze rise. A full moon had just broken through a group of oaks on the vacant lot across from the drive-in. ''Ellis has to have a twin, and he's out there somewhere. It's my bet he doesn't know we found his blood at the Peña scene.''

''Sounds logical.''

He looked back at Sky. The casual observer might think she looked totally relaxed sitting there, her back against the passenger door, her dark hair shifting softly in the breeze from the overhead fans. But Grant's observation wasn't casual, and he saw clearly the remnants of the haunted look that had filled her eyes earlier.

He tightened his hand on the steering wheel. The thought of how some gutter-scum rapist had come up from behind and grabbed her had anger stirring just below the surface of his control. The emotion grew hotter when he thought about how *he'd* done the same thing. True, he hadn't known any details of what her attacker had done, but he'd known she'd survived a rape. He'd been careless to even lightly taunt her at the gym the way he had. That was one mistake he wouldn't make again.

The one positive thing that had come from the incident was that she'd opened up to him. Minutely, he acknowledged, but at least the barrier had shifted. Considering they'd had zero communication during the past six months, he would take what he could get and be satisfied.

He glanced at the ceiling fan that spun lazily overhead, then shifted his gaze to the drive-in's paint-chipped building with the faded handmade sign in the window that advertised Giant Gulp Shakes. Sam had insisted they eat lunch here at least once a week, and on those days Grant had opted for iced tea and left the cholesterol to his partner.

Now that Sam was dead, Grant hadn't imagined he'd ever show his face again at this hole-in-the-wall. He'd been wrong. He was here now because there was no way he would have left Sky after she'd opened up to him. Standing there in the parking lot of the Training Center with her face pale and her hands jammed into the pockets of her shorts, she'd looked vulnerable and exposed, as if she might break into a thousand pieces if he touched her.

It had undone him to see her like that. He'd wanted to gather her close, swear he'd never let anybody hurt her again. Instinct had told him her nerves were too raw for her to welcome the gesture. Told him, too, the last thing he should do was try to get her into the closed confines of his not-so-spacious Porsche. So when the idea of this far-from-elegant drive-in popped into his head, he went with it.

He pursed his lips, mulling. If he thought Sky would make a habit of coming with him, he'd eat here every day and say to hell with the cholesterol. But she wouldn't come, he reminded himself. He'd been lucky tonight. She hadn't meant to walk back into his life for even a few hours, but here she was. The realization came slowly, stunningly that he had no intention of letting her walk out again. She was the only woman he was compelled to be with. The only woman he'd ever considered the possibility of a future with. The only one he'd spent uncountable nights with her face lodged in his dreams. The only one whose loss he'd grieved. He would not—*could* not—let her leave again.

"Your next step is to go to Austin?"

Her soft voice jolted him out of his thoughts. "Right," he said, and paused until the emotion that had flooded into his chest eased. "There's no guarantee the judge will let me have a look at Whitebear's adoption records, but I've run into a brick wall trying to get a line on his twin." As he spoke, Grant scooped up the sack with the remnants of their meal and tossed it into a nearby trash container. "I called our state pen. Other than the indigent defense fund lawyer assigned to Whitebear, the only person who's visited him since he's been there is his son. The twin brother hasn't shown his face."

"Maybe he writes to Ellis," Sky ventured.

"I checked. The whole time he's been in slam, he hasn't received one piece of mail. Hasn't sent any that the guard knows about. Of course, it's possible his son, or some other inmate, helps Ellis communicate with his twin."

"Are you going to question Whitebear or his son about the twin brother?"

"Not unless I have to. I don't want to tip my hand at this point and let them know I'm on to them." Grant turned the key in the ignition; the Porsche's engine purred to life. "I need to run everything down to the lieutenant in the morning. As soon as Ryan approves my going to Austin, I'll hit the road."

They made the trip back to the Training Center in less than five minutes. Grant nosed the Porsche into the space beside Sky's Blazer and left the engine running. He didn't want to spook her, didn't want to make her think he was going to try anything. What he wanted was her trust.

She smiled. "Thanks for dinner. The shake was awesome." In the glow of the parking lot's lights, her face was all intriguing angles and planes.

"You're welcome."

"Drive careful."

"I will."

She climbed out and shut the door.

"Sky," he said softly, then waited for her to turn back and meet his gaze.

"Yes?"

"I appreciate you telling me why you reacted the way you did in the gym."

Emotion flickered in her eyes. "I owed you an explanation."

"You can trust me. I'll never hurt you."

Her lips parted. He sensed her hesitation. Finally she nodded. "I know." She turned, unlocked the Blazer and climbed inside.

A minute later, Grant watched the taillights of her vehicle disappear into the night. "You know," he said quietly, "but you still don't trust me, not enough to let me into your life."

A blade, long and sharp and deadly flashed before Sky's eyes. The thick fist slammed into her from behind, exploding air out of her lungs. She went down hard and fast, and before she could scramble up, he was on her. Pain, blinding, numbing, mixed with her terror; a scream tore from her throat in the same instant her eyes flew open.

"Oh, God. Oh, God." She scrambled onto her knees, her legs tangling in the sheets as she dragged in quick gulps of air.

Lungs heaving, pulse pounding, she flailed for the lamp on her nightstand. Squinting against the light, her eyes swept the room. Her ivory robe was where she'd left it, looking like a shimmering ghost draped on the arm of her grandmother's wooden rocking chair. The neat stack of scientific journals she needed to scan sat undisturbed on the antique desk angled in one corner. On the nightstand, her glasses still lay on top of the thick paperback she'd used to lull herself toward sleep only hours ago. Everything in the room was as it should be.

Everything but me, she thought, scrubbing her palms across her sweat-drenched face. "It wasn't real," she whispered. "Wasn't real."

Trembling beneath her thin nightgown, she waited on the bed only until she felt certain her legs would support her. Then she fumbled for her glasses, shoved them on and fled down the hall, switching on every light as she went.

When she stepped into the bathroom and looked in the mirror, she winced. Her eyes were swollen from lack of sleep, her skin as pale as a corpse's, her mouth grim.

She splashed icy water on her face, toweled off, then

continued to the living room, switching on every lamp. Two nights ago, she had decided Streisand's was the best music to stay awake by. Fickle, last night she'd changed to the Stones. She clicked on the stereo, engaged the CD player.

Now a graveled-voiced blues singer assured her she could lean on him.

"I'd love to," she said in a shaky voice. "Come on over." She closed her eyes and waited for the soothing notes to erase the remnants of the terror that had grabbed her by the throat and squeezed.

"It wasn't real," she whispered again. To verify, she looked across her shoulder at the alarm panel beside the front door. A red light glowed, indicating the system she'd activated before going to bed had not been breached.

That knowledge did little to calm her. After all, the monster hadn't crashed through the door. It had been inside her all the time.

Just the simple gesture of shoving her hair behind her shoulders proved difficult with her hands shaking so badly. Her hands weren't the only unsteady thing about her. Her legs trembled, her heart stuttered against her ribs and her teeth chattered at intervals.

She was an expert in self-defense, but there was no defense against this internal monster. Like cells gone mad, it had grown and gathered strength, finally forcing itself back into her consciousness after so many years.

Nine, she thought dazedly. It had been nine years since the rape. The horrifying nightmare had started days after, had lasted months. But the monster had faded and eventually gone away. Forever, she had thought. Hoped.

It had returned violently three nights ago. She'd had dinner with Grant, come home, showered, then fallen into bed and slept. Hours later, the terror had slammed into her. She had tried to use logic to shake off the nightmare's stunning effects, telling herself that by confiding a few details of the attack to Grant, she had stirred everything up.

After the second night of hell, she'd called Dr. Mirren. In her typical soothing manner, the psychiatrist had assured Sky that the nightmare was a result of her recent attempts to come to grips with the rape. After a lengthy discussion, the doctor had offered to prescribe a mild sedative, but Sky had declined. Her problem wasn't getting to sleep. It was what happened after she got there.

Her flesh had turned to ice; she wished she'd taken the time to put on her robe. She gave a wary glance down the brightly lit hallway. The nightmare was still too real for her to venture back into the bedroom. Instead, she wrapped her arms around her waist and tried to get her breathing under control.

Over the past six months, she had begun to believe she'd made progress. Grown stronger. That maybe the part of her that had shattered would mend—not completely, but enough so that an intimate relationship could be more than just what other people had. No, she realized, she was back where she'd been nine years ago, vulnerable and afraid.

Because she was too shaken to maintain the usual tight control on her thoughts, she found herself suddenly aching for Grant. For the feel of his arms around her. For the soothing sweep of his warm breath as he whispered soft words against her cheek. She pulled in a slow breath. Not only was he *not* there to do any of those things, she didn't even know if he was in the state. Two days ago, she'd returned to the lab after a meeting at the M.E.'s office and found a message that he'd called to say he was leaving for Austin. Was he still there, searching for a lead on Ellis Whitebear's twin brother? If so, for how much longer? Or had he already returned and just hadn't bothered letting her know?

Biting her lip, she reminded herself that he'd had no

obligation to tell her he was leaving, much less contact her
when he got back. *If you care about me, you'll let me go.*
She'd made her feelings clear to him six months ago.

He had let her go.

Now she had a monster to face, and she had to deal with
it. Alone.

Her gaze went to the sofa upholstered in pale, muted
shades and scattered with earth-tone throw pillows and a
wool-soft comforter. She had spent the previous two nights
huddled there, fighting sleep. Tonight would be the third.

In what was fast becoming habit, she padded into the
kitchen, the sparkling white ceramic tiles cold against her
bare feet. The digital clock on the coffeemaker glowed
1:02 a.m. Now that the terror was receding, she could feel
fatigue settle in her legs and back. She knew the only way
she'd stay awake was with a double kick of caffeine. She
dumped an extra scoop of coffee into a filter, filled the pot
with water, poured it into the machine, then switched it on.

Just as she reached for a mug, the phone on the counter
trilled, nearly sending her out of her skin. "Get a grip.
You're on call," she muttered, perturbed at her skittishness
over the simple ringing of the phone. She grabbed the re-
ceiver. No matter how perverse, she welcomed the distraction of working a crime scene.

"Milano." Sliding automatically into chemist mode, she
reached for the pen and pad she habitually kept by the
phone.

"It's Grant. We need to talk about the case."

Something low in her belly tightened at the sound of his
voice. "Are you back in town?"

"Just drove in."

"Did you find Ellis Whitebear's twin brother?"

"That's one subject we need to cover." His voice came
over the phone in a level slide that told her nothing. She

furrowed her forehead, trying to remember her schedule. "Tomorrow morning I have a nine o'clock meeting at—"

"Now. We need to talk now."

"Okay," she said slowly, thinking about her earlier yearning to step into his arms. "Where do you want me to meet you?"

"Open your front door, Milano. I'm right outside."

Sky made him wait in the hallway long enough for her to pull on jeans and a shapeless T-shirt, and sweep her hair back with a clip. She punched in the access code to deactivate the alarm, hoping the second barrage of cold water she'd splashed on her face had put some color in her cheeks.

She knew it hadn't when she swung the door open and Grant's eyes narrowed. "What's wrong?" he asked as he stepped inside.

"It's the middle of the night, Pierce. Give a girl a break." She couldn't tell him that the few details she'd given him about the rape had resurrected her nightmare. Even now, the thought of the throat-clenching terror she'd experienced the past three nights nudged her toward panic. She didn't trust herself to tell him without losing control. She had fallen apart once in front of Grant, and she wasn't going to put either of them through that again. The fact that the nightmare had returned after nine years, as crippling as ever, cemented the agonizing knowledge that she could offer him nothing.

"I usually don't try for the runway model look until after the sun's up," she added, forcing lightness into her voice.

He didn't smile, just gave her a long, hard look that made her want to squirm. "I don't like the runway model look," he finally said. He turned, scanned the living room where the blues singer crooned that he'd keep her safe and warm in the arms of love. Grant shifted his gaze to the brightly lit hallway that led to her bedroom. "You alone?"

"What?" She stared up at him, incredulous. Did he really think she was entertaining some other man?

He turned, eyed her steadily. "Are you alone?"

"Yes."

"Hard to tell. I was on my way home and didn't plan to stop. When I saw your apartment lit up like searchlights on a helicopter, I figured you weren't asleep."

"Oh." She'd forgotten she had switched on every light in the place in an attempt to ward off the shadows. Uncomfortable under his assessing gaze, she arched an eyebrow. "You took this route to get home? Since when is my apartment on the way to the snooty part of town?"

This time he did smile. "I went a little out of my way."

"About five miles." She flicked a wrist in the direction of the breakfast bar where her briefcase and purse sat. "I'm up because I brought home lab files to review." It wasn't exactly a lie, she told herself. She'd finished going over the files before she'd gone to bed.

"It's hell when you have to bring work home," he commented easily, then nodded toward the kitchen. "Do I smell coffee?"

"I just made a pot." She turned, glad for any excuse to avoid the steely gray eyes that made her feel as if he could see right through her. That was the problem with cops, she thought. They didn't take anything at face value. "Want some?" she asked as she walked around the counter and into the kitchen.

"Sure."

"Black, right?"

"Good memory, Milano."

"Austin's a good five hours from here," she said, pulling two mugs out of the cabinet. "Did you drive straight through?"

"I was in a hurry to get here."

Here, she wondered, or just back to the city? Out of the corner of her eye, she watched him peel off his cream-colored jacket, then lay it across a high-back stool on the counter's opposite side. The gold badge on his belt beside his holstered weapon glinted in the light as he moved. He had spent hours in his car, yet his loose pullover and pleated linen slacks looked fresh and neat.

The lines of utter fatigue at the corners of his mouth and eyes revealed just how tired he was. She filled two mugs, left them untouched beside the coffeepot while her hands curled into fists. God, what she'd give to be free to walk around the counter and press her palm against his cheek.

"Something on your mind, Milano?"

"No." Heat crept up the back of her neck when she realized he'd begun watching her again.

She came around the counter, handed him a mug. "Have a seat," she said across her shoulder as he trailed her into the living room.

"Think I'll stand." He wandered over to the dark fireplace, leaned a shoulder against the mantel. "Need to get the kinks out."

Sky slid onto the cushions of the wing chair that sat angled at one end of the sofa. "Did you find Ellis Whitebear's twin brother?"

"No." Grant sipped his coffee, blinked hard. "Stuff's got a punch," he commented, then set the mug on the mantel.

"I made it a little strong."

"If you drink that entire cup, it'll keep you awake through next week."

That was the idea, she thought. "I can add some water to yours."

"Forget it. Let's talk about Ellis."

"So, you didn't find his twin," she said, then sipped.

The coffee went down hot and strong, and sent a welcome jolt of caffeine through her system.

"That's right, I didn't."

Something in Grant's voice stiffened her spine. "Did you at least get a lead on him?"

"A hell of one. I can positively say that Ellis Whitebear doesn't have a twin brother."

Sky sat unmoving while the words sank in. "There has to be a twin, an identical twin," she reasoned slowly. "That's the only logical way to explain the DNA found at the second murder scene."

"There is no twin."

"You saw Whitebear's adoption records?"

"No." The hand Grant shoved through his blond hair left it looking appealingly rumpled. "I got nowhere with the judge. He turned down my request to unseal the records."

"The brother's name could be in there."

"It's not."

She set her cup down with a snap. "If you didn't see the records, how can you be sure?"

His mouth curved into a sardonic arch. "Turns out I've got a lot in common with the case worker who handled the adoption. She didn't let me look at the records, but she slipped me the name of Ellis's birth mother and the address in Plano where she lived when she put him up for adoption."

Sky furrowed her forehead. "What do you and the case worker have in common?"

"Neither of us have any use for men who slit women's throats." Grant lifted a shoulder. "I drove to Plano and checked around the neighborhood. A midwife delivered Ellis. She still lives across the street from the house where he was born, still delivers babies. She swears there's no twin brother."

"Ellis Whitebear is in his late forties," Sky pointed out. "The woman could have delivered hundreds of babies since he was born. Do you trust her memory?"

"I trust her journals. She keeps a record of all the babies she delivers. Records their name, weight, length, even takes a snapshot. She showed me Whitebear's page. I saw a picture of Ellis, buck naked when he was about ten minutes old. Lovely sight. There's no twin brother."

Sky rose, her mind whirring as she began to pace. "Whitebear is locked in a cell. Even though his DNA is at the crime scene, we *know* he wasn't. He didn't commit the second murder."

"That's a fact."

She felt like a specimen under a microscope, pacing the living room while Grant examined her with unreadable gray eyes.

"The only explanation is the bandage," she reasoned. "Ellis had to have bled on it, and the killer left it under Carmen Peña's body."

"We went through that scenario, Sky. It doesn't make a whole hell of a lot of sense. Tell me about the controls you use in the lab."

She froze. She knew her blood had drained from her face. That wasn't something she could control. But she could keep her voice level and hard. "You're thinking the only other explanation is that I messed up the blood work on the first case. That my testimony sent the wrong man to prison. And another woman is dead because of me."

"No," Grant said evenly as he walked to her. "The Benjamin case was mine and Sam's. We conducted the investigation, worked the evidence. The outcome was our responsibility." He stared down at her. "In the morning I have to brief Ryan on what I found out in Texas. The lieutenant will ask the same question I just asked you. I'd like to have an answer for him. Tell me about the controls in the lab, Sky," he repeated. "How stringent are they?"

"Like steel." Punchy with exhaustion, she struggled to think. "All evidence that's logged in gets a specific case number. The evidence from each case is kept separate from all other evidence. Always separate." She dragged the heel of her palm across her forehead. "Before I start on a DNA profile, I label my vials with that case number, put tape over the label so the information won't get wiped off. I change gloves after each step of the process. Change my lab coat before I move from each room so nothing can get contaminated. After I've purified the DNA sample, I mix the reagents from the typing kit with that sample. I've got a certain window of time to do that." She heard the nerves that had crept into her voice, hated them. "The chief could call, and I wouldn't talk to him until I got done," she continued. "I keep notes every step. I log everything—"

Grant placed his hand on her arm. "It's all right—"

She stepped back. "No, it's not."

Was it possible she'd somehow made a mistake and her testimony had put the wrong man in prison? Had Sam and Grant and the DA put faith in her that wasn't justified? "If I somehow made a mistake that cost Carmen Peña her life, it's not all right."

"We don't know that you made a mistake." Grant paused. "What's the chance of two unrelated people having the same DNA?"

"One in five billion," she said automatically. "As far as anyone knows, you've got to have identical twins to get an exact DNA match." Grant's warm, musky scent curled into her lungs. Because she was tempted to reach for him for comfort, she took another step back.

He slid a hand into the pocket of his slacks. "The obvious key to this is the bandage with Whitebear's DNA left at the second crime scene. I don't care if Whitebear's sitting in a cell. He's involved somehow in the murder.''

She gave a quick shake of her head. "You said you discounted that scenario.''

"I said it didn't make a whole hell of a lot of *sense*. If the bandage was left as a means to clear Whitebear, the same MO should have been used at both scenes.''

"It wasn't. The MO was different. So it still doesn't make sense.''

Grant angled his head. "I've worked a lot of murders, Sky. I'm not sure any of them made sense.'' He swiped a hand across the back of his neck. "Everything that relates to the first murder needs to be rechecked. That includes all the evidence, every witness's statement, everything.''

"The victim's blood,'' Sky said, beginning her own mental list. "The suspect's. All the blood samples taken from the maintenance men who worked at the apartment complex...'' She fought back a swift surge of nausea that rose in her throat. "Oh, God.''

"What?''

"What if...?''

"What if what?'' Grant prodded.

She pressed her hand against her forehead. "The day after the first murder I went to the apartment complex. I took a vial of blood from each male employee to check against the suspect blood found at the crime scene.''

"I remember.''

"What if the vial with Whitebear's name on it actually contains blood from one of the other men?'' She stiffened her spine against the possibility that somehow, some way, blood samples had gotten mixed up, that vials had been mislabeled. That she'd made a terrible mistake that led to another woman's death. A mistake that could end her career, and damage Grant's.

"What if the real killer is one of the other employees?''

she asked. "That could explain the matching DNA at both scenes."

She shivered against the cold realization that crept beneath her flesh. "I don't believe this is happening."

Grant stood inches away, looking calm. Controlled. "Whitebear had the means, the opportunity and the motive to murder Mavis Benjamin. The jury considered more than just your testimony when they found him guilty."

The possibilities looming in her head notched up the sick feeling in the pit of her stomach. "I need to talk to my captain first thing in the morning and let her know what's going on. I'll recommend she assign Gilchrist to run a second DNA profile on all the blood samples I took on this case. Every vial. My work needs to be verified."

Grant nodded. "I know that needs to be done to eliminate any questions. Still, my gut tells me Gilchrist will get the same results as you." He fell silent, staring into the darkened fireplace. "Whitebear holds the key to this. I just wish to hell I knew what that was."

"You'll have to go to the state pen. Interview him again."

"If he'll talk to me." Grant shrugged. "He's on death row. I can't exactly hang the threat of prison over his head to get him to cooperate."

"You can tell him that giving us more of his blood might get him freed." Sky pulled in air, hating the desperation in her voice. "All along he claimed he was innocent. Grant, what if he is? What if I got vials switched and that wasn't his blood at the first crime scene? The only way to resolve this is to know for sure if it was his blood or not. Another chemist needs to draw a sample from him. Check it—"

"You, Sky." Grant took a step toward her. "*You* need to draw it. Check it."

She shook her head. "I might have messed up—"

"You might not have. You're the best damn chemist in

this department. Just because things don't seem to add up right now doesn't mean your work can't be trusted.''

"*I* have to trust it," she said fiercely. "I testify in court. What I say can lead to a person's execution. How can I do that when I'm standing here right now feeling totally uncertain of everything?" She heard her voice hitch, attempted to level it. "I hate this. I hate losing control."

"You haven't lost control. And you don't have to deal with this alone."

She closed her eyes against the gentleness of his tone. It was so hard to fight the promise of comfort she heard there.

"You'd better go," she said, her voice an unsteady whisper. "I need to think this through."

He stared down at her, a muscle working in his jaw as his eyes darkened to the color of tarnished pewter. "You figure you'll just take all this on your own shoulders and waltz me out of here?"

"No—"

"Like before?"

Everything inside her went still. "Before was personal."

"And this is business. The Benjamin case is mine, mine and Sam's. I'm responsible. That means I'm calling the shots. Something's gone haywire, and we need to figure out what it is. Together." He reached out a hand, slid it to her nape and kept it there when she stiffened. "Just like there was something wrong when I first walked in here. Suppose you tell me why you're really up this late."

Her eyes widened. "I told you. I have lab files to review."

"Your briefcase is sitting on the kitchen counter next to your purse."

She gave him a wary look. "So?"

"You're a creature of habit, Milano. I remember from before that when you brought work home, you always put your briefcase on the coffee table so you could spread everything out there. You never put your briefcase on the counter until you finished your work.''

Heat crept up her neck, pooled in her flesh beneath his fingers. ''Habits change—''

''Every light in this place is on.''

She stepped back, forcing him to drop his hand. ''The electric company loves me.''

''Then there's the coffee.''

''So, it's strong—''

''It's one o'clock in the morning. Why are you drinking coffee with enough caffeine to keep you climbing the walls for a week?''

''I couldn't sleep.''

''Why?''

Feeling cornered, she took another step back. After losing so much sleep, she wasn't in any condition to accept probing. ''It's just one of those nights.''

''One?'' he persisted. ''You look near exhaustion. You've got shadows under your eyes the color of slate, and a haunted look that says you've lost a hell of a lot more than one night's sleep.''

''It doesn't matter.''

''It matters.''

When she didn't answer, he eased a step closer and wrapped his hand around hers. ''Talk to me, Sky.'' He lifted her hand to his lips, placed a soft kiss against her knuckles. ''Let me in.''

Her pulse skipped, and she had the fleeting sense of how good her hand felt in his.

''I…'' Her throat knotted. Talking to him about the rape had sparked the nightmare back to life. Telling him that would cause him guilt and hurt he didn't deserve. One thing she was sure of, the *only* thing she was sure of, was she'd hurt Grant Pierce enough for one lifetime.

''It's something *I* have to deal with. Alone.''

"Why? Why alone?"

"It's best."

"For whom?"

"Both of us."

"That may be true." He turned her hand over, watched her eyes as he traced a fingertip along the length of her palm. Her heart stopped, then did a slow roll.

"Problem is, I'm not willing to stand back and find out," he continued quietly. "Six months ago you forced me out of your life. The way I saw it then, I had no choice but to let you. Now there's business between us, and there's no forcing me out. You're not dealing with this alone." His eyes locked with hers. "None of it."

"Grant, I can't—"

He raised her hand, pressed his firm lips deep in the center of her palm. Her eyelids fluttered shut for a brief instant while her stomach dropped to her toes.

"Someday you'll let me in, Sky. Someday you'll trust me enough."

Chapter 4

"How did you convince Ellis Whitebear to give us a blood sample so fast?" Sky asked forty-eight hours later.

"It wasn't fast," Grant stated, momentarily sliding his gaze off Interstate 40 and onto Sky. "Not in my book. It took me two days to convince his attorney, Marcia Davis, that it was in her client's best interest to give up some blood. I should have had her eating out of my hand in one day, tops. I must be getting rusty."

Sky angled her chin. "The legendary Pierce charm not what it used to be?"

"You tell me, Milano," he said, flashing her a grin while he passed a slower stream of traffic. "You're the one who climbed into my car at the mention of a double-chocolate giant gulp shake. I figure I was pretty charming."

"You did okay."

Grant heard the thread of emotion in her voice, saw the change in her eyes before she shifted her attention out the passenger window. Her gaze seemed to lock on a highway sign serving notice that the first exit for McAlester, Oklahoma, was one mile away.

He frowned. After they'd passed frequency range, he'd switched off the police radio; now, cool, silent air and Sky's light, tempting scent surrounded him as he studied her out of the corner of his eye.

She looked calm and relaxed, sitting with her legs crossed demurely in the passenger seat of the detective cruiser. Her dark hair was pulled back into its usual prim bun; wire-rims perched high on her perfectly shaped nose. The crisp cotton blouse and dove-gray slacks she wore magnified the image of a poised professional.

The casual exterior didn't fool Grant. He noted the way nerves had her right foot jiggling at intervals. Saw, too, the white-knuckled grip she had on the handle of the tackle-box-size evidence collection kit she'd placed between them on the front seat. She looked, he decided, about as relaxed as a coiled spring.

Something had happened. Between the time she'd stood outside the Training Center and opened up to him about her rape and a couple of nights later when he'd returned from Texas, something had happened. His frown deepened as he reviewed in his mind how he'd walked into her apartment and found every light in the place switched on, music blaring and a jittery chemist about to consume a pot of radioactive coffee that could have kept an entire task force awake for a week.

Whatever it was that had Sky climbing the walls two nights ago had not eased its grip.

Silently Grant studied her profile, taking in the shadow of weariness at the corner of her eye, the fatigue that turned her face pale. An air of vulnerability pulsed off her flesh in faint, tense waves.

During the drive, he had asked her what was wrong.

Several times. Each time, she had shaken her head in denial. Each time, the wary strain in her eyes had deepened.

He rolled his shoulders in a vain attempt to loosen the muscles that had knotted there. He would wager half his stock options that the Benjamin/Peña cases were only a part of the reason she was so uptight.

Sky and another chemist had worked grueling hours over the past two days, rechecking and verifying every test result on the evidence from Mavis Benjamin's homicide. Then the recent Peña murder. While the chemists had slaved over their instruments, Grant had tracked down and reinterviewed all the witnesses who'd testified in Ellis Whitebear's trail. So far, all test results, all witnesses' statements—*everything*—had checked out.

They would know soon enough if vials of blood had somehow been mislabeled two years ago when samples were taken of all the maintenance workers at the apartment complex Mavis Benjamin had managed. Grant's cop instincts told him that wasn't the case. Sky was too good a chemist, too organized and meticulous in her work habits for a glitch like that to have happened. Because his gut told him that she'd labeled the vials correctly from the start, he was back to asking the question of how a death row inmate's DNA had shown up on a bandage at a recent homicide?

No matter how long it took, no matter the number of chess pieces he had to shuffle around on a mental game board, he'd find the answer. Just as he would dig until he knew what had happened after Sky opened up to him about the rape, and why her gaze now went instantly wary whenever he got within five feet of her. It didn't take a rocket scientist to see that she'd reinforced the barrier she'd built between them six months ago.

Dammit, Grant thought as he pushed the cruiser forward in a burst of speed, she could reinforce all she wanted, but it wasn't going to work. Not this time. She wasn't shoving him out of her life again when this investigation ended.

He tightened his grip on the steering wheel as conflicting needs waged a battle inside him. She'd survived the worst kind of hell a woman could endure; he understood that. He didn't want her hurt further by his conjuring up pain-filled memories. Still, he and Sky deserved the chance to find out exactly what they could come to mean to each other.

He wanted the chance anyway, Grant amended, holding back a sardonic laugh at the irony of it all. He'd never had the inclination to dip below the surface with any woman…until he'd met Sky. She was the one woman whose thoughts he wanted to share, and couldn't. Whose trust he'd asked for, then been denied even a crumb of that trust.

Biting back frustration, he slid his gaze across the cruiser's front seat. She had no way of knowing that he'd set more than just the goal of getting Whitebear's blood during this day trip to the state prison. He was also determined to find out what had caused her to block off a part of herself again.

Once he knew the reason, he would get a handle on how to deal with it.

He jabbed a hand through his hair, barely aware of the eighteen-wheeler that shot by at breakneck speed. His other immediate goal was to get a handle on exactly what was going on inside *him*.

He'd lost count of the times he'd asked himself that very question since he'd pressed his lips to Sky's palm and urged her to trust him, to let him back into her life.

Why, he wondered, was he so ready to give her another shot at his heart?

Maybe losing Sam was the reason, Grant mused. He dealt with death every day, but those deaths weren't personal. When Sam died, Grant had lost a partner he respected and cared for. Nothing Grant could do would bring Sam back. Sky, on the other hand, was alive, and he wasn't going to step back and lose her, too.

He wasn't a fool. No way did he intend to leave himself wide-open again. Still, those few moments when he'd held her hand and felt the alluring jump in her pulse played in his mind far too often for him to ignore the knowledge that he couldn't just stand by and let her push him away again. And he wouldn't—by God, he wouldn't—let her walk away from him. Not unless they'd dealt with whatever was between them, and decided it wasn't enough.

Maybe that was the decision they would make; maybe it wasn't. Just how deep the emotions went on either side, he didn't know. This time, he planned on hanging around until they both had a chance to find out.

"What did you tell Whitebear's attorney?" Sky asked. She moved her hand from the evidence collection kit, then twisted her fingers in her lap. Grant could almost see her nerves pulsing. "Marcia Davis has to be suspicious of why you've asked for more of Whitebear's blood."

"She is." Easing out a slow breath, Grant forced his mind to business. Talking about the case was preferable to the silence that had hung between them during the four-hour drive. "I reminded her that the DNA we found at the crime scene is her client's. That's why a jury sent him to death row. But something's come up on another case, and I want to double-check a few facts."

Sky furrowed her brow. "She accepted that at face value?"

"No way. But I pointed out that Whitebear's position can't get much worse, no matter what samples he gives over. She couldn't argue that."

Grant clicked on the blinker, then swung onto the McAlester exit. "At first, Davis told me she had to think about letting Whitebear give us more blood, then she hung up. What she did after that was make a few calls to see if she could find out what I'm up to. The people she contacted clued me in on that. Since you and Lieutenant Ryan are the only ones who know all the details, Davis struck out. That's when she agreed to our taking the blood sample."

Grant steered around a corner. A huge banner stretched across the sunbaked road, welcoming them to McAlester's 48th Annual Prison Rodeo.

"I was in high school the last time I made it to the prison rodeo," he commented as he headed the cruiser in the direction of the state prison. "Have you ever been?"

"No." Sky shifted her gaze from the banner to give him a speculative look. "I'm having a hard time picturing you at a rodeo."

"Why's that?"

"Upbringing, Pierce. You've got all those blue-blooded genes coursing through your veins. I figure rich kids like you grow up attending the symphony and assorted fund-raisers on breaks from private school."

"I admit I did my fair share of hanging out at the country club," he commented, then cocked his head. From the moment they'd met, it had been so easy, so comfortable to slide into a give-and-take banter with Sky. "Then one night I tagged along with my brother, Nathan, and a few of his pals when they hit a country-western bar. I not only got introduced to some great music, I developed a true appreciation for women wearing skin-tight jeans and cowboy boots."

"Nothing like a well-rounded patron of *all* the arts," Sky murmured.

"That's me. Nathan and I came to the prison rodeo a couple of years running. Everybody has a good time, a few get a little rowdy, then everybody goes home at the end of the weekend."

"Except the inmates," Sky pointed out as the sprawling prison came into view.

"So true."

Under the glaring noonday sun, the whitewashed buildings gleamed like a peaceful oasis in a mirage. The ten-foot-high chain-link fence topped with swirling coils of razor wire and gun towers placed at intervals were stern reminders that murderers and assorted other morally bankrupt humans inhabited the surreal setting.

"You and I played a major part in putting Whitebear in this place," Grant stated. "As far as he's concerned, our visit today will be about one point more popular than that of the guy who brings him his last meal."

"If it turns out I made a mistake and he doesn't belong here, he'll be glad we came."

"I get the feeling nobody made a mistake," Grant stated, his brow furrowing.

"I hope you're right." Sky raised a hand, palm up. "If you are, we'll just need to figure out how Whitebear's blood wound up at the Peña crime scene."

"Yeah." Grant pulled the cruiser to a halt in the prison's visitors' parking lot. He opened his door and stepped into the oppressive summer heat that nearly took his breath away. Leaning back inside the car, he retrieved his suit coat, then hooked it over his shoulder with one finger.

"Ready?" he asked, slipping on his dark glasses as he walked around the cruiser to Sky's side.

"Ready." When she replaced her wire-rims with sunglasses, Grant noted that the dark lenses made her skin even paler in contrast. He fought the maddening need to grab her shoulders, shake her, demand she tell him what had put the hollow look on her face and wariness in her eyes.

Instead, he set his jaw and walked beside her in silence along the tree-shaded sidewalk toward the prison's double front doors.

As she moved, Sky shifted the evidence kit from one hand to the other. *Tools of her trade,* Grant thought. He knew the kit held syringes with sterile blood collection tubes and specially treated index-card-size absorbent paper onto which blood could be transferred so no refrigeration was needed. Also in the kit were alcohol swabs, combs, paper bindles, bandages, even smelling salts for use on the occasional squeamish donor.

As they neared the entrance, they came abreast of several well-kept wooden houses that had once been residences, but now served as offices for some of the prison's staff. Looming over the homey structures were the whitewashed buildings that made up the prison's main body.

Grant pulled open one of the double entrance doors, welcoming the blast of cool air that gushed out. Sky stepped past him through the door; her tantalizing scent drifted out from her flesh and wrapped around his senses.

"Sky," he said quietly.

Pausing, she traded glasses, then turned to face him. "Yes?"

The weariness in her blue eyes pulled at him. "When we're done here, let's stop and get something cold to drink." *And talk,* Grant added silently.

"I want to get back to my lab as soon as possible."

The knots he only now realized had been in his stomach since they started their drive tightened.

"I'll get you back." He walked toward her, keeping his eyes locked on hers. "But we're going to have a talk first."

Her face went deadly pale. "No, I—"

"Help you?" asked a uniformed female guard behind the glass-fronted visitor's desk.

Grant caught the stiffening in Sky's shoulders beneath her crisp white blouse as she turned and walked to the desk. There they informed the guard of their business, then showed their identification. Sky handed her purse to the guard; Grant unclipped his holstered 9 mm Glock from his belt. He removed the clip, unchambered the remaining round, then passed the automatic and ammunition through the small security window. The purse, weapon and ammunition went into a locker behind the desk. A second guard with a thick gray mustache and sharp eyes went through Sky's evidence kit. Satisfied there were no concealed weapons or contraband inside, he handed it back to her.

Grant followed Sky through a metal detector, then down a ramp and through two sets of sliding steel doors. Their shoes sounded hollow echoes along the short hallway where a heavyset guard with a flat stare unlocked a door to a small room that was routinely used for attorney-client visits.

Grant nodded to the woman with a hip propped against the small table in the center of the room. "Counselor," he stated.

"Hello, Pierce."

Marcia Davis was a slim, compact woman in her mid-fifties with salt-and-pepper hair cut in a short, no-frills bob. She met Grant's gaze with dark brown eyes that gave no hint at her thoughts. He had dealt with the attorney from the indigent defense fund on several other cases, and he knew her to be intelligent and stealthy. As always, Grant planned to watch what he said in her presence.

He lifted a hand in Sky's direction. "Sky Milano, meet Marcia Davis."

The attorney pushed away from the table, giving a slight nod. "You testified in one of my cases last year," Davis stated, returning Sky's handshake. "The Tobias case."

"I remember."

The attorney glanced across her shoulder at the guard who stood waiting at the room's entrance. "Has Jason

Whitebear signed in yet? He wanted a few words with his father before we got started.''

''No, ma'am,'' the guard stated.

Davis checked her watch. ''I've got another appointment in Tulsa in a couple of hours, so we won't wait. We're ready for you to bring in Ellis Whitebear.''

The guard nodded. The thick metal door with a small window in its upper half closed behind him with a firm thud.

''One thing, Pierce, before my client gets here,'' the attorney said, crossing her arms over her chest.

Here it comes, Grant thought, meeting her gaze squarely. ''What's that?''

''Why don't you tell me the real reason you need more of my client's blood?''

Out of the corner of his eye, Grant watched Sky move to the far side of the table, then open the lid of her evidence kit. With efficient ease, she pulled on a pair of thin surgical gloves.

''I told you the reason,'' he stated, focusing his attention firmly on the attorney. ''Something's come up on another case, and I want to double-check a few facts.''

''Hogwash,'' Davis returned evenly, sliding her sharp gaze Sky's way. ''Something's come up on *this* case or you and your chemist wouldn't be here right now.''

Grant raised a shoulder. ''Your client's guilty, or he wouldn't be here right now.''

''Is he?''

''His DNA was on a dead woman's dress.''

Davis kept her eyes on Sky. ''*Was* it Whitebear's DNA on Mavis Benjamin's sleeve?''

''Yes,'' Grant said, then waited until the lawyer shifted her gaze back to him. ''It was.'' Until a test told him different, it was.

"Do you have new evidence that impacts my client's case?"

"No." Grant kept his eyes locked with hers. As a police officer, he had an obligation to report *evidence,* not rumor, innuendo or hypotheses. At this point, he wasn't sure what the hell he had regarding the two-year-old homicide case.

Pursing her lips, the attorney tucked a wayward strand of salt-and-pepper hair behind one ear. "I'll tell you what, Pierce. You and Sam have always been upfront with me."

"Sam's dead," Grant countered instantly, then set his jaw against the now-familiar curl of regret that settled inside him.

"I'm sorry about that," Davis continued. "He was the best homicide cop I've ever dealt with. Sam once told me the way he proved someone guilty was to try to prove them innocent. Every step he took where he couldn't do that made that person's guilt more likely."

Grant arched an eyebrow. Sam had pounded that philosophy into his head when they'd first partnered in Homicide. "Your point, Counselor?"

"My point is that I had a great respect for Sam and I figure you learned from him, or he wouldn't have kept you on as a partner very long. I've always known you to tell the truth, Pierce, even if it might not advance your own case. Whatever's going on that involves my client, I trust you to do what's right."

Trust, Sky thought as she pulled a folded form from her evidence kit. Two nights ago at her apartment, Grant had pressed a kiss against her palm and asked her to trust him.

The raw emotion she'd seen shimmering in his eyes had ripped her heart in two.

What he didn't understand was that she *did* trust him. She had always trusted him. She just didn't trust herself.

With unsteady hands, she unfolded the form, laid it on the table, then closed her eyes for a brief instant.

Five nights, she thought dully. For the past five nights the vicious monster lurking in her subconscious had flung her back to the most terrorizing moments of her life. She'd thought the months of therapy with Dr. Mirren had given her the strength to free herself, to get on with her life.

Fool, she silently chided.

She stared down at her gloved hands, impotent to stop the slight tremor that surged through them. The dream came all the time now. All the time. There was nothing to stop it. *Except the day,* she reminded herself, twisting her fingers together. Her monster didn't lurk during the day, so she wouldn't let herself conjure up the feel of the blade against her throat, the smell of the hand that clamped over her mouth to smother her screams. She wouldn't remember, wouldn't let the panic arrow through her, not right now, not here in this brightly lit room that smelled vaguely of prisoners' sweat and fear. Not while Grant was only a few feet away. She had fallen apart in front of him once.

That was enough for one lifetime.

Standing in silence, she studied him though a veil of dark lashes while he conferred with Marcia Davis. How had it happened? Sky wondered. How had this whipcord-lean cop with the whisky-edged voice and appealing sandy blond hair stepped back into her life? She had pushed him away, turned her back on him. Hurt him. Yet, here he was. Granted, it was work that had brought them together again, but there was more.

He knew. Not about the nightmare specifically, but he knew something was wrong. She raised a hand, rubbed a latex-sheathed index finger against her furrowed forehead. Of course he knew. She had seen the shadows beneath her eyes and the hollow look in her face this morning in her bathroom mirror. She'd lost so much rest that makeup no longer did anything to hide the ravages of insomnia. Of course he knew.

He had asked her what was wrong. Several times he'd asked. How she wished she could tell him. Just rest her head against the warm comfort of his shoulder and tell him. She didn't dare, she reminded herself. She was holding on to control by only a thin thread and she didn't dare do anything around him that might make her lose hold of that thread.

Expelling a breath, she suddenly realized Grant's gaze had shifted and was now locked onto her face.

The sharp assessment she'd felt throughout the four-hour drive to the prison sliced through her once more. She now knew what it was like to be a specimen under the lens of one of her microscopes, to be not just looked *at,* but *into.*

His all-too-personal study unnerved her further, had her shifting her gaze to the nearest drab gray wall. Her already-clenched fingers tightened around each other. She had to get away from him, had to put some space between them. She didn't want to go somewhere for a cold drink and conversation after they were done here. She wanted to lock herself in her lab's cool, controlled confines. *Hide.*

Her shoulders stiffened against the thought. She couldn't hide. If she'd made a mistake in her lab, if she'd mislabeled vials of blood, that meant her testimony had helped put the wrong man on death row, and resulted in Carmen Peña's death. She had to get to the truth. Had to find out if she was at fault and, if so, try to repair some of the damage.

To do that, she had to work with Grant.

The sound of the heavy metal door swinging inward had Sky's head jerking sideways.

She'd last seen Ellis Whitebear two years ago in a courtroom, the day the jury convicted him of Mavis Benjamin's murder. He'd changed little since then, Sky thought as she watched the man shuffle through the door in cuffs and leg irons, a guard on his heels. Whitebear was big, broad shouldered, heavy topped, flat bellied. His straight hair flowed over his ears, thick and black, lapping over the collar of his white T-shirt. His copper-tinted skin stretched taut over high cheekbones that attested to his Native American heritage.

"Ellis, you remember Detective Pierce and Sky Milano," Marcia Davis stated as the guard escorted his charge to the table where Sky stood.

"Yeah."

Sky was aware that Grant had moved to her side before Whitebear fully settled into a chair.

"How you doing, Whitebear?" Grant asked levelly while the guard took his position just inside the locked door.

Ignoring the question, the prisoner stared at Grant. Moments later, the man's eyes shifted, then settled on Sky. "You want to stick me again."

Grant leaned in. "That's right."

"Ellis," Marcia Davis began, propping a hip against the table. "As I told you, something's come up on another case that Detective Pierce is working." She flicked a cool look at Grant before shifting her gaze back to her client. "The detective tells me he needs another sample of your blood to double-check a few facts."

The silver cuffs surrounding Whitebear's meaty wrists clacked against the tabletop when he shifted his hands. "What facts?"

"I'm not at liberty to get into that right now," Grant advised, his gaze steady on the inmate's face. "All I can say is that things can't get much worse for you. Even if they could, I'm not looking to make them worse."

Whitebear sneered. "I didn't kill that bitch. You put me here, and I didn't kill her." His narrowed gaze slid to Sky. Her throat tightened at the flicker of pure hatred in the dark eyes that locked on her face. "Both of you lied—"

"We told the facts as we knew them to be," Grant

stated, his voice intense, unwavering. "If there's more that needs to be looked at, now's the time."

"He's right, Ellis," Davis added. "As I told you, we can use Detective Pierce as a free investigator who might make a positive difference in our situation. He sure can't make a negative one. We've got nothing to lose by cooperating with him, and everything to gain."

"Ain't much to gain by rottin' in a cell the way I have for two years."

"That's right," Davis answered, raising a shoulder. "Ellis, it's my duty to remind you that this is up to you. The police don't have a search warrant or a court order. You don't have to let Ms. Milano take a sample of your blood. You don't have to do anything but go back to your cell."

To Sky, it seemed as if the air in the small room grew heavy while the man sat in silence, staring down at his cuffed wrists. Just when she was certain he was about to tell her and Grant what they could do with their request, Whitebear raised his head and met her gaze.

"Stick me, then get the hell out of here."

Nodding, Sky pulled a small rubber ball, tourniquet and syringe from her kit.

Grant picked up the form she'd laid on the table. "Before we get started, we need you to sign a Waiver of Search of Body form," he said, then pulled a pen out of the inside pocket of his suit coat.

Whitebear shot a contemptuous look at the paper Grant laid in front of him. "I don't read much."

Davis stepped forward. "Read it out loud, Sergeant."

Using the tip of a finger, Grant turned the form his way. "'I, Ellis Whitebear, after having been advised of my right not to have a search made of my body…'"

When Grant finished reading the form, he handed Whitebear his pen, watched the inmate scribble his name.

Sky retrieved several sealed packets of alcohol swabs

and a blood collection tube from the kit. As incongruous as it seemed, she was glad for the distraction. It was easier for her to remain outwardly composed when she had a specific task to do.

She had taken blood from uncountable suspects and prisoners, could nearly do it with her eyes closed. As she swabbed alcohol across the inside of Whitebear's arm, she knew the pinpricks of tension that probed at the back of her neck were not due to the task at hand. It was the thought that this man had possibly spent two years in prison due to a mistake she'd made.

"Squeeze this," she stated, handing Whitebear the rubber ball. With brisk efficiency, she wrapped the tourniquet around his thick upper arm, then slid the needle into his vein.

"You can stop squeezing now," she said after a moment.

She had performed this task hundreds of times, she thought as she placed a bandage on Whitebear's arm. Yet this was the first time her hands had been unsteady while doing it. The first time tension at the back of her head had built into an ache.

"Thank you, Mr. Whitebear," she said quietly.

The man stared up at her through dark, hooded eyes. "Ain't nobody called me that in two years."

Sky nodded as she retrieved an ink pad and small card from her kit. "I need your right thumbprint on this card," she stated. Before she and Grant left the prison, she would go to the clinic and transfer the blood she had drawn onto four areas of the specially treated card. After the blood dried, she would seal the card in an evidence envelope and slip it into her kit to transport back to her lab.

After Sky rolled Whitebear's print, the guard approached the table. "Let's go, Whitebear," he stated, tapping the prisoner on the shoulder.

While Marcia Davis followed her client out the door, Sky

dropped the sealed tube filled with blood into a plastic specimen bag that displayed an orange-and-black bio-hazard emblem. The used alcohol swabs, bandage wrappings and gloves went into a separate pouch in the bag. She stowed the bag, the card with Whitebear's thumbprint and the signed form into her kit, then turned to Grant.

"I need to finish up in the clinic."

He nodded, his gaze intent. "I'll wait for you out front. We passed a café on the way in. We'll stop there and get something to drink. And talk."

She lifted her chin. "We can get our drinks to go," she said levelly. "I want to get this sample back to my lab."

He took a step toward her. "Dammit, Sky—"

"Don't push me." The words lashed out, edged with the searing fatigue and frustration that swirled inside her. The knots of tension in the back of her neck clenched. She couldn't afford to tell him. Couldn't afford to risk even one more second of the debilitating nightmare. "I have to…"

When her voice wavered, his gray eyes glistened behind their sandy lashes. "Have to what?" he asked, his words deathly quiet on the cool, still air.

"Deal with this case. Just this case. I can't deal with you. I can't."

Legs unsteady, she grabbed her evidence kit and headed out the door.

Chapter 5

When Sky appeared in the prison's reception area thirty minutes later, Grant was still steaming over what she'd said in the interview room.

He waited until they were outside and at the edge of the parking lot before he snagged her wrist and spun her to face him. "You're going to have to deal with me, so live with it, Milano."

"On this case." Her right hand clenched the handle of the evidence kit so tightly, he could see the white of her knuckles beneath flesh. "Outside of it, you and I have nothing to deal with, so *you* live with it, Pierce."

"Like hell."

She raised the evidence kit to eye level. "I need to do the DNA profile on Whitebear's blood sample. We have a four-hour drive back to the lab. Let's get started."

The leaden heat of the afternoon sun hung in the air, yet her voice was cool enough to chill Grant's flesh.

"Darlin', we started a long time ago." With the dull roar

of anger filling his head, he glanced around the parking lot for something to tear apart with his bare hands. Seeing nothing but rows of cars, he settled on grinding his teeth. "Why won't you tell me what's wrong?"

She blinked. "Nothing—"

"*Everything's* wrong! You've got shadows under your eyes, lines of fatigue at the corners of your mouth, and your hands weren't quite steady when you stuck that needle into Whitebear's arm."

Her chin went up as she jerked her wrist free of his grasp. "I didn't hurt him."

"I didn't say you did."

When she took a step back, Grant took one forward. All of his instincts told him if he backed down now she would walk away, for good this time. The past six months had shown him what his life would be without her. The memory of how it had felt to lose her settled a clawing ache in his stomach. He had no intention of reliving that experience, not if he could help it.

"You know what annoys me the most, Milano?" he persisted. "People who lie to me. So I suggest you start telling the truth before I get really annoyed."

"I'm not…"

When her voice broke, the fist around his heart tightened, instantly defusing his anger.

Shaking her head, she turned her back to him and stared out at the parking lot. Beneath her white blouse, her shoulders looked board-stiff.

"Sky." His hands weren't quite steady when he cupped her shoulders and gently turned her around. Her face was even paler than before, the shadows under her eyes like flaws in marble.

"Don't," she said, making a halfhearted attempt to shrug from his grasp. "Please don't…"

"Tell me why you've put the wall back up between us."

"It never went down."

"It did." Beneath his palms, her shoulders felt like high-tension wires. "The other day at the Training Center, when you told me about how the guy who attacked you grabbed you from behind, you let that wall down. Not much, but some. Do you know how that felt? Do you know how it felt to have you open up to me?"

"I had to tell you." She closed her eyes for an instant, opened them. "I flipped you when you grabbed me. I had to explain why."

The edgy desperation in her voice had Grant furrowing his forehead. "Then we went to dinner and started talking."

"About the case—"

"We started talking. For the first time in months we talked." He had felt something relax between them—he wasn't mistaken about that. "When I got back from Texas two nights later, you'd put up the wall again." His eyes probed her face. He wanted answers. *Needed* them. "Did I say something wrong? Did I hurt you in some way?"

She winced, then looked away. "No, Grant. No."

"Okay, so nothing happened," he stated. "I didn't say anything to hurt you. You just shut me out again. I want to know why."

When she didn't answer, he cupped a finger under her chin and forced her gaze back to his. "I've developed a big dislike for that wall, Sky. I'll climb over it, tunnel under it or just knock a hole through it. Whatever way, it's coming down."

She stared up at him through despair-darkened eyes. "I don't want it to come down."

"Tell me why," he countered. "If it's a good enough reason, maybe I'll walk away."

"I want you to walk. That's all the reason you need."

Slashing knives of hurt stabbed at his heart. He hadn't known those words would bring this kind of pain.

"Dammit, I need more. I *want* more," he added through his teeth. "Why do you want me out of your life? Because you don't care about me? If so, say it, and I'll be gone."

"We...can't work." She looked as though she might come apart in his hands at any second. "We didn't work six months ago, and we can't work now."

The fact that she'd avoided answering his question had a tingle of relief loosening the tightness in his chest. "Do you want me out of your life because you don't care about me?"

"As a friend." She pulled her bottom lip between her teeth. "I care about you as a friend. That's all."

He remembered the way the pulse in her wrist had jumped, then pounded like a hammer when he'd pressed a kiss to the center of her palm. *Desire.* It had been there, probably buried between layers of conflicting emotion, but there all the same. Maybe that was it, he thought. Maybe the desire she'd felt was responsible for the edge of panic he now saw in her eyes.

"The rape," he said, his voice quiet and level. "I don't know what you went through because you haven't told me. But I've been a cop long enough to know how bad it could have been."

Her eyes flashed, then went dark. "I don't want to talk about it."

"Fine, so listen while I talk. We both know I have a reputation around the department," he continued. "Probably ninety percent of it is talk. If I'd done half the partying I've heard I've done, I'd be six feet under. But I do admit that all I've ever wanted out of a relationship was fun, games and no complications. Until now."

He traced his finger along the slope of her chin before dropping his hand and taking a step back. "Maybe that's part of what's put the panic in your eyes. I'm not saying I won't have a tough time keeping my hands off you. I will. But I'll do it. You'll be the one calling the shots on this, Sky. I won't touch you until you're ready. You have my word."

"I'll never be ready. Never."

He narrowed his eyes. Why did it matter so much to him to prove her wrong? Why did *she* matter? At this point he didn't have a clue. She just did.

"You need time," he said softly. "And care. And patience. I understand that. I'm offering those things. All I want is for you to trust me enough to let me be a part of your life."

"It's not you." She turned and took a few halting steps toward the parked cruiser before swinging back to face him. The tears welling in her eyes put a knot in his throat. "It's me, Grant. Can't you understand? It's *me.*"

"Make me understand, dammit." He walked toward her, his eyes locked with hers. "What is it about you that makes you want to shut me out of your life? Tell me, Sky. *Tell me.*"

"I can't." Shaking her head, she took a deep breath. Then another. "Just take me back—"

The sudden roar of an engine drowned out her words.

Their heads jerked in unison when a faded blue pickup going to rust shot into the lot, its bald tires squealing on the sun-beaten pavement. Seconds later, the pickup braked to a halt and a tall, wiry man in his twenties with shoulder-length black hair and fury in his eyes shoved open the door.

Grant's mind scrolled back two years to Ellis Whitebear's trial. The man now stalking their way with a can of soda gripped in one hand had pleaded with the jury during the sentencing phase to show leniency toward his father.

"You stuck him already, didn't you?" Jason Whitebear demanded. He clenched his fists, crumpling the soda can before tossing it aside.

Shoving Sky behind him, Grant noted the grease-stained work shirt with an oval patch sporting the name Spider in its center. Worn, faded jeans encased the man's long, lanky legs. A greasy red work rag hung from one clenched fist.

"That's right." Grant was well over six feet tall, but he had to lift his chin to look Spider in the eye. "*We* took a blood sample."

"I told that woman lawyer to keep you away from my old man."

"Wasn't your decision to make…Spider."

"Wasn't yours, either."

"Correct," Grant agreed smoothly. "It was your father's. He agreed to give us a blood sample, so we took it. Now, back off."

Color swept into the dark tanned skin that stretched over sharp, high cheekbones as Spider took a step sideways and locked his gaze onto Sky. "You lied at his trial. Wasn't putting him on death row enough? What the hell you trying to frame him with this time?"

"I didn't lie." When Sky stepped around him, Grant set his jaw. "No one lied."

"You got up there, swore on a Bible, then spouted some fancy scientific talk that impressed the hell out of the jury. Doesn't change the fact that you lied through your teeth."

"No—"

Spider lunged for the evidence kit so fast that Grant had no time to stop him from clamping his hand over Sky's. The same instant Grant grabbed Spider's wrist and twisted,

Sky smashed her heel against the top of the man's scuffed boot.

The solid jolt had Spider jerking back. He released her with such suddenness that Sky stumbled sideways, the evidence kit still clenched in her hand. The anger and frustration simmering in Grant zeroed to flash point. He plowed into the man's chest, slamming him backward against the cruiser.

Body coiled, Grant pressed his forearm against the man's throat. "Touch her again, I'll break every bone in your hand."

Grant's gaze sliced to Sky. She had regained her balance and now stood a few feet away, the evidence kit tucked beneath one arm. She flexed, then unflexed the hand Spider had grabbed.

"You okay?"

Sun glinted off her wire-rims when she nodded. "I got some grease on me, is all." Her voice was even, controlled.

"Meant no harm." With Grant's arm pressing into his windpipe, Spider croaked the words.

"Tell that to the judge," Grant stated, his voice icily calm. "I'm hauling you in on assault." He flicked a look at the crumpled soda can. "And littering."

"Go ahead, lock me up," Spider grated. "That won't keep me quiet about you trying to pin something else on my old man."

Grant narrowed his eyes as he eased pressure off the man's windpipe. "What the hell makes you think we're trying to pin anything on Ellis?"

"You cops got quotas. What happened? You go through some of your old cases and find one you think you can blame on him, too?"

"We're not here to make your father's situation worse." Although Grant eased his weight back, the anger in the dark

eyes that drilled into his prompted him to keep one palm
flat against Spider's chest.

"Worse?" Spider hissed, his fists cocked. "You want to
tell me how it could get *worse?*" He moved his gaze to
the prison's whitewashed facade. "My old man can't do
nothing on his own in there. They tell him when to wake
up, when to go to sleep, when to eat, what to eat. He can't
go outside. Can't sit in the sun if he wants. He didn't do
nothing, and he's locked in a cage. In a few years, they'll
slide one last needle into his vein."

"He's here because he murdered Mavis Benjamin,"
Grant stated. Beneath his palm, Spider's chest felt like a
solid plane of sinew and muscle.

Spider cut his gaze sideways, doing a slow study of Sky.
"So you say."

"So says the evidence," Grant pointed out levelly.

"I don't give a flying flip what you claim it says. It's
wrong. You're wrong."

When Grant dropped his palm and took a step back, he
noted Spider was favoring the booted foot Sky had
stomped. "Okay, Whitebear, have your say. Why do you
think the evidence is wrong?"

"I know my old man." Using a forearm, Spider swiped
at the sweat that beaded his tanned brow. "Sure, he hated
that bitch apartment manager. Everybody knew it. But hating her doesn't mean he killed her."

Grant had lost count of the guilty people who had looked
him straight in the eye and sworn their innocence. Still, he
glanced at the evidence kit in Sky's hand. He couldn't help
but wonder at the outcome of the test she would soon do
on Whitebear Senior's blood sample.

Still, no matter the result, he had to go with what they
had at this point. "A jury heard all the evidence and decided your father killed her."

"The jury was wrong." Dropping his gaze, Spider scrubbed the red rag against the palm of one hand. "I was out north of town on a job," he muttered. "Got stuck in rodeo traffic, then had a flat." He stuffed the rag into the back pocket of his jeans. "If I'd been here, you wouldn't have stuck another needle in him."

Grant leaned in. "Your father gave us permission to take his blood. That's all we needed."

Spider sneered. "You going to arrest me or not?"

Grant let out a slow breath. He could make an arrest, haul Jason, aka Spider, to McAlester PD, then have one of the locals do the paperwork. That would take a couple of hours. Spider would probably bond out long before he and Sky got back to Oklahoma City.

"Not this time."

Spider pushed away from the cruiser. Passing by Sky without a look, he limped along the shade-covered sidewalk toward the prison's front doors.

As the adrenaline drained out of him, Grant scrubbed a palm over his face, then turned to Sky. "You're sure he didn't hurt you?"

"I'm sure."

"You want to go back inside and wash the grease off your hands?"

Her gaze tracked Spider until he pulled open the prison's front door and disappeared inside. "I think we've had enough of the Whitebears for one day, and vice versa." She looked back at Grant. "I'll wash my hands when we stop for something to drink."

Nodding, he gave her a long, silent inspection. His heart wasn't safe around her. And something was keeping Sky from letting him get close to hers. Maybe she never would.

His mood darkened like storm clouds.

"We'll get the drinks to go." He turned and stabbed a

key into the lock on the cruiser's door. "After that, I'll take
you back to the lab."

He hadn't spoken more than a few words since they'd
left the prison. With fingers of tension curling around her
stomach, Sky glanced across the cruiser's front seat.
Grant's mouth was set, his eyes narrowed behind the lenses
of his sunglasses. He had one arm propped against the window; the other hand gripped the steering wheel tight
enough to make the veins on the back of his hand strain
against his tanned flesh.

Easing out a quiet sigh, she sipped soda through a straw
and shifted her gaze out the passenger window, taking little
notice of the scenery blipping by as the cruiser headed west
on Interstate 40. At the café where they'd stopped, she had
washed the grease off her hands while Grant waited in a
line of rodeo fans for a waitress to bag two sodas. Now, as
the cruiser sped west out of McAlester, Sky wondered if
they would make the entire four-hour drive back to
Oklahoma City in the uneasy silence that hung around
them.

Probably best if they did, she decided, feeling a sense of
resignation sliding through the aching fatigue that held her
in its grip. She and Grant had said everything there was to
say, outside the prison before Jason Whitebear showed up.

The cool soda she sipped did little to ease the dry throat
that came with the memory of how, when Whitebear
grabbed her hand, Grant's eyes had turned to glass. The
kind of glass that left jagged gashes on flesh. For the first
time she had seen the inner core of hard, immovable
strength behind Grant's outer, almost careless self-ease.

A protector. Although she had the training to defend herself, inside her stirred a basic, instinctive need for a man
who could be counted on to keep her safe. A white knight

to shield her. A defender. What woman didn't want a man who fit that bill?

And that was the problem, Sky acknowledged. She wanted what she couldn't have.

Without warning, tears welled up and she blinked them furiously away. In her mind, she replayed Grant's assurances that he would give her the care and time she needed. He would wait until she was ready. His words had simply melted her heart...then broken it.

He could give her all the time and care in the world, but that wouldn't change things. Six months in therapy with Dr. Mirren hadn't altered anything. Not really. Nothing, Sky was now convinced, would keep the demon inside her at bay, except silence. If she didn't talk about the rape, didn't stir things up further, the horrifying nightmare would subside—she had to believe that. Had to believe that the monster would creep back into her subconscious where it had lurked for the past nine years.

Then maybe she could sleep. And begin thinking again with some sort of clarity.

Sliding her gaze sideways, she studied Grant's face. In the deepening afternoon shadows, his profile was a study of sharp lines and determined angles. Her chest ached with the knowledge that his need for her to open up, to let him into her life was the one thing she couldn't give. Didn't dare try to give.

Resting her head back against the upholstered seat, she closed her eyes. In less than four hours she'd be back in the controlled confines of her lab. Safe and shielded. For the past nine years, work had been her haven, her solace. It was all she needed.

It would have to be.

A few minutes later, the loud sputter of the engine had

her eyelids popping open. The cruiser coughed, jerked, then shimmied.

Grant swore viciously, eased out of traffic and steered the wheezing cruiser to the highway's shoulder. The engine heaved one last, gripping shudder then died.

"Out of gas?" Sky hazarded.

"We've got half a tank." Scowling, Grant turned the key, pumped the pedal and was rewarded with a metallic grinding that made Sky wince.

"Should have driven my Porsche," he muttered. Seconds later, he shoved open the door, climbed out, then slammed the door behind him for good measure.

"Hafta' say you folks are lucky."

Grant shot a dark look at the man steering the wrecker through the thickening traffic on McAlester's main street. Sky sat between him and the driver, her evidence kit and purse piled in her lap, her gaze focused straight ahead out the windshield that displayed the smashed remains of an uncountable number of bugs.

Without the benefit of air-conditioning, the inside of the wrecker felt like a sauna. Grant set his jaw at the feel of sweat trickling down his spine, pooling at the small of his back. The immediate prospect of one of the spongy springs in the seat beneath him shooting up through his backside did nothing to lighten his mood. Nor did Sky's soft, subtle scent that wafted on the heated air, creeping into his senses and tightening his gut.

"How is it you think we're lucky?" he ground out.

The driver shot him a mile-wide, nicotine-stained grin. "The police dispatcher's call came through just as I was closin' shop." He nodded at the line of traffic out the windshield. "Rodeo starts this evening."

"Yeah." Grant fisted his hands against his thighs. "Just

drop us off at the nearest garage so someone can take a look at the car…Hank,'' he added, noting the name on the front of the worn ball cap from which peeked strands of wiry gray hair.

"Well, now, I can drop you and your car off at Wade's Garage,'' Hank drawled, using the tip of his thumb to shove up the cap's brim. "Ain't gonna do you or your car much good, though.''

"Closed for the rodeo?'' Grant speculated.

"Yep. Until first thing in the morning. This here's the first night of the rodeo. Nobody wants to miss the fun.''

Frustration churned in Grant's stomach. "I don't guess there's another garage open?''

"Nope. Like I said, nobody wants to miss the fun.''

Grant shoved a hand through his sweat-dampened hair. How much better could this get? He'd already used his cell phone to call his office. Lieutenant Ryan had advised that there was no way the city would pay to send a wrecker on a two-way run that would take over eight hours. Not unless a vehicle was beyond repair. Grant twisted in his seat, shot a killing look at the hulk of city-issue scrap metal winched behind the wrecker.

"Here's the deal, Hank. I'll pay you to drive us and the car to Oklahoma City.'' Out of the corner of his eye, he saw Sky slide him a hopeful look.

"Well, I might've just taken you up on that, but I promised the wife I'd take her and the kids to the rodeo.'' Hank raised a bony shoulder. "It's the first night, you know.''

"I heard that somewhere.'' Grant took a deep breath, which only pulled more of Sky's scent into his lungs. "Any other wreckers in town?''

"Nope. I've got me a monopoly on the service.''

"If that's the case, we'll need a place to stay.'' He and

Sky were sitting so close, there was no way Grant could have missed her body's instant stiffening.

"Stay?" she asked. "We have to spend the night here?"

"No, Milano, we'll start back," he stated, jerking his thumb toward the wrecker's back window. "Just as soon as you pop the hood on the cruiser and fix whatever the hell's wrong."

She shoved her wire-rims higher up on her nose. "I don't know anything about cars."

Grant scowled at the smudges of grease that had appeared on the sleeve of his linen shirt after he'd spent thirty futile minutes fiddling with the cruiser's dead engine. "And I don't know enough about them to figure out what's wrong with that piece of junk. So we're stuck here until Wade— who's making merry at the rodeo's opening night—shows up at his garage in the morning."

"Well, that's settled," Hank mused, rubbing his grizzled chin. "Seein' as how this is you folks' lucky day, I don't expect you'll have to spend the night in your car."

Sky jerked her head his way and gaped. "In the car?"

"Rodeo." Hank nodded toward the other side of the street where three cars vied for one parking space. "Motels're booked. But I know one that's got a room you could rent. All I gotta do is convince my cousin Delbert that you're not gonna raise a fuss about a little musty smell and bare floors."

"A room?" Sky asked. "*One* room?"

The thread of unsteadiness in her voice had Grant biting back a curse. He thought without smugness of the women who regularly tossed offers at him to join them in bed. The one woman he wanted to spend time with panicked at the thought of being in the same room with him.

Hank shot her a speculative look. "Well, Del's got two rooms at his place, if that's what you folks want."

"It is." Propping an arm on the dash, Grant leaned as far forward in the seat as the spongy springs allowed. "If everything else is booked, how come Del has two vacant rooms?"

"Well, there's a story there," Hank stated, then dove into a lengthy tale of exploding water pipes, dissolving Sheetrock and soggy carpet. "Me 'n' Del redid the Sheetrock last night. Plan to tape and paint the walls tomorrow. Some hitch came up about gettin' the carpet steamed and stretched. Won't be done for a day or two. Del wasn't happy when he heard that. He was hopin' to rent out both rooms during the rodeo."

Sky nodded. "You'll tell him it doesn't matter to us, right? We won't complain about unpainted walls and bare floors."

Hank sent her a wink. "Leave Del to me, ma'am. He's got two hefty teenage boys who'll have the furniture back in those rooms in no time."

Two hours later, Sky sat in a booth at Darcy's Diner, the evidence kit on the seat beside her and a piece of warm apple pie in front of her. The big red plastic cup that held the lemonade she'd ordered with her dinner was half-empty, a ring of sweat pooling on the paper place mat beneath it.

Across from her, Grant leaned back in the booth, his expression closed, his gray eyes unreadable as he worked through his second beer. The sleeves of his linen shirt were rolled up, emphasizing tanned forearms with corded muscles. Seconds before, he'd shoved his fingers through his sandy hair, leaving it appealingly rumpled.

Because her fingers itched to smooth that sandy thickness, Sky balled her hands into her lap. She kept her gaze on her pie and off of the rodeo fans who packed every table, booth and stool at the counter. She'd long ago had her fill of the admiring looks Grant had garnered from every female in the place.

She had no right to feel that way, she reminded herself as despair pressed against her heart. She and Grant had no future because her past wouldn't let her go. It was as simple as that. And each moment she spent in his presence, all the more devastating.

She checked the cat-shaped clock with moving eyes and shifting tail that hung over the diner's big, wide-pane front window. By now, the motel owner's two hefty sons would have finished lugging furniture into the rooms she and Grant had rented after a quick glance inside. Hank, the wrecker driver, had made short work of convincing his cousin Delbert that the "police folks" from Oklahoma City wouldn't complain about carpetless floors and unpainted walls. With that assurance, Delbert had happily swiped Grant's gold credit card through the reader.

Sky raised her glass and sipped the tart lemonade. She knew she should suggest they go back to the motel and lock themselves in their separate rooms. Still, she lingered over her half-eaten pie. Just a few more minutes, she thought, and considered dropping a quarter into the small jukebox at the booth and punching in the three selections it would buy her. Anything would be better than the strained silence that had hung between them since they'd left the prison.

"Need some change?"

She looked away from the jukebox to find Grant studying her with an intensity that made her toes curl. "I guess the noise level in here is already high enough," she said over the clink of glassware and heady din of conversation.

Behind his sandy lashes, his dove-gray eyes did a slow sweep of the crowded diner that sported yellowed linoleum tiles, red vinyl booths and homemade pies in a three-tiered stand on one end of the counter. "Yeah."

Sky's throat ached. Although she had little appetite, she lifted her fork and sliced off a bite of pie. "I'd forgotten about Jason Whitebear."

Grant shot her a look at the change of subject. "Jason, aka Spider, was at his dad's trial every day," Grant finally stated, then took a sip of his beer. "Sam ran the background check on him. I plan to go back to the file and take a look at it."

Sky tilted her head. "Does Jason have a record?"

"Nothing serious, or Sam would have done more checking on him."

"Jason wasn't happy about my taking another blood sample."

"On that point we agree."

Ignoring the dry edge in Grant's voice, she took another bite of pie. "I've been trying to put myself in his place. Wondering how I would feel if it were my father on death row and some chemist showed up to stab a needle into his vein."

Grant shifted, settled back into the seat. "How would you feel?"

"If I thought it would help my father's situation, relief."

"And if you suspected the cops were there to set him up to take the fall for some other crime?"

"I'd be furious, just like Jason."

"The question is," Grant began, idly tracing an index finger along the rim of his glass, "why would we try to set up someone already on death row? What would be the point?"

Sky picked up her glass, swirled her lemonade and felt her nerves begin to calm. The case was common ground. Something she and Grant could discuss without emotion getting in the way. "Like Jason said, we want to clear an old case by hanging the blame on his father."

"That's lame." Grant angled his head. "Why do you think he made a grab for your evidence kit?"

Sky glanced down at the plastic case on the seat beside her. "He doesn't know we now transfer collected blood onto cards and work from a dried sample. He thinks Ellis's blood is still in a vial, which would break if I dropped the kit and contaminate the sample so it couldn't be used."

"Exactly. Why?"

"For the principle of it?" Sky ventured. "Jason thinks we're harassing Ellis, so he wants to harass us."

"Could be."

Just then, the middle-age waitress with blond hair teased into a severe beehive appeared beside the booth. A round, laminated button pinned to her frilly white blouse urged them to Attend The McAlester Prison Rodeo.

"Enjoy your meal?" she asked automatically. Without waiting for a response, she ripped off the check from her pad, slipped it onto the table near Grant, then hurried off to see to other customers.

Grant took the check, raising a hand in a "Don't argue" gesture when Sky reached for her purse.

"I owe you for my motel room and now this meal," she stated, watching him pull his money clip out of his pocket.

"Forget it." Eyeing her, he slid a few bills onto the table.

Sky shifted her shoulders. "When we get back, I'll do the paperwork so the department will reimburse—"

"You have a crumb on your lip."

"Oh." She reached for her napkin.

"Let me," he said softly.

When he reached across the table, the pad of his thumb hovered at the corner of her mouth. Hours...or maybe seconds later, his thumb did a slow, lazy sweep across the curve of her bottom lip.

Sky's breath froze in her lungs while her heart bounded straight into her throat, then back-flipped.

His fingers curved. With infinite gentleness they cupped her chin as his thumb continued its seductive trace of her mouth.

Desire pooled, thickening round her like a gossamer spider's web.

She knew she should pull back. Knew she should shove his hand away. Still, she sat there, staring into the depths of his gray eyes while the noise of the diner faded into nothingness. Every thought, every feeling, every need focused on his touch. Her lips parted. The warm, musky taste of his flesh flooded her senses. Deep inside her, heat spiraled, stirring a deep-seated, basic physical need. She wanted to touch. Wanted to feel. Wanted *him*.

Oh, how she wanted.

She couldn't, she reminded herself, trying to think past the hard, thick throbbing of her pulse. Couldn't chance intimacy. Couldn't risk again stepping into Grant's arms, then falling to pieces when panic clawed through her. She couldn't. *Wouldn't*.

But, oh, how she wanted.

She jolted when he released her chin, breaking the spell. Studying her with a thorough, unapologetic intensity, he held up his thumb for her inspection. "Got it," he said quietly.

With her blood still swimming in her head, Sky slid the tip of her tongue across lips that seemed to have burst into flame. "It?"

"The crumb." His mouth tightened. "Don't ever play poker, Sky. Your eyes mirror your thoughts."

Heat ricocheted into her cheeks. "I..." Her heart was hammering too fast to allow her to think, much less speak.

He rose, gazed down at her. "Ready?"

Her hand trembling, she grabbed the evidence kit, then slid out of the booth. Her legs weren't quite steady. "I'm going to take a shower, then turn in." It took every ounce of effort to keep her voice even.

He raised an eyebrow. "It's barely seven o'clock."

"I know." If he could stir her by a mere light touch when they were in a diner full of people, she was well aware of what might happen if they wound up alone. "It's been a long day."

"That's another point we agree on."

As they wove their way through a maze of tables and milling customers, Sky tried not to notice all the appreciative female gazes glued to Grant's backside.

She wanted him.

Grant stood in the motel's parking lot, staring through his sunglasses at the door Sky had closed—*and bolted*—seconds before. The next instant, the air-conditioning unit that poked out beneath the room's front window churned on.

He shoved his hands into his pockets and scowled. Back in the diner, he hadn't intended to touch her. Hadn't meant to slide that crumb from her lip. Her mouth had been ripe and full and naked and too tempting not to touch. In that brief, heart-stopping instant when he'd indulged himself with a slow trace of her lips, he had watched color flood her cheeks and her eyes go wide and smoky with desire. She wanted him, yet she was doing everything in her power to deny that emotion.

Muttering an oath, he turned away from the bolted door. Instead of heading to the room next to Sky's, he started across the black-topped parking lot that, even with the sun slipping toward the horizon, exhaled the searing heat of the day. Since he was without a car, the minimart on the other side of Main Street would have to do as a place to get a couple of toothbrushes, toothpaste and a razor. Grant added a paperback to his mental list, knowing he had a long, sleepless night ahead of him. And while he was shopping, he would do his damnedest to decide what to do about the fact that the woman he wanted in his life climbed the walls whenever he got near.

All of his senses told him it was more than just the rape that had put the recent tormented look in Sky's eyes. Something more.

At the edge of the street, he waited for a break in the traffic, then jogged to the other side through a plume of heated road dust.

It had been his insatiable curiosity and boundless patience that had helped land him in Homicide. Sometimes a part of the job was waiting for a killer to make a mistake. Grant knew how to watch and listen and wait. He could also be relentless when he went after something he wanted.

The something he wanted now was a chance at the relationship that had barely gotten started six months ago before Sky ended it.

Pulling open the door of the minimart, Grant gave thanks for the blast of cool air that greeted him. Deep in thought, he walked down an aisle where cans of bean dip nestled beside rolls of antacids. He knew in order to get to that relationship, he had to peel away the defensive layers Sky had built around herself. Get to the heart of her secrets. He would, he resolved. No matter what it took, no matter how long, he would get there.

What Sky had yet to understand was that this time, things

were different. This time, he had no intention of letting her go.

Fifteen minutes later, Grant strode back toward the motel, his purchases in the plastic sack dangling from his fingertips. The heated evening air had sweat trickling down his back as he walked past a dozen closed numbered doors. He turned a corner and headed down the shaded walkway that led to the far end of the motel. When Sky's room came into view, the sweat against Grant's flesh turned to ice. His heart shot into his throat.

The drapes inside Sky's room billowed in scarlet tongues of flames that licked the inside of the wide window. Dark gray smoke swirled behind the flames, plumed from beneath the door.

Grant couldn't stop the terror from singing in his head. "Sky!"

Tossing aside the plastic sack, he smashed his shoulder against the locked door.

Chapter 6

Grant yelled Sky's name over and over as he slammed his shoulder against the motel room door. From somewhere down the walkway, a man hollered.

"Fire! Get help!" Grant shouted just as the door gave way beneath the brute force of his weight. Black, acrid smoke billowed out as he dashed inside.

"Sky!"

She had to be all right, he thought frantically, his gaze sweeping the small room from wall to wall. He had one moment of unspeakable horror when he saw that flames had already engulfed the mattress. *She's not there,* he told himself, forcing control back in place. She wasn't anywhere in the room, he realized the next instant. Nor was her evidence kit which, due to chain-of-custody requirements, she kept with her at all times when the kit contained evidence.

Eyes slitted, forearm pressed against his mouth and nose, he moved past the bed and small nightstand that flames had leapt onto. The thin wedge of light beneath the bathroom door drew him like a beacon of hope.

"Sky!"

When he flung open the door, a burst of steamy air hit his face. The movement he spied behind the pink plastic shower curtain sent relief sweeping through him.

"Fire!" he shouted over the rush of water. Out of the corner of his eye he saw her purse and the evidence kit sitting beside the sink. He grabbed a towel off the room's only rod, then whipped back the shower curtain.

His mind had time to register inviting curves and yards of water-slicked flesh before Sky's bare foot slammed squarely into his chest. The blow sent him stumbling backward, his leather soles nearly going out from under him on the floor's smooth tiles. The momentum from the blow smashed him into the wall; the towel rod bit into his back as his breath escaped from his lungs in a grunting rush.

"Grant...?" Face red, eyes wide, Sky clutched the pink curtain around her like a protective shield while gaping at him through rivulets of water and wet hair.

"This place is on fire!" He panted the warning past the tight throb in his chest while sweeping one hand toward the door where smoke rolled in to join the shower's steam. Pushing off the wall, he held the towel spread out in front of him as he rushed toward her. "We've got to get out of here."

"I need my clothes," she sputtered when he wrapped the towel around her and the shower curtain, then swept her into his arms.

"Were they on the bed?"

"Yes."

"They're toast."

When he spun around, the curtain ripped from the rod.

Over the rush of water and hiss of flames, Grant heard the little metal hooks jingling against the rod.

"Wait!" Sky leaned, nearly sending him off balance on the now-wet tiles when she grabbed the evidence kit and her purse, then clutched them to her chest.

He bolted for the door, cognizant now of the wail of sirens. In the outer room, flames danced across the bed and the few pieces of furniture, lending an eerie orange sheen to the scalding air.

Sky gave a compulsive jerk as if she'd been singed by the flames. "Dear Lord," she murmured, tucking herself closer to his chest.

Grant tightened his arms around her. As he moved, thick smoke swirled, stinging his eyes, piercing his lungs.

Seconds later he darted out the door into a blessed spray of water.

Firefighters continued muscling equipment off a fire engine as he moved swiftly to the outer edges of the parking lot where a police car, an ambulance and sightseers crowded. Farther off, the traffic on Main Street had come to a standstill. Some drivers stood beside their idling cars, watching the drama unfold.

Sky craned her neck to get a look at what had been her room. "I don't...believe this," she said, her uneven words filled with dismay. "I didn't even smell smoke...when I was in the shower. Didn't hear... Grant, I..." She shivered. "I don't..."

"You're okay. Everything's okay." The soothing words were meant to comfort, but saying them didn't make his hands any steadier. He shut his eyes against the knowledge of how close he'd come to losing her. Too close.

A tall, sandy-haired man wearing a white shirt sporting an ambulance company logo jogged over. "You folks hurt?'' he asked, transferring a bright red rescue equipment box from one hand to the other.

Grant inched his head back to get a good look at Sky. Her long, dark hair was slicked off her face, making her blue eyes look extraordinarily wide, her cheeks pale. He was deliriously relieved that he saw no signs of shock. Still, that didn't mean the enormity of what she had survived wouldn't avalanche on her in a few minutes.

''Why don't you let him check you out?'' he suggested quietly.

''No.'' Gripping the evidence kit and her purse, she shook her head. ''No EMT, doctor or hospital. I'm fine, Grant. Just fine.''

''You sure about that, ma'am?'' Narrowing his eyes, the EMT peered at her face. ''Wouldn't take me no time at all to check your vitals.''

''No, thanks. I'm okay.''

Lifting a shoulder, Grant met the man's gaze while managing to take his first full breath since he'd spotted the flames in Sky's room. ''I'll keep a close eye on her.''

''We'll be here a while longer,'' the EMT advised. ''Holler if you need me,'' he said, then headed back toward the ambulance.

''I'm okay,'' Sky repeated over the thrumming of the fire engine's pump. ''Really.''

''Glad to hear it.'' Grant pressed a kiss against her damp hair, pulling in the twin scents of shampoo and smoke. ''You gave me a scare. A big one.'' Now that the adrenaline had begun to seep out of him, he was aware of the soft, damp thigh against his arm, the nearness of the bare throat and shoulders where water still beaded.

''Grant?''

He pulled his gaze from her glistening flesh. ''What?''

"You saved me," she said, the solemn tone in her voice matching the look in her eyes. "You saved my life."

He angled his chin, making a snap decision on the best way to remove the strain from her face. "You know, Milano, that's a first for me."

"The first time you've saved someone's life?"

He grinned. "First time I've ever saved a woman wrapped in a shower curtain the color of a plastic yard flamingo."

"Oh." She looked down, her face turning as pink as the curtain. "I need some clothes."

"I'd say that's an accurate statement," he said, then headed across the parking lot.

"Where are we going?"

"To the motel's office. Delbert might have some clothes to loan you."

Sky blinked. "If there's a Mrs. Delbert, her clothes would probably fit me better."

"No luck," Grant said as they neared the office. "When we checked in, Delbert mentioned he's a widower. But I caught a glimpse of his teenage daughter. She's about the same size as you."

Grant used a shoulder to shove through the office door into the small lobby that had room for only a few serviceable chairs and tables. The hatch at one end of the registration counter was raised, as if whoever had been on duty had rushed out in a hurry.

"Delbert's probably outside in the crowd of bystanders watching your room burn," Grant commented.

Gripping the curtain, her purse and evidence kit against her breasts, Sky began to squirm. "You don't need to keep carrying me around. Put me down so I can look for some clothes."

"Yes, ma'am." Grinning, he set her gently on her feet.

In the office's dim light, he gave her a considering once-over. "You know, Milano, you look pretty good the way you are."

She tossed her long damp hair back. "Half-drowned and wearing a shower curtain?" she asked, a line forming between her eyebrows.

A sudden chill, very brief but very real, ran through Grant's blood as he brushed a fingertip down her cheek. His grin faded.

He'd come so close to losing her.

"Alive," he managed after a moment. A tremor worked its way into his heart, tightening his chest. He realized then that his feelings for her went far deeper than he'd been willing to admit. How deep, he wasn't sure. All he knew was that he would do whatever it took to keep her in his life.

"You look real good alive," he stated softly, then wrapped an arm around her shoulders and gathered her close.

Two hours later, Sky sat on the edge of Grant's bed, staring out the window of his motel room. It was dark now; the lights that dotted the parking lot reflected off the water from the fire hoses still pooled on the pavement. Grant stood beneath one of those lights with the fire chief and Delbert, the motel owner, who looked decidedly harassed.

He had every right, Sky thought. The room she'd rented had been reduced to a charred, sour-smelling mess that was now cordoned off with yellow tape. With little effort, the fire chief had determined that a short in the air conditioner, which Sky had switched on moments before taking her shower, had caused the blaze.

Her gaze lowered to the purring air-conditioning unit beneath the window in front of her. A shiver ran through her and she wrapped her arms around her waist.

Dressed the way she was, it was no surprise she had goose bumps. With all of the stores closed for the rodeo, she'd been grateful when Delbert's teenage daughter had offered to lend her some clothes. That gratitude transformed to heated embarrassment when Sky got a look at herself in the bathroom mirror and saw how snug the cutoffs and white halter top fit. The appreciative male glances she'd garnered from firefighters, cops and Grant had notched up her discomfort.

Grant. What was she going to do about Grant?

Her gaze shifted back to where he stood, deep in conversation with the other two men. The murky spill of light from overhead turned his tall, lean torso into an alluring arrangement of masculine planes and shadows.

She could love him. The thought had her stomach quivering. No, she couldn't, she corrected, as an ache settled in her heart. Her past stood in the way. Despite six months of therapy, regardless of Dr. Mirren's assurances that she would again someday be ready to enter into a physical relationship, Sky knew the truth. The terrorizing memories inside her wouldn't let go.

She closed her eyes against a longing so deep, it cut into her soul. All she had to do was rest her head on Grant's shoulder, and his arms would slide around her to hold, to comfort. She only had to make the move.

But she couldn't.

The tears she'd fought all day swam dangerously close to the surface. She pulled off her glasses, placed them on the nightstand, then settled back against the bed's headboard and pressed her fingers to her eyes.

Why had fate, in the form of a few drops of blood, thrown her and Grant back together? She thought of Ellis

Whitebear's dried blood sample now stored in her evidence kit. If a killer hadn't left a bandage at a recent crime scene, if she hadn't made a possible mistake in her lab on a two-year-old case, she and Grant never would have made this morning's trip to the state penitentiary. And she wouldn't now be propped up in his bed with her nerves stretched razor-sharp.

A mind-numbing fatigue settled over her and she struggled to hold it back. She desperately needed rest. Yet she didn't dare go to sleep, not tonight. Just the thought of fighting her way out of the tortuous nightmare in Grant's presence sent another chill through her. She leaned her head against the headboard and stared up at the ceiling. If she stayed awake, there was no danger of the monster roaring to life. No chance her subconscious would conjure up the shadowy form that had loomed over her in the dark all those years ago. Or the scent of cologne she would carry with her to the grave. Or the blade that had pierced her flesh. Or the terror.

None of those things would happen, as long as she stayed awake.

She was asleep when Grant unlocked the door to the motel room a half hour later. A fitful sleep, he decided as he stood at the edge of the bed and gazed down at her. She was lying on her side, one hand fisted against the pillow. In the soft glow of the bedside lamp, her skin looked stunningly pale against the rumpled white sheet that had slid down to her waist. When her head jerked, then turned, her long, dark hair spread against the pillow like a pool of rich mink.

He curled his hands against his thighs while he waited for the need that clawed in his stomach to ease. Everything in his life had come easy for him, except this one woman.

And he was at a loss to know what to do about her. He wanted her to trust him. Wanted her to open her heart to him. He knew none of that was going to happen, not when she wouldn't even tell him what it was that put the shadows under her eyes and turned her sleep so fitful.

Letting out a long breath, he clicked off the bedside lamp, turned and walked into the bathroom. Somehow, some way he would reach her. No matter how long it took, he would get through that wall.

He had to.

Light glinted in a shimmering arc as the blade swept in front of Sky's eyes.

"No!" The word ripped from her throat. Bolting upright, she flailed blindly at the dark surrounding her.

"No!" In terrorized panic she scrambled onto her knees, her legs tangling in the sheet and bedspread as she sucked in air to scream.

"Sky." The deep male voice came from a space just inches away. So close. *Too close.*

"No!" She lashed out wildly with her fists against the hands that settled on her shoulders.

"Sky, it's Grant. Sky, look at me."

Still caught in the terrorizing grip of the nightmare, she saw only the sharp, vicious blade. "No!"

"Look at me." He cupped his palm to her cheek as she cowered against the headboard. "You had a nightmare." His voice was gentle, but firm enough to pull her out of the dark, suffocating pit. "You're okay now."

"Grant?" Her heart hammered against her ribs in fast, hard blows; her lungs burned and her face was wet with sweat and tears. She was afraid to move for fear she would crack and shatter into a dozen pieces.

"You're okay." The mattress shifted with his weight when he settled beside her.

Dim light from the bathroom's half-open door wedged across the bed. Blinking, she focused on Grant's face, saw the concern in his gray eyes, the deep lines at the corners of his mouth.

Choking back a sob, she shoved her damp hair away from her face with trembling hands. "Oh, God." The pressure in her chest was unbearable. "I can't... God, Grant."

"Let me hold you."

She shuddered once, then curved into him when he inched her forward. His arms came around her in a firm, comforting embrace. Instinctively she turned her face into his throat while the heat of his body seeped into her frozen flesh.

"This is it, isn't it?" He pressed a kiss against her hair. "This nightmare. It's the thing you've been dealing with."

"Yes." She felt a wave of nausea rising from within, and gulped in huge breaths to hold it back.

"Why couldn't you tell me?"

"It was more than just that tonight," she blurted, and found that just saying the words made her already-raw throat ache. "I need... Could I have some water?"

"Sure." He tipped her head back to study her face with quiet intensity before he rose. "Do you want more light?" he asked, inclining his head toward the lamp at the side of the bed.

"No." From experience, she knew it would take time for color to seep back into her face and the glassy fright to fade from her eyes. She didn't want him to see her like this. "The bathroom light is fine."

"Okay. I'll be right back."

The skimpy cutoffs and halter top did nothing to dispel the desperate cold that had settled inside her. She brought her knees up close to her chest and wrapped her arms around her legs. Taking long, even breaths, she concentrated on the sound of running water.

"Here's your water," Grant said seconds later.

"Thanks." She was trembling so badly that she used both hands to reach for the glass.

Without comment, Grant cupped his fingers around hers and lifted the glass to her lips. "You're freezing."

"I'm warming up." The water eased the ache in her throat. "Thanks."

"You don't have to thank me." He set the glass on the nightstand, unbuttoned his shirt and shrugged it off. "This will help warm you up," he said. "Lean forward."

Too shaky to protest, Sky did as instructed, slipping her arms into the sleeves when he settled the shirt around her shoulders. The linen held the warmth of his body, the calm, soothing scent of his cologne. The fist that had settled in her chest loosened its hold by one notch.

"Why couldn't you tell me?" Grant asked, resettling onto the edge of the bed. "Why couldn't you tell me about the nightmares?"

"Nightmare. Just one." She clenched her hands in her lap. "The same one. Always the same."

"About the rape?"

"Yes." Without warning, the terror bubbled back into her brain. Gritting her teeth to hold back a whimper, she forced herself to concentrate on the hard, shadowed lines of Grant's face. "It was… Tonight it was more. It was a flashback. I was there. *He* was there." Something sharp and cold clawed at her stomach. "It was real. Too real."

"You can't keep this inside you." Grant settled his hands around her clenched fists. "I want to help you, but I can't unless I know what you're dealing with. Unless you tell me—"

"I have to tell you." The terror that had swept her into a black pit while she'd slept sounded in her voice. "I have to get it out of me, I have to get him out of me."

"You're safe." Grant stroked his thumb across her knuckles. "I won't let anything or anyone hurt you."

"I know." She wouldn't tell him that even now she had the sensation of a hand clamping brutally over her mouth. "I can't breathe here," she said, pulling from his grip. "I need to get up for a minute."

"All right."

She caught the furrow of his brow as she slid her legs from the tangled bed linen and rose. She paced to the door, then back again, the bare floor cool beneath her feet. Her stomach muscles trembled as she forced her mind back to that night over nine years ago.

"It happened during my senior year of college. His name was Kirk Adams. He was a star wrestler. Senior class president."

She didn't have to close her eyes to picture the athlete's handsome face with its strong, finely drawn features and dark eyes.

"Each time I saw him on campus he had a different girl on his arm," she continued after a moment. "Never the same girl."

"How well did you know him?"

Sky paused in her pacing to turn and face the bed where Grant had remained seated. In the dim light coming from the bathroom his eyes were intense, unwavering.

"Not well. He was a pharmacy major. We took the same chemistry class, and the professor paired us on a lab project. Adams asked me out a couple of times. I said no." She dragged the heel of her palm across her forehead. "He was too smug, too sure of himself. Something told me to keep my distance."

"That personality type doesn't take rejection well."

"You're right, he didn't." Sky felt a river of ice creep up her spine. "Although I didn't know that about him because he didn't make a big deal of my turning him down." She resumed pacing from one wall to the other, then back again. "One Saturday night, a girlfriend asked me to go to a party at her boyfriend's fraternity house. She and I had been studying most of the day and a break sounded good. One hour wouldn't hurt, I told myself. One drink wouldn't hurt. Some people I knew would be at the party so it was safer than going to a bar." She'd been wrong. "I thought it was safe."

"Adams showed up at the party?" Grant prompted when she remained silent.

"Yes. I didn't know he belonged to that fraternity until he walked up, handed me a fresh drink and said he had some questions about our lab project. He was smiling, polite. We talked about fifteen minutes, then he excused himself. A few minutes later I started feeling woozy."

Her legs suddenly shaky, Sky settled into the room's lone chair and met Grant's gaze across the twisted span of sheet and bedspread.

"At first I just felt lightheaded, and thought all the studying I'd done had gotten to me. I figured if I got some fresh air I'd be okay. I looked for my girlfriend to tell her I'd wait for her in her car, but there were too many people and I couldn't find her. By then I was really dizzy. I stumbled into some guy and spilled his drink all over me." She stared down at her hands, fisted in her lap. She could still smell it, the sickening stench of Jack Daniel's that had soaked the front of her dress. "I know he thought I was drunk. When I tried to tell him I was sorry, I couldn't get the words out. My brain wouldn't send the right message.

That's when I knew Adams had put something in my drink.''

"A pharmacy major," Grant said quietly. "Easy for someone with his knowledge to know what to use."

Looking up, she nodded. "Too easy." She swallowed hard, forced herself to continue. "When I got outside, everything was tilting—the house, the parking lot, the cars. I kept thinking if I could just lie down, the dizziness would pass. Right when I got to my girlfriend's car, a hand came from behind me, clamped over my mouth and jerked me off my feet.'' A trembling breath escaped her lips. "I tried to scream, but nothing would come out. Tried to get away. He was too big, too strong. He shoved me into the back of a dark-colored van, then slammed the door shut."

She closed her eyes against the haunting memories. "Either the van was the kind with no windows in the back, or it had curtains, because inside it was pitch-black. By then the drug had wiped out my equilibrium and I couldn't tell which way was up, so I crawled around on my hands and knees. I remember feeling a wool blanket beneath me...."

She raised an unsteady hand to rub at the ache that had settled in her throat. "It was dark. I was so afraid. Terrified. I heard the engine turn over. The van started moving. Then I passed out."

Grant stood abruptly, jammed his hands into the pockets of his slacks, pulled them out again, then crossed to where she sat. The palm he placed against her cheek was gentle, but his eyes resembled steel. "You don't have to finish this."

"Yes, I do." She thought of the vicious edge of reality the flashback had put on the nightmare. "I tried to keep it inside me, but I can't. I can't."

"All right." He sat on the bed inches from her chair, his eyes locked with hers. "Go on."

"When I came to, he was straddling me, ripping at my clothes. I started struggling. He grabbed both of my wrists with one hand and jerked my arms over my head. Then I heard a metallic sound. I didn't know what it was until I felt a blade against my neck."

"A switchblade."

Sky nodded dully. "He pressed the tip in, just enough to make me bleed. He told me if I fought, he would slice my face. I didn't know how to defend myself then. I was so messed up from the drug that even if I had gotten away I couldn't have run far. So I did what he said." She closed her eyes. Remembering was like walking barefoot over hot coals. "I've always wondered what would have happened if I had fought."

"He'd have cut you, maybe killed you." Leaning closer, Grant linked the fingers of one of his hands with hers. "You did the most important thing, Sky. You stayed alive."

"I kept telling myself it wasn't me he was touching." Though she fought to keep her voice calm, it shook as the horror of the night intensified. "Even when it felt like everything inside me was tearing apart, I told myself it wasn't happening to me."

Grant's fingers jerked, then tightened around hers. When he turned his head and stared across the room, she saw the muscle working in his jaw.

"It was so dark, I never saw his face," she continued quietly. "But at one point he lowered his head. That's when I smelled his cologne. It was the same scent Kirk Adams always wore when we worked in the lab. Always. That's how I knew for sure it was him."

Muttering a quiet oath, Grant shifted his gaze back to hers. "During the whole time, you never got a look at his face?"

"No. When he was done, he drove to a secluded part of the campus and told me to get out. He turned off the lights so I couldn't see the license tag when he drove off. Later, a campus cop found me staggering down the middle of the street. My dress was ripped and smelled like a distillery. I was crying, in shock and still so impaired from the drug that I couldn't get out what had happened. I couldn't even tell him my name."

Grant angled his head. She could almost see his mind working behind those sharp gray eyes. "Campus cops aren't the most experienced or professional group around. Because you were staggering and he could smell booze on you, he assumed you were drunk, right?"

"Yes."

"You weren't driving, so he had no reason to do a blood alcohol test."

"He figured I'd been partying with some guy, and when things didn't go his way he'd gotten rough, then ditched me. After the cop put me in his car, I blacked out. He took me to the campus infirmary and told the student nurse on duty that he'd come back to take a report after I sobered up. When I finally came to, the drug had worn off enough for me to tell her I'd been raped. She phoned the doctor on call. He was a new resident on contract to the university who had never taken a vaginal swab for a rape kit before." Sky raised a hand, let it drop back into her lap. "He mishandled the sample and contaminated it."

A grim realization settled in Grant's eyes. "You never saw Adams's face, just smelled his cologne. The worst lawyer on earth could make a joke out of an ID like that in court."

"Things never got that far. The information I gave about the cologne was enough for the police to interview Adams, but not arrest him. He claimed he didn't know anything bout what happened to me after we talked at the party. The police found out one of his fraternity brothers owned a black van that had no windows in the back. It was common knowledge that he always left the keys in the ignition. No one saw the van leave or return to the lot during the party.''

''What about the wool blanket you felt on the van's floor? Did the cops find it?''

''No. The owner said the blanket he always kept in the back had disappeared. He had no idea how long it had been gone.''

Mouth tight, Grant said nothing, just waited for her to continue.

''Adams drove back to the fraternity house after he got rid of me,'' Sky said quietly. ''A girl there admitted to spending the night with him. She'd been partying hard, so she had no idea what time they hooked up. It was her impression that Adams was as drunk as she was.''

''An act to strengthen his alibi,'' Grant said, his voice deathly quiet. ''An inept doctor screwed up whatever evidence was on you. Adams got rid of the blanket from the van and, along with it, more evidence. Since the cops had nothing to compare body samples to, they couldn't get a search warrant to force Adams to give samples. It was your word against his.''

''Yes. It was rough, knowing he was laughing while my entire world crumbled.''

''I wish I had been there to take care of you.'' Grant raised a hand, tucked a wayward strand of hair behind her ear. ''What happened after you found out he was going to walk?''

''The nightmare started.'' She stared down at the hand Grant had linked with hers. Now that she'd told him about the rape, now that she'd gotten it out, she could feel hot tears boiling up inside her. She hadn't cried. In all the time since that terrible night she hadn't allowed herself to cry. She had told herself if she did, she might never stop.

Taking a deep breath, she waited until she steadied. "My family doesn't have a lot of money. I was going to school on a scholarship and working part-time to earn money for expenses. I couldn't afford private counseling. The college had a male therapist on staff whom I could see for free, so I made an appointment. The man had no clue what rape was all about. The first question he asked me was how I provoked the attack. I walked out and never went back."

Grant nodded slowly. "And never dealt with the rape. Then when I touched you, it all came back."

"After the rape, after I knew Adams wasn't going to pay, I handled things the best way I could. I was so afraid, constantly looking over my shoulder, and I hated that. So I took lessons and learned to defend myself. I couldn't do anything about the fact that evidence in my case had been contaminated, but I could do something about other cases. I changed my major from forensic anthropology to forensic chemistry. That meant staying in school two more semesters and taking out some hefty loans, but that was something I had to do."

A tear spilled down her cheek and she swiped it away with an unsteady hand. "But you're right, Grant, I never dealt with the rape itself. I shut myself in a nice, safe lab and told myself my job was the only thing I needed in my life. Then I met you, and you made me want more. I thought I could deal with a relationship. I was wrong. I hurt you. I'm so sorry, Grant. I'm so…"

"Sky—"

"I wouldn't…" Her voice hitched; tears streamed down her cheeks. "Wouldn't…let myself cry. I haven't, not since that night. Not since…'' She broke, simply broke. Covering her face with her hands, she began to sob.

"You need to cry," Grant murmured, and scooped her into his arms. He carried her to the bed, slid onto the mattress and settled back against the headboard with her cradled in his lap.

"Let it out." His voice was as soft as the hand he used to stroke her hair, her cheek. "Let it all out."

He had given her his shirt, so her hot, desperate tears pooled across his bare shoulder. The arms that cradled her were strong, warm and comforting.

"I didn't mean to hurt you," she managed after the tide began to stem.

"I got hurt because you didn't trust me enough to tell me what was wrong."

She raised her head, met his gaze through wet, spiky lashes. "It was me I didn't trust, never you. I had convinced myself I'd dealt with the rape. Then I stepped into your arms and had a panic attack. That's when I knew I hadn't really dealt with anything. I couldn't trust myself not to go to pieces on you again."

"So you walked away."

"I had to." She dropped her gaze. "I called a rape crisis center and they referred me to Dr. Mirren."

"Dr. Mirren?"

"A psychiatrist. She's helped."

"You're still having the nightmare."

"I…" Sky let her voice drift off. "It stopped for years. It came back the other night."

Grant's eyes narrowed. "What night?"

"After I told you that Adams grabbed me from behind. That night." She gave an uncontrollable shudder. "And every night since."

"Which explains why you were climbing the walls when

I drove in from Texas and stopped by your apartment,'' Grant reasoned. ''And because the nightmare returned after so long, you decided we shouldn't be together.''

''I didn't want to chance breaking down on you again. I don't want to hurt you—''

He cupped a finger under her chin, nudged it up until her gaze met his. ''The only way you can hurt me is to lock me out of your life. You matter to me, Sky. Maybe I haven't figured out exactly how much, but you do.''

She lifted her hand, placed her palm against the firm line of his jaw. ''I don't know if I can give you what you need.''

''What I need is you.'' He brushed a light kiss across her lips. ''Giving ourselves a second chance is what matters right now. As long as that's what we both want, everything else is workable.''

She nested her head against his shoulder, drew in his scent and let herself absorb the sensations. It had been so long since she'd felt the comfort of an embrace. So long since she'd been held. *Only you,* she thought as she listened to the steady rhythm of Grant's heart. She knew with unerring certainty he was the only man with whom she would ever feel this sense of trust. The only man.

Tonight she'd done what she had thought impossible. She had told him about the worst experience of her life. A quiet sureness settled over her, and she knew she was close to burying her past. For the first time in years, no shadow hung over her future.

''Our being together,'' she said quietly. ''It's what I want, too, Grant.''

''Then we'll be together.''

For the second time that night, Grant stood beside the bed and watched Sky sleep. She lay in the middle of the mattress, her dark hair tumbling down her back, one well-toned arm stretched across the pillow where he'd lain when she drifted to sleep. He watched her, and felt a kaleidoscope of emotions. Anger. Relief. Horror. They were all there, swirling inside him, as hot as the flames he'd carried her through hours earlier. He could still hear her terrorized scream when she'd jolted out of the nightmare. Still feel the scalding outrage that had built inside him as she related the sick things Kirk Adams had subjected her to.

She'd been drugged. Kidnapped. Raped. She'd endured a degradation so horrific, she'd denied herself the right to cry.

As he gazed down at her face, Grant could find no trace of the vulnerability that had seemed to emanate from her the past few days. Now, a healthy color tinted her cheeks, her breathing was slow, even, relaxed. It was as if by finally telling him what she'd suffered, she'd purged herself of the last vestiges of being a victim.

He wanted to rip Kirk Adams apart.

Grant's hands curled into fists against his thighs. He wanted to get his hands on the sleaze, tear him limb from limb for what he'd done to her. For the things he had stolen from her. From them.

Grant set his jaw. He had been careful to hide the rage that had burned inside him while Sky was awake. The rape wasn't about him, it was about her. He understood that. But after she fell asleep, his real emotions had spewed to the surface, hot and molten. Now that rage had transformed into iced fury.

It was not just the cop in him, but the man who wanted to hunt down the sadistic bastard and dole out the justice Sky had been denied. It would be easy, Grant thought. With the connections available to him, it would take little effort to find Adams. No trouble at all to pay him a visit.

When his clenched hands began to tremble, Grant turned

away from the bed and walked to the room's lone window. There, he parted the curtain and stared out at the sky that the weak light of a new dawn had transformed to pewter.

By telling him her darkest secrets, Sky had given him more than just her absolute trust. She had offered a part of herself that she'd given to no other man. A part that was sacred.

His fingers tightened on the curtain as emotion flooded into his chest. He had thought there was no deeper intimacy than sex that a man and a woman could share. Tonight, Sky had shown him there was. In all but the physical sense, she had become his.

Possessiveness coiled deep within him, a fierce, primitive thing that shocked him with its strength. He had spent the past six months wanting her, aching for her. That they had agreed to give their relationship a second chance should be enough for now. It should be, he knew that.

After what she had told him tonight, he wasn't sure it could be enough.

He'd been a cop a long time. He was rarely surprised, sickened, shocked or saddened by the cases that came across his desk. Still, when the victim was someone he knew and cared about, it made a difference. He cared about Sky. Now that he'd heard the horrific details of what she'd endured, it made a hell of a lot of difference.

Grant stood in silence, staring out at the horizon flooded with the pinks and yellows of a new sunrise. He didn't have to look back across his shoulder to picture his holstered Glock and gold badge that lay side by side on top of the chest of drawers. In the past, he had used the power of both to exact justice.

Kirk Adams was beyond reach of the badge.

Not the Glock.

Grant closed his eyes against a thought so alien that it

sent a black, boiling nausea lurching into his stomach. Better, he thought, to think about consequences. Using the weapon without the badge went against everything he believed. Everything that was right. He knew that. Logically he knew.

Still, in a deep, dark place inside him, he wanted— *needed*— to exact justice for Sky.

It was a need that all of his instincts warned he rid himself of. Completely. Totally.

He just wasn't sure he could.

Chapter 7

Sky woke to the muted sound of running water. Fuzzy-headed, it took her a minute to remember why she was in a room in which an air-conditioning unit chugged softly beneath a window where sunlight slanted through a gap in the curtains. *Grant's motel room.*

Her eyes popped open. Rising on one elbow, she shoved her sleep-tumbled hair out of her face. The running water was the shower, she realized. Grant was in the shower.

Slowly she pushed from beneath the rumpled sheet and bedspread, then propped her back against the plump pillows. Yesterday he had carried her from a burning motel room and saved her life. Last night he had pulled her from the terrorizing grip of the nightmare and saved her in a totally different way.

She'd told him about the rape. Sky nibbled at her bottom lip while the memories of the night swept over her. Grant had listened while she purged her soul of the horror, then he'd held her, rocked her, soothed her. Then she'd fallen into a deep, fathomless sleep that erased the mind-numbing fatigue that had plagued her since the nightmare returned.

The demon would not come back. She knew that as sure as she knew the events of the past twenty-four hours had refocused her life from the path it had taken since the rape. She felt cleansed. Purified. Whole. In control. And no longer afraid.

Healing, Dr. Mirren had said, came in many guises. The psychiatrist was right, Sky thought. It had taken more than just the passage of time for her to heal. She had needed to deal with not only the physical violation, but the emotional one. The healing process had begun six months ago when she started therapy. Last night with Grant she had taken another monumental step.

Sky closed her eyes against the emotion that flooded her chest. Who else but Grant? What other man could she have trusted enough? No one. Only him.

The irony of the thought that followed had her mouth curving. His dead partner had nicknamed him Pretty Boy because of Grant's heart-stopping effect on women. He was a man who would know all the tricks, be adept at every slow, subtle move of seduction. Yet, he had been content to hold her—just hold her—while she fell into an obliterating sleep in his bed. How, she mused, had his ego handled that?

Her quiet thoughts scattered when the bathroom door swung open. A blast of steamy air emerged, along with Grant. Sky's eyes widened when she saw he wore only his pleated linen slacks, and a white hand towel looped around his neck. His wet, sandy hair was slicked back, emphasizing strong cheekbones and the firm angle of his jaw.

She sat motionless on the rumpled bed that was still steeped in shadow while her lips parted and her heart did a slow roll. She didn't need her glasses to make out the broad, muscled chest scattered by gold-tipped hair that veed down the center of his flat stomach then disappeared beneath the waistband of his slacks.

He retrieved his designer watch from the top of the chest of drawers and checked the time. As he slid the band onto his wrist, his gaze flicked to the bed. When he turned toward her, a glint of hard steel disappeared so quickly from his eyes that Sky wondered if she'd imagined it.

"Good morning," he said quietly.

Now that he was facing her, she saw the fatigue in his face, the lines of exhaustion that etched his cheeks and mouth. "Morning. Did you get any sleep?"

He raised a shoulder. "I had some things on my mind to work through." His mouth curved. "You, on the other hand, slept like a rock."

Nodding, she shoved her hair behind her shoulders, and realized for the first time she was still wearing his shirt. She stared down at the hopelessly wrinkled flaps of linen that lapped over her borrowed halter top and cutoffs. "I think we both need a change of clothes."

"While you get cleaned up, I'll check on the cruiser." He walked to the window, spread the curtain and looked out. "If it's ready, I'll pick you up, then we can find a store. We'll get something to eat after that."

The hard, almost unnatural tone in his voice had Sky's spine straightening. "Grant, is something wrong?"

He hesitated for a split second, then turned and met her gaze. His eyes betrayed nothing. "I'm just trying to figure out the fastest way to get back to the city." As he spoke, he pulled the towel from around his neck then lobbed it back into the bathroom. "I'm as anxious as you to find out the DNA results on Whitebear's blood sample."

"Uh-huh." Sky was no longer paying attention to what

he said. Her concentration had centered on the dark bruise that mottled the right side of his chest.

"I kicked you." She scrambled out of bed and walked to where he stood, the movement sending his shirt drooping off one shoulder. "When you ran into the bathroom to save me from the fire, I kicked you against the wall."

His eyebrows rose as he stared down at her. "I nearly wound up on my butt, just like when you flipped me at the gym. You pack one hell of a kick, Milano."

Without knowing she was going to, Sky raised a hand and gently fingered the plum-colored bruise. "I'm sorry I hurt you."

"No harm done." He placed his hand lightly over hers so that her palm rested against the bruise. Beneath her hand, she felt the steady beat of his heart. "One thing's for sure. I don't have to worry about you being able to defend yourself."

"No." Her breathing shallowed as the warmth of his flesh seeped into hers. She became aware of the sinewy strength beneath her fingers, of his heady masculine scent, with undertones of soap from his shower. Her body seemed to soften like hot wax as it responded in ways that were instinctive and fundamentally feminine.

When he tucked a stray wisp of hair behind one of her ears, her throat tightened. "Grant, I..."

"You're not ready, I know."

"I want to be ready." She could feel the cool bare floor beneath her feet, a shivery contrast to the heat flooding her veins. "I want to be."

"When the time's right." He lowered his head, dropped a light kiss against her forehead. "No pressure," he murmured. "Remember, you're calling the shots."

Even after he dropped his hand from hers, she kept her palm against his bruised chest. When no skitter of panic welled up inside her, she released the breath she realized she'd been holding.

"I think maybe it would be okay…"

When her voice drifted off, he angled his chin. "What, Sky? What would be okay?"

"For you to kiss me." This wouldn't be their first, after all. During the short time they'd dated six months before, they had shared a few friendly kisses. It was when their relationship was about to take a long stride past friendly that she'd panicked and fallen apart.

His eyes stayed on hers as he used a fingertip to trace the line of her earlobe, then idly stroke the small gold hoop she wore. "You think a kiss would be okay?"

Her heartbeat thickened when his fingers grazed the side of her throat. She remembered his taste, the dark, male tang of his mouth. Silvery-edged anticipation had her pulse thudding hard and thick at the base of her throat. "Yes, I think so."

"Well, then."

When he lowered his head, she felt herself stiffen, instinctively searching for the smallest sign of the heightened anxiety that had presaged her previous panic attack. Now, all she felt was the rush of sensual expectation.

His lips brushed against hers lightly, gently, and her eyes fluttered closed. His lips touched hers again, lingered with a slow, seductive ease that curled sensation after sensation down her spine, her legs, all the way to the tips of her toes.

This time it wasn't sharp, terrifying anxiety that tightened her insides, but desire.

"Still okay?" he murmured against her mouth.

She dragged in a deep breath and found that the air around her had heated and taken on density. "More than okay," she managed over a suddenly dry throat.

Her hand slid from his chest up to his shoulder as she inched closer, closing the space between them.

She felt a mix of longing, restraint and carefully leashed passion when his mouth took hers again. The intimate privacy of the small, shadowy motel room added to her sense of security, but she knew it was Grant who made her feel safe.

One of his hands settled on her hip, the other cupped the side of her neck. She knew he was taking care to make sure she could step away if she suddenly felt trapped.

She didn't feel trapped. She felt as if she were on the verge of freedom. She wanted to give. To take. To bask in the feel of Grant's arms around her now that fear had receded into a hazy memory.

Her hand moved, explored the smooth, hard planes of his shoulder. She marveled at the iron-hard tension she felt there, reveled at her response to his heated flesh. She could hear her own heartbeat raging in her chest, felt his heart pounding an answering echo against her breasts. His body was against hers, hard and lean; she felt his arousal against her belly.

Need shot through her like a bolt of electricity, stunning her in its intensity.

His mouth moved from hers to feast down the length of her throat with slow, cool, devastating control. His name escaped her lips in a soft moan.

Too much, she thought dimly as her legs began to tremble. Too much, too fast. Still, it had been so long since she'd felt—just *felt*—that she couldn't bring herself to step away. When his mouth found hers again, her fingers dug into his shoulder as much for balance as in response to the sharp-edged mix of emotions that raged inside her.

It was Grant who eased out of the kiss. His gray gaze rested on her face with an unreadable intensity as he slid her clenched hand from his shoulder and pressed a soft kiss to her knuckles. "You're not ready," he said, his voice soft and husky.

She looked up at him, shaken, yearning and just a little dismayed of what was happening inside her. "Not because I'm afraid."

"Good." His eyes, dark and unreadable, stayed locked with hers as he slowly, carefully opened her fist, then pressed his mouth against her palm. "I won't ever hurt you, Sky."

"I know." She dragged in a ragged breath, trying to absorb the flood of sensation. Her head was spinning and she was pretty sure her lips were vibrating. "But you're right. I'm not ready…to go beyond this. Not yet."

He rested his forehead against hers while he pulled his drooping shirt up and settled it on her shoulders. His movements were so slow and smoothly deliberate that she barely felt the unsteadiness in his hands.

"When you are ready, all you have to do is let me know."

She pressed a hand to her stomach where a hard ball of need had lodged. "Believe me, you'll be the first."

He wasn't going to be able to let it go.

The thought echoed through Grant's brain as he shut the door to the motel room behind him. He stood unmoving in the still morning air in which the heat was already edging toward oppressive. Sky's soft scent clung to his wrinkled shirt, filling his senses while the need to protect, to deliver some sort of justice for her deepened inside him.

He shoved his fingers through his hair. He had the taste of her in his mouth, could still feel the soft silk of her flesh on his hands. The kisses they'd shared minutes before had left her trembling and, yes, wary. *Of him.*

His teeth tightened on a curse as he thought about the abrupt vulnerability that had her digging her fingers into his shoulder. She was so sure of herself in her work, and so uncertain of the most basic aspect of her femininity. No matter how long it took, no matter *what* it took, he would make her sure again, give her back what that gutter-slime Kirk Adams had taken from her.

Shoving his hands into the pockets of his slacks, Grant stared unseeingly across the parking lot at the heavy flow of traffic headed toward the turnoff for the prison rodeo. Until the moment he'd touched Sky, he had thought he had managed to snap control back into place. Thought he had convinced himself that the need to give Adams a taste of justice had been just knee-jerk reaction at hearing what the bastard had done to her. The intimacy he and Sky had just shared told him otherwise.

He closed his eyes, hoping to shut out the memory of the previous night. Of the scream that had torn her out of the nightmare. Of her pale-as-death face. Of the ragged sobs that had wracked her body while she clung to him. Instead, the horror she'd suffered swam even more vividly in his brain.

He felt his blood heat all over again and he struggled against the fury that intensified with a sense of his own impotence. It was as if the closer he and Sky became, the stronger his need to do something—*anything*—to right the wrongs she'd suffered.

Shoving on his sunglasses, Grant stalked across the motel's parking lot. The main legacy of yesterday evening's fire was the lingering smell of doused ash, sour and acrid, that hung in the still air and left a taste in his mouth. His thoughts were just as bitter.

Somehow he needed to regain his objectivity. Needed to push away the anger and deal with the *facts* of what Sky had suffered. He and Sam hadn't closed every homicide case they'd worked. Most, but not all. Sometimes they'd *known* who the bad guy was, but the evidence wasn't there, so the do-wrong walked. That was a reality a cop had to accept and live with on an all-too-frequent basis. Always before, Grant had managed to put that aspect of the job into perspective, managed to shuffle the sense of injustice into a part of his brain where emotion played no part.

He was pretty sure no amount of shuffling was going to strip his emotions from what Sky had endured. *Something.* Dammit, he had to do *something.*

The thought pounded in his head, masking the sound of the traffic as he jogged across McAlester's main street.

He wished he could talk to Sam. Wished his partner was around to help establish rules for the mental chess game that had lodged itself in Grant's mind. Sam had taught him to use people's predictability to determine their moves, but in this case it was his own future moves Grant couldn't seem to get a bead on. He needed to balance the anger that churned inside him with the code of behavior he'd sworn to uphold when he pinned on the badge. Problem was, he didn't know how to do that.

He let out a long breath into the hot summer morning. If Sam was in a position to listen to the mental war waging inside him, his deceased partner wasn't sending any advice on how to win that war.

"Thanks, buddy," Grant muttered.

He needed time to regroup, he told himself as he walked across the parking lot of the convenience store where he'd bought supplies the previous evening. With time, his perspective would level out. Objectivity would return. His icy fury would diminish, his stomach would unknot. He had to trust that.

He passed the diner where he and Sky had eaten dinner.

Glancing through the big front window, Grant noted that the place was packed. As were the drugstore and barbershop he passed.

He checked his watch as he turned a corner and a white cinder-block building came into view. The hand-painted sign that stretched across the building's front read Wade's Garage. The two overhead doors were up, revealing a large workshop from which raucous country music blasted. In one stall, a mechanic wearing brown overalls twisted a wrench beneath the underbelly of a dusty black pickup truck suspended on a hydraulic lift. Beside the building, there was a large wire-fenced compound where jobs done or waiting sat in haphazard rows. The unmarked cruiser was parked in the compound near the gate, sunlight reflecting off its brown roof.

Grant hoped the fact that the car was parked in the compound signaled that work on it had already been completed.

The mechanic glanced across his shoulder and gave a nod to acknowledge Grant's presence. Setting the wrench on top of a rolling toolbox, the man walked out into the sunlight. Grant got three instant physical impressions: carrot-colored hair, freckles, beer belly.

"Help you?" the man asked, wiping one hand on the thigh of his grease-stained overalls. Wade was embroidered in dingy red across the chest pocket.

Grant introduced himself, then swept a hand in the direction of the cruiser. "That's my car. When Hank towed it in last night, he said he would leave you a note to check it first thing this morning."

"He did." Wade scratched his mop of hair that looked even more reddish orange beneath the bright sun. "I did."

"What was wrong?"

"What was wrong still's wrong. Can't fix her."

Grant silently cursed the city's stringent budget that so

often obliged cops to settle for ancient, less-than-efficient equipment. "Is there a part you need?"

"Yeah." Rubbing his protruding belly, Wade looked at the cruiser in grim assessment. "A new engine. That'll do the trick, but it'll take a lot of time and money to get her going."

Grant's eyes narrowed behind the lenses of his sunglasses. "The car needs a *new* engine?"

"Yep. I got a look at the radio in the dash. You're a cop, right?"

"Right."

Wade nodded. "Somebody poured sugar into the carburetor. Maybe someone who doesn't like cops walked by the car and saw the radio. She's got a city government tag on her, you know."

"Yes, I know."

Wade held up a grimy hand. "Yesterday you started her up, she drove okay for a few miles, then she went into a coughing fit, right?"

Grant planted a hand on his hip. In deference to the heat, he'd left his sport coat and gun in the motel room. His badge was in his back pocket. "Right."

"Once the engine cooled, the sugar caramelized. Stuff's all through it, just like sludge. When I opened the hood this morning, it smelled like somebody'd burnt dessert. I checked the carburetor, unhooked the fuel line. Looks like someone poured caramel into it."

"Sugar..." While he formulated a time line in his head, Grant shifted his gaze across the street to the post office where the flag in front hung limp in the still, hot air.

"How long would the car have run after the sugar was poured in the carburetor?" he asked, shifting his gaze back to Wade.

"Depends on how much sugar they used. At most, a

couple of miles.'' Wade lifted a shoulder. ''I suppose it could've been kids that done it. Last Halloween we had a couple of cars wind up here with sweet insides. The cops never did catch 'em. The owners of the cars were plenty mad about it, I tell you.''

''You don't have to tell me,'' Grant said through his teeth, his thoughts shifting to the previous afternoon. The cruiser had run without a hitch on the drive from the city, had shown no sign of engine trouble when he and Sky left the state prison. After that, they'd stopped at a café. The parking lot there had been full, so he'd parked the cruiser in the back. He and Sky had both gone inside; he'd stood in line to buy soft drinks while she washed off the grease she'd gotten on her hands when Jason Whitebear made a grab for her evidence kit.

The evidence kit that had barely survived the fire…along with Sky.

Suddenly, yesterday's bizarre string of events took on a darker, more sinister tint. For the first time, Grant turned a suspicious eye toward the fire. The fire chief had determined the cause was a short in the air-conditioning unit in Sky's room. A room she wouldn't have been in if the cruiser hadn't broken down. Had the air-conditioning unit malfunctioned, or been purposely sabotaged? If so, by whom? Someone who had a reason to want Ellis Whitebear's blood sample destroyed? Worse, someone who wanted Sky hurt or dead? A combination of both?

The possibilities shot a sudden, profound wariness into Grant's system. ''I'm going to have a lab tech go over that cruiser. Don't let anybody else touch it.''

When he glanced back at the wire-fenced compound, Wade raised a hand to shield his eyes from the sun's glare. ''Don't guess I know anybody else who'd want to touch it.''

Making a mental list of what needed to be done, Grant turned and jogged back in the direction of the motel. His first priority was to get back to Sky. Fast.

"Someone poured sugar in the cruiser's carburetor?" Sky asked as she dropped her contact lens case into her purse that sat on the unmade bed.

"Yeah." From where he stood, Grant could smell the tang of the soap she'd used in the shower. He took a deep breath and realized he was still feeling the effects of the relief that had rolled over him when he opened the motel room door and found her safe.

She wrinkled her nose. "What sort of damage does that do to a car?"

"Gums up the system," he answered. "To an engine, it's the mechanical equivalent of a blood clot."

"But who...?"

"I don't know." Turning abruptly, he strode to the chest of drawers, retrieved the holstered Glock and jammed it onto his belt. "But I'm damn well going to find out."

Sky lowered onto the edge of the bed, frowning as she pleated the edge of the sheet between her fingers. "I guess what Wade said could be right—that some kids played a prank."

"Yeah. Problem is, my gut tells me otherwise." Grant stared across the room at her, his jaw set. "I need to call Lieutenant Ryan and give him a rundown on what's happened. After that, we'll check out. I'm going to make sure Delbert puts that burned air-conditioning unit into storage until someone from the State Fire Marshal's Office can get here to check it."

Sky's fingers froze against the sheet. "Why? The fire chief here said a short in the unit started the fire."

''That's probably what happened. I want to know exactly why the unit shorted out.''

''You mean…? You think the fire might not have been an accident?''

His jaw tightened when he saw the color drain out of her face. The last thing he wanted to do was frighten her.

''Is that what you think, Grant?'' she asked when he remained silent.

''Dammit, I don't know what to think. About *anything*.'' The words came out on a new crest of anger he hadn't realized had been building inside him.

''The rape included.'' She raised a hand, let it fall back into her lap. Her pale skin lent an air of fragileness to the delicate lines of her face. ''I saw it in your eyes this morning. You don't know what to think about the rape.''

His hands clenched against his thighs. ''I know exactly what to think about the rape,'' he said quietly.

''I don't blame you.'' Her eyes had gone as dull as her voice. ''I understand.''

Her statement had him hesitating. No way was he going to share with her the violent thoughts he'd had about Kirk Adams. If she knew what was raging through his mind where that bastard was concerned, it would scare her. Hell, it scared him.

He took a cautious step toward her, then another. ''What is it you think you understand?''

She turned her head and stared out the room's lone window. The dark fall of her hair streamed across her shoulders, a stark contrast against the white halter top. ''I learned in my therapy sessions that some men are unable to handle a relationship with a woman who's been raped. Maybe you're one of those men.''

A blow to the side of his head would have had less impact. ''Sky, that's not—''

"I...understand if you are." She remet his gaze. "There are people—men and women—who can't help but wonder how a rape victim could get herself into such a situation, or if maybe, just maybe, she provoked the attack." When she spoke again, her voice was thick with the tears that glistened in her eyes. "They may even wonder if she enjoyed the experience."

Grant closed the distance between them, pulled her to her feet and gathered her close. "You were drugged, for God's sake! Kidnapped." He had to fight to keep his voice even, struggled to keep the hand steady that he stroked down the long fall of her dark hair. "Totally defenseless. You were a victim, Sky. A smart one. You survived."

When he felt her body tremble, he leaned his head back. As he thumbed a stray tear from her cheek, he silently cursed himself. He'd had a lot of dealings, both on and off the job, with women caught up in traumas, but with Sky things were different. She'd knocked him off balance to the extent that he was stumbling around like an inept idiot.

"I've been thinking a lot about what you told me last night," he said quietly. "What I'm trying to come to terms with is the fact that no one was there to protect you. That you never got justice."

"I accepted that a long time ago. I had to."

He pressed a kiss against her temple as he continued to comb his hand through her hair. "Something like that is hard for a cop to deal with. I'm used to the bad guy getting caught. And punished."

She settled her cheek against his shoulder, slid her arms around his waist. "That didn't happen in my case. I had to learn to live with it."

Grant closed his eyes against the vision of her battered and bloodied. At that instant, he knew he would never be able to shake that image—just like he hadn't been able to shake his feelings for her during the past six months. He'd tried. God knew, he'd tried.

"I have to figure out in my head how to deal with what happened to you," he said carefully.

This time it was Sky who leaned back and gazed up at him with blue eyes that still shimmered with tears. "I guess we both have things to work out."

"Yeah." His unsettled emotions tightened his mouth. "But I do know one thing."

"What?"

"No one is ever going to hurt you again. I swear it."

Chapter 8

"I think I finally have this espresso maker figured out," Judith Mirren said, raising her voice over the hissing and bubbling emanating from the gleaming black machine tucked into an alcove on her kitchen counter. Looking over her shoulder, the psychiatrist gave Sky a smile. "On the phone you sounded rested and happy. You look that way, too."

"I am." Sky set her purse on the tile floor and eased onto a long-legged stool at the kitchen's center island. "A lot has happened in the past day and a half."

As she spoke, movement caught Sky's eye. Sigmund slunk out of nowhere and began brushing back and forth against his mistress's legs, arching his back and purring like a little motorboat.

"Patience, Sigmund," Mirren stated as she put the finishing touches on the lattes. "You'll get your dinner when Sky and I are done."

As if aiming blame for the delay of his food, Sigmund

shot Sky a yellow-eyed glare while twitching his furry gray tail back and forth in jittery little arcs.

"You mentioned on the phone that you told Grant about the rape," Mirren said as she turned. Her honey-brown-and-gray hair was scooped up in the usual attractive top-knot. A tidy black pantsuit with a paisley silk scarf tied at the neck enhanced the doctor's air of professional competence.

"Yes, I told him." Sky thought about the nightmare that had seemed so real, and swallowed hard. "I thought I could never do that."

"Move now." Using one foot, Mirren gently plowed the tomcat aside, then carried two oversize cups across the kitchen. Angling her head, she slid onto the stool beside Sky's. "What changed your mind about telling Grant?"

Sky tasted the latte. It was warm and rich and rejuvenating. Between sips she explained what had happened after Grant pulled her from the grip of the nightmare.

"How did he react?" the doctor asked.

"He was caring and kind," Sky answered, staring at the cheerful pots of herbs that lined the windowsill over the sink. Her chest tightened with the knowledge that what she'd felt for Grant six months ago had deepened a hundredfold over the past few days. Those feelings were all so new. Overwhelming.

"Compassionate," she added, meeting the older woman's waiting gaze. "There's no other man I could have told. Only Grant."

"He sounds special." Eyes filled with ready understanding, Mirren sipped from her cup. "More than special."

"He is." Sky ran a fingertip around her cup's rim. Despite the contentment she felt, a nagging memory had her furrowing her forehead. "While I told Grant about the rape, I sensed him getting angry. He didn't want me to see his reaction, I could tell. But he couldn't keep his feelings out of his eyes.''

Sky paused. Nerves had made her palms damp, and she rubbed them down her trousered thighs. ''It's as if, while I talked about the rape, Grant could see inside me, could *feel* how awful it was.'' Even now that she had purged the worst of the black, ragged memories, she felt her eyes begin to fill with tears, and blinked them back. ''The next morning, I realized he was still angry. Maybe even angrier.''

''Some time has passed since then,'' Mirren commented after a moment. ''How is he handling that anger now?''

''I'm not sure.'' Sky shifted her gaze across the kitchen. Sigmund had taken up sentry duty in front of a set of French doors, his slitted gaze fixed beyond the glass on a sparrow hopping around on the wooden deck. ''While we were in McAlester, some things happened on two cases Grant and I are working. Demanding cases. He—we both have a lot to deal with where work's concerned.''

Like the fire that might not have been an accident, Sky thought. And the sugar someone dumped into the cruiser's carburetor. The lab tech who'd dusted the cruiser found only smudged fingerprints under the hood. When Sky had spoken to Grant a few hours ago, he had yet to hear from the State Fire Marshal's office about the results of their inspection of the air-conditioning unit that had sparked the fire. But, Sky reminded herself, none of that had anything to do with her past...and Grant's feelings about the rape.

''When I saw the next morning how upset Grant still was, I thought maybe he'd discovered he couldn't handle a relationship with a rape victim,'' Sky explained, pushing away her cup. Caffeine wasn't helping calm the nerves tingling at the base of her neck. She folded her hands on the island's granite surface to keep them still. ''I told him I would understand if he couldn't.''

Mirren arched a slim eyebrow. "What was his response?"

Sky closed her eyes against a wave of regret. "It hurt him that I even considered he might feel that way." She shook her head. "Six months ago I hurt him when I couldn't confide in him about the rape. Now I've told him, and I still managed to hurt him."

"Sky, don't be so hard on yourself. The trauma of a rape integrates itself into every aspect of a woman's life. Learning to deal with that is a struggle." The doctor linked her long, neat fingers together beside her cup. "Did Grant explain his anger?"

"Yes." Sky let out a breath. "He said he was trying to come to terms with the fact that no one was there to protect me. That I never got the justice I deserve."

"That's more than understandable. A sense of helplessness is hard for a man to deal with. It can be overwhelming to men who are in positions of authority, such as police officers. The fact that your rapist is free, and shouldn't be, goes against the basic beliefs of Grant's profession."

"True." Sky shifted on the padded stool, trying to twitch the feeling of unease out of her shoulders. She couldn't put her finger on why the tension had settled there yesterday after Grant had assured her that he just needed to figure out how to deal with what she'd suffered. Nor could she name the reason that the prickly feeling had stayed with her during the trip back to Oklahoma City after they'd rented a car in McAlester. Now, twenty-four hours later, she had no idea why the pinpricks of unease still danced up her spine.

"Sky?"

She suddenly realized Judith Mirren had asked her a question. "I'm sorry. What?"

However complacent they were, the doctor's eyes were sharp and searching. "Would you like another latte?"

"No, thanks." Sky glanced at her watch. "I have to get back to the lab."

"Working overtime this evening?"

"Yes." In a little over two hours, the hybridization period would be complete on the blood sample she'd taken the day before yesterday from Ellis Whitebear. This evening she planned to photograph the strips she'd prepared with the amplified DNA and interpret the results. She would know then if she'd made a terrible mistake two years ago that had put the wrong man on death row. A mistake that had allowed a killer to go free and had cost Carmen Peña her life.

"I'm glad you found time to drop by." The psychiatrist leaned back on her stool. "Is there something else you wanted to talk to me about?"

Sky shook her head. "No. I..." She bit back on a restlessness that made her feel as if everything in her world was just a half beat out of sync. A lot of it was due to the Whitebear case, she knew. But her relationship with Grant was the reason she was sitting in Dr. Mirren's kitchen.

"I guess I'm nervous because I've spent the past nine years deliberately keeping people at a distance. Grant and I have agreed to give our relationship a second chance." She raised a shoulder. "That's what we both want."

"But?"

"To have a man so close, feeling so protective on my behalf is a little overwhelming, that's all."

"As is the knowledge that your relationship might soon shift into intimacy."

"Yes." The memory of the soul-deep kisses she and Grant had shared sent a quick jolt to Sky's stomach. She didn't think she was ready to take that last step, not yet. Still, just thinking about what it might have been like if she'd given herself to Grant in that dimly lit motel room made her breath hitch and filled her with an undeniable longing.

"Time will help you sort out things," the doctor continued, her mouth curving into an easy smile as she squeezed Sky's hand. "Remember, you're not the only one who needs some breathing room. You've had years to deal with the trauma of the rape. Grant has had a little over a day. You're ready to move on, but he needs to come to terms with the residual feelings associated with your being assaulted, just as you did. Give each other time and understanding, and your relationship can evolve into something wonderful."

Sky sat in silence as the doctor slid off the stool and collected the cups. Until that moment she had not known how desperately she wanted a future with Grant.

While Sky was saying her goodbyes to Dr. Mirren, Grant was walking into the office of the Oklahoma State Board of Pharmacy. Smith Casteel, a decorated OCPD lieutenant whose sudden resignation six months ago had sent shock waves through the department, let him into the four-story building.

"Thanks for waiting until I could get here," Grant said as they shook hands. "Traffic was hell."

"Not a problem," Casteel said. With his shirtsleeves rolled up and his tie loose, he didn't look as if he was in a hurry to leave. "I had some paperwork to catch up on." Turning, Casteel led the way through a maze of dim, tiled hallways with dark offices on either side.

At the end of one of those hallways, he stopped at a doorway and motioned Grant inside. "Make yourself comfortable. I can probably find some coffee if you want a cup. We brew the same battery acid here as at the PD."

"I'll pass."

Grant lowered onto the chair nearest the door and took in the roomy paneled office with a desk, two visitors' chairs and credenza. His gaze lingered on the framed photograph of a striking brunette angled on one end of the credenza. Kathy Casteel had been an up-and-coming public defender when she was attacked by a robbery suspect whose acquittal she'd gained. That had been months ago and the last Grant had heard, she was still in a coma.

"Sorry to hear about Sam," Casteel stated as he settled into the high-backed leather chair behind his desk. "He and I worked a couple of cases together during my stint in Homicide. I learned a hell of a lot from Sam Rogers."

"So did I." Grant had only a nodding acquaintance with Smith Casteel—he'd been promoted to Vice while Grant still rode the streets. Still, Casteel had once carried a badge and his current job of conducting background and compliance investigations for the Oklahoma State Board of Pharmacy enabled Grant to sidestep the red tape—and hard-edged questions he knew he would encounter—if he tried to get what he wanted through the DEA.

Casteel propped his forearms on the desk. He was a tall, lean man in his late thirties, with dark eyes that looked a little harder than the floor beneath Grant's feet. "I don't guess you're here to trade stories about Sam."

"No. I have a couple of questions about a man who may be a licensed pharmacist in this state." As he spoke, Grant slid a folded piece of paper from the inside pocket of his sport coat. "Here's a copy of what the Department of Public Safety has on him," Grant added, leaning forward to hand the paper across the desk.

Also in his pocket was the copy he'd run of Kirk Adams's photo from the yearbook he'd pulled off a shelf in the library at the University of Oklahoma. After one look, the bastard's handsome face and cocky grin had branded itself in Grant's brain.

"When he renewed his driver's license two years ago, Adams lived in Ventress, Oklahoma," Grant stated. "He hasn't filed a change of address with the DPS. The information may be current. I'd like to find out for sure."

Casteel studied the paper, then slowly lifted his gaze. "Is Adams a suspect in a homicide?"

"No, his name came up in a conversation, is all. He's the type of guy who has no qualms about breaking rules, and he thumbs his nose at authority."

"Not the preferred qualities of someone who dispenses pharmaceutical narcotics for a living," Casteel observed.

"True, and those are Adams's good traits," Grant stated. "He's known to victimize women, and he's slick enough to get away with it."

Casteel's eyes narrowed. "Do tell."

"If the pharmaceutical board's received complaints on him, he's someone you should take a close look at," Grant continued. "The complaints are probably righteous."

"I'll make a note of that." Casteel pursed his lips. "Once you get confirmation of his address, do you plan to pay Mr. Adams a visit?"

"That's not on my agenda." It was the truth. At this point, Grant didn't know what, if anything, he would do once he knew Adams's whereabouts. The mental chess game now playing in Grant's head required planning, long-term strategy, and it was far from over. All he knew at this point was there was a dark, dangerous something inside him driving him to get all the information he could on the slime.

Raising a hand, Grant rubbed his gritty eyes. He'd spent the previous night pacing a path in his living room carpet, telling himself that the fact Sky had survived the rape, that she had let him back into her life was enough. For the first time in his life, a woman had him thinking serious thoughts of futures and tomorrows. Dammit, that ought to be enough. For a few minutes he had almost believed it could be. But the past—*her* past—wouldn't loosen its hold on his thoughts. The image of Sky, drugged, terrorized and bleeding haunted him. During the remainder of the night, a plan had played in his head, growing and expanding until it took on a sense of reality that Grant wasn't sure he knew how to control. All he knew was that *if* he paid Adams a visit, he would be in and out before the bastard knew he was there. He'd worked Homicide long enough to know how to take care of trash without leaving a trace.

"So, Pierce," Casteel began, "since you've got nothing solid on Adams, I can view your visit as unofficial. That means I'm not required to fill out a report on what you've just told me."

Grant gave a slight nod. "I wouldn't want to cause you unnecessary paperwork."

"I appreciate that." Shifting his hooded gaze, Casteel slid a keyboard from beneath the center of his desk and typed in data. A moment later, he nodded at the monitor angled at his left. "So, your boy is one of *those* Adamses."

Grant frowned. "What exactly does that mean?"

"Kirkland Adams, aka Kirk Adams, is the son of Warner Adams, who owns just about every pharmacy in the southeastern part of this state. The family is stinking rich. It's doubtful Kirk's ever pulled a shift behind a drugstore counter, even though he's a licensed pharmacist. He's probably solely management, working under the old man's thumb." Casteel flicked a look at Grant. "Kirk's home address is the same as on his SDL."

Nodding, Grant felt his throat tighten. Ventress, Oklahoma, was two hours away by car. "Ever had any complaints filed on him?"

"Kirk looks squeaky clean," Casteel said, his gaze skimming the monitor. "His old man has his finger on the political pulse of about ten counties. If Junior's ever encountered any trouble, Pop has probably bought him out of it."

"Yeah." Grant set his jaw. He had hoped to find *something.* Some reason to get to Adams through legal channels, but he knew now that wasn't going to happen. The bastard didn't even have an unpaid parking ticket. Grant readily acknowledged that work-related complaints and unpaid tickets wouldn't begin to avenge what Adams had done to Sky. But at least the slime would be forced to answer for *something,* Grant thought. Then, maybe the wrongness of the plan formulating in his mind would overshadow the rightness.

"Anything else?" Casteel asked.

"No. I appreciate your help."

"Anytime."

As Grant rose, he felt a light vibration against his waist. He shoved back the flap of his sport coat, pulled his pager off his belt and checked its display. "This is a call I've been expecting from the Fire Marshal," he said, remeeting Casteel's gaze. "Mind if I use your phone before I head out?"

"Help yourself," Casteel said.

Sky sat motionless at her work counter in the forensics lab, staring at the photograph she'd taken of Ellis Whitebear's latest DNA profile. If her heart was still beating, she couldn't tell. She doubted there was any blood pumping through her veins, because her flesh had turned to ice beneath her white lab coat.

It was close to eight o'clock; this late, she was the only

person in the lab with its U-shaped counters lined with beakers, trays of test tubes and stands holding glass pipettes at rigid attention. Behind her, the evidence refrigerator sitting next to the emergency shower clicked on and hummed.

She'd lost track of how many times she'd reread the notes she had compiled since she'd walked into the lab yesterday with Ellis Whitebear's blood sample in her evidence kit. Now she forced her dazed mind to picture each of those steps, to determine if somehow, some way she'd made a mistake.

In an unconscious gesture, she started to push her glasses higher up on her nose, then realized she wasn't wearing them—she'd put in her contacts that morning.

Over the past hours, she had drunk an entire pot of coffee, and her stomach was burning worse than her eyes. Her shoulders and back muscles felt like high-tension wires; her world, which had seemed just a half beat out of sync hours earlier, now threatened to spin crazily out of control.

If she were called into court this minute, she would have to testify that Ellis Whitebear's DNA did not match the man's who killed Mavis Benjamin two years ago.

But it *had,* Sky reminded herself, while the muscles in her stomach contracted like a fist. At one time it *had* matched. That was why Whitebear was sitting on death row for the murder.

The pressure in her chest threatened to spread as she swiveled on her stool and checked the clock on the far wall. Its thin, red second hand swept soundlessly around the dial. Why she was checking the time, she didn't know. It didn't matter how late it was, she had to tell Grant the results of the DNA profile. With a shiver of deep uncertainty chilling her to the bone, she reached for the phone.

When his pager went off, Grant was pounding his way up the station's back stairs. He recognized the number of the forensics lab on the pager's display. He already knew Sky was working late—before leaving the Fire Marshal's office he'd called the Homicide sergeant on duty and told him to look in on her to make sure she was okay.

Clenching his jaw, Grant swiped his ID card through the scanner on the stairwell's third-floor landing, then jerked open the door. He knew without a doubt the fire that had destroyed Sky's motel room had been no accident, and he planned to keep her in his sights until he got his hands on whoever had set it.

Minutes later, he slid his ID card through another scanner, then strode into the lab, passing through the unmanned reception area without a glance. The light in Sky's office was on, as was the computer terminal, but she wasn't at her neat-as-a-pin desk. Veering right, Grant headed down a long, dimly lit hallway.

"Sky?"

When she swiveled on her stool, he saw instantly that she was holding herself as rigid as marble.

"What's wrong?" he asked, advancing across the tiled floor to her work counter. Up close, her face was a little less pale than her white lab coat.

"I...don't believe this."

"What don't you believe?"

"His DNA's not the same, and that's not possible. I don't understand it. How could this happen? Actually, it *can't* happen." In the rush to get out, her words bumped and tumbled over each other. "Grant, it's *not* possible."

"Slow down." He settled a hand on her shoulder, felt the tenseness there. His gaze flicked across her work counter littered with a haphazard jumble of papers, file folders and computer printouts. A mug filled with coffee tilted half-on, half-off a cork coaster. In all the time he'd known Sky, he had never seen her work area anything but precise and tidy, with papers, files and even test tubes in exact order. He understood now that her work environment had been the one place in her life where she could always guarantee order and control.

''Take a deep breath.'' He repositioned the coffee mug while using a foot to maneuver a long-legged stool next to hers. ''Are you talking about Ellis Whitebear's DNA?''

''Yes,'' she said as he settled onto his stool. ''He doesn't have the same DNA he had two years ago.'' She scrubbed the heel of her palm across her forehead. ''That sounds crazy, doesn't it? I drew his blood then. I drew it again the day before yesterday.'' A line formed between her brows. ''How could he not have the same blood DNA?''

Grant frowned. ''It has to be the same, doesn't it?''

''Yes.'' She swept up two photographs of what looked like rows of thick, shadowed lines interspersed with dark blots. Grant saw that one photo displayed a date two years past. The other carried the date of his and Sky's visit to the state pen.

''That's my point,'' she said, shoving the photographs into his hands. ''Whitebear's DNA has to be the same, but as you can clearly see, it's not.''

Grant raised an eyebrow as he stared down at the photographs. Where this sort of scientific data was concerned, he was lost. But he did know how to backtrack and dig through facts to find answers.

''Okay,'' he began, setting the photographs on the counter beside a small biological waste container. ''Let's go over the steps you've taken. Before we went to Mc-Alester, you and another chemist took a second blood sample from all the men who'd worked at the apartment complex at the time of Mavis Benjamin's murder. You confirmed that all samples had been labeled correctly two years ago, and that no labels got switched.''

Sky ran a finger up and down the bridge of her nose. ''Yes, Gilchrist and I verified everything.''

''It was, without a doubt, Ellis Whitebear's blood in the vial that had his name on the label.''

''Yes. Through process of elimination, it had to be.''

''You and I know the blood you took the day before yesterday is for sure Whitebear's.''

''For sure.''

Grant nodded. ''What you're telling me now is that those two blood samples, taken from the same man two years apart, don't match.''

''That's right. They have different DNA.''

''Okay.'' Grant rubbed a hand across his face. ''Taking all that into account, logic tells me that something happened between the time you took the first blood sample and the second to change Whitebear's DNA.''

''That's like saying someone's fingerprints changed.'' Raising her hands, Sky stared down at her palms. ''DNA is the equivalent of a person's molecular fingerprint. You can't alter your DNA any more than you can the loops, swirls and whirls on the tips of your fingers.''

Baffled, Grant shoved a hand through his hair. ''So much for the logic angle. And, to add more mystery to this mix, we found a bloodstained bandage at the Peña crime scene with blood that matches one of those DNA samples.''

''The first sample,'' Sky said. ''The blood on the bandage matches the sample I took from Whitebear two years ago.'' She shook her head. ''This makes no sense.''

''I agree,'' Grant said, his gaze going to the counter across the lab where a boxy instrument with more dials than a radarscope sat. ''But at least we can now say that the man who slit Carmen Peña's throat a couple of weeks ago isn't sitting in a cell on death row.''

"Yes, we can say that." The frustration in Sky's voice had Grant shifting his gaze back to her. "I'm missing something, Grant." She fisted her hands in her lap. "Something's gotten by me and I don't know what it is."

"I know how you feel," he said, and leaned back on his stool. He had seen her only in passing since they'd returned from McAlester, and he wanted a moment to take her in. Gone was the prim bun at her nape. Now her dark hair was done up in a casual twist that allowed little wispy tendrils to flutter around her cheeks. The trendy wire-rims had disappeared in favor of contact lenses, and the eyes that stared into his were as blue as the flame on the lab's gas burners.

He forced his breathing to remain even while a knot of emotion tightened his chest. After years of coolly romancing a number of women, it was still foreign to him that he could find this one woman so quietly appealing, so deeply arousing, when it had nothing to do with sex.

Because he wanted to touch her, he balled his hands against his thighs. He already knew that she fit in his arms the way no woman ever had, or would, fit again. Had already accepted that the depth of his feelings for her would only intensify. As would his innate need to protect her both from past and future threat.

Setting his jaw, he shoved back thoughts of the dark, lapping waters of vengeance that had slowly eroded the edges of his control since the night she told him about the rape. Soon he would have to decide just how he was going to deal with those feelings. Right now he had a more urgent issue to address.

"Something's gotten by me, too," he said quietly.

Her brow furrowed. "About Whitebear's DNA?"

"No, about the fire in your motel room. Sky, it was no accident."

He watched the color drain from her cheeks as her eyes widened. "You're sure?"

"I spent the last two hours at the State Fire Marshal's office. One of their techs checked the air-conditioning unit from your room. I've got his report with a whole lot of technical electrical jargon in it, but the bottom line is that someone switched a couple of wires, which caused the unit to short out about five minutes after you turned it on."

Falling silent, she gnawed her bottom lip. Grant could almost see her mind working behind those vibrant blue eyes.

When she finally spoke, her voice was steady. "The tech can verify that the wires were switched. But there's no way of knowing when that was done, right?"

"Wrong," Grant countered. "While I was with the tech, I called Del, the motel manager. He said the air-conditioning unit was new, installed the day before we checked in. The electrician who did the work tested it, and the unit worked without a hitch. You were the next person to turn it on, just before you got into the shower."

"And almost got burned alive." She swiped a hand against the back of her neck. "We had no idea we'd wind up spending the night there. How would somebody know ahead of time where you and I would be?"

"After we checked in, we both used our separate keys to take a look at our rooms. Anyone watching would know which room was yours." Regret settled inside him for having put the wariness in her eyes, but she needed to know the truth. "Then you and I walked to the diner and ate dinner. That gave someone plenty of time to slip into your room and switch the wires in the air conditioner."

Grant paused, curving his fingers around the hand she'd

fisted in her lap. "Sky, has Corrections notified you recently about someone you've testified against being released? Someone who might hold a grudge?"

"No. No one."

"Gotten any hang-up phone calls? Maybe a call here at the lab that seemed hinky?"

"Nothing like that." Her gaze went to the papers spread across her workbench. "The only strange thing going on has to do with Ellis Whitebear."

Grant nodded. "Whose blood sample you just happened to have in your room at the time of the fire. And whose son was superannoyed that you'd gotten that sample in the first place."

She remet his gaze. "You're thinking Jason Whitebear sabotaged the air conditioner."

"It's not just a thought, it's a suspicion. Remember, we saw Jason, aka Spider, walk through the prison's front door before we drove off. Just because he did that doesn't mean he stayed there—that's something I plan to check out. He could have waited until we drove off, then followed us to the café. We parked in the back because the front lot was full. He would have had time to dump some sugar in the cruiser's carburetor."

Sky angled her chin. "You think Spider had a bag of sugar in his pickup truck?"

"Hell, I don't know," Grant answered. "There's a convenience store next door to the café. Maybe he ran in there and bought a bag. In any case, dumping sugar in the cruiser's carburetor was a guaranteed way for Spider to keep us in town long enough to try to get rid of his father's blood sample."

"Okay, let's suppose Spider did that. What reason would he have to destroy the sample and…"

"Burn you alive in the process?" Grant finished when her voice drifted off.

"Yes," she answered, then swallowed hard.

"That's one of the questions I want answered. Just like you want to know how the hell his father's DNA could have magically transformed."

"DNA doesn't do that."

"Ellis's seems to have," Grant pointed out, then raised a shoulder. "While you're working on figuring that out, I plan on taking a good look at Spider. I've already called Communications and ordered a run on him. I want to know everything he's been up to since the check Sam ran on him two years ago." Grant's eyes narrowed. "I also want to know where he was the night Carmen Peña disappeared from her job at the convenience store."

"It was his father's DNA at that crime scene," Sky pointed out, then frowned. "At least it used to be. And his father's the one on death row for Mavis Benjamin's murder."

"Things are getting more curious by the minute," Grant commented. "That's why you and I are heading back to McAlester tomorrow to pay Ellis an impromptu visit. It's his blood that's thrown a wrench in the works. I figure he's the one who can give us some answers."

Sky shook her head. "His lawyer won't like us talking to him without her knowing."

"She'll know. I'll call Marcia Davis from the prison and tell her we're there to chat with Ellis. She already knows we can't collect evidence against him, so there's no downside to her agreeing to our seeing him again. I just don't want to give her advance notice of what we're doing. She let Spider know we were coming the first time, which was her right. I don't intend for him to know about tomorrow's visit."

"Even so, aren't you worried about what might happen to the cruiser we drive?"

"We're taking my Porsche. It's got an alarm."

Nodding, Sky swiveled her stool and began straightening the papers on the counter. "It sounds like you've got things under control, Sergeant."

Grant gave a quick thought to the folded pages of information on Kirk Adams inside the pocket of his sport coat. Some things, he was no longer sure he could control. "I'm doing my best," he said quietly.

"I need to call my captain and let her know we're going back to the prison tomorrow." Sky took one last look at the photographs, then slid them into a file folder. "This is driving me nuts. Maybe if I get my mind off DNA for a few hours, something logical will come to me."

"Here's something that'll do the trick." Grant placed a hand on her arm and turned her back to face him. The scent she wore reminded him of dark, mossy glades. "You and I are spending the night together."

He thought that if he had coldcocked her, she couldn't have looked more shocked. "Grant, I…"

He took her hands in his. "Whether the blood sample was the target of the fire or not, the fact is that someone tried to burn you alive. If he decides to take another shot at you, he'll have to deal with me. That means you've got a roommate until I get my hands on him."

Sky stared at him for a long moment. "My apartment has a state-of-the-art security system."

"Security systems have been known to be breached."

"You might remember that I'm pretty good at taking care of myself."

"I'm not likely to forget." At the police gym, she'd flicked her arm and sent him airborne. Then in McAlester, she'd slammed him into a wall with one expertly placed kick. Feeling a tic of pride in her ability, Grant slid a hand beneath the lapel of his sport coat to rub his chest where the bruise still lingered. "Humor me, Milano, it's a macho thing."

"What about your clothes? You'd need a change of clothes."

"I've got my gym bag in my Porsche with my shaving stuff inside. I went by the cleaner's today, so I've got a fresh suit and shirt for tomorrow."

"I can see you've got this all thought out."

He grinned. "I'm like the Boy Scouts—always prepared."

Her eyes stayed locked with his as she ran her tongue over her lips. The gesture went straight to his gut, then shot lower. Her taste was in his system, the feel of her in his arms branded into his memory. He had never felt such raw-edged want of a woman as he felt for her. He also knew he had to let her call the shots if their relationship had a chance of moving into intimacy.

"A roommate," she murmured, dropping her gaze.

With one finger, he nudged her chin up until her eyes met his. "You've got a couch, Sky. I'll sleep there. If, and when, that location changes, you'll be the one making the decision. I'm not doing this to pressure you. I'm doing this to make sure no one has a chance to hurt you again."

Her mouth curved at the edges. "I've never had a white knight before."

"You do now."

She took a deep breath. "Grant, about us sleeping together. It's something I want, I'm just…"

Afraid. She didn't have to say the word, he could see the nerves swimming in her eyes. He clenched his jaw, forcing back thoughts of the scum who had put fear inside her. Those thoughts he would address later.

Moving his hand from her chin, he cupped her cheek. "You need to understand something, Milano. I don't want to sleep with you."

"Oh." With color flooding her cheeks, she began to lean away.

He slid his palm to the side of her throat, held her still. "I want to seduce you, very slowly, then make love with you."

Beneath his palm, he felt the quick jerk and scramble of her pulse.

With her blue eyes locked on his, she raised a hand and circled her fingers around his wrist. "That sounds wonderful."

"It will be. When you're ready, it will be."

Chapter 9

Sky stood in the small interview room at the state penitentiary where she'd drawn Ellis Whitebear's blood three days before. This time she'd left her evidence kit back in the lab—her tests had already revealed all the scientific data they could about the man's blood. She and Grant had come today to try to find the answers to the secrets that lurked in that blood.

The death row inmate had yet to be escorted into the room where the vague scent of sweat and fear hung in the air, so Sky allowed her gaze to linger on Grant. He stood near the gunmetal-gray door with its barred window, talking in low tones to a guard who pointed to information on a clipboard.

Grant's summer-weight silk-and-linen suit looked as if it had been made for him, which was probably the case. The same was true of his pearl-gray shirt and matching tie, and maybe even his Italian leather shoes.

As she studied him, Sky felt her mouth go dry. He had

not looked nearly so polished after spending the night on her couch.

A quiet breath escaped her lips while she pictured how he'd looked early that morning when he'd wandered into her kitchen. She'd been pouring water into her coffeemaker when she'd looked up and saw him leaning against the doorjamb, clad only in a pair of low-slung gym shorts. His sandy hair had been sleep-tumbled and a night's growth of beard shadowed his chin. The surge of need that had shot through her had been so immediate, so powerful that she'd sloshed water across the countertop and onto her bare toes. While she sponged up the mess with unsteady hands, the unrepentant grin he'd flashed her had kicked her nerves into high gear. If they hadn't had important, out-of-town business to tend to, she would have forced away the last skitters of disquiet that lingered inside her, and stepped into Grant's arms.

Even now, hours later, desire thudded with unexpected force in the pit of her stomach.

Tonight, she thought with a sudden realization that had her shoving her hands into the pockets of her slacks, then pulling them out again. Tonight, she would take that last step. She was ready. She had not known, *really known,* how ready until this moment. She felt indecision slide away to be replaced by a heady anticipation that had her palms going damp.

The sound of the heavy metal door swinging open pulled both her gaze and her thoughts across the room. Just as he had three days ago, Ellis Whitebear shuffled through the door in handcuffs and leg irons, a guard close behind him. His thick, black hair still lapped over the collar of his white T-shirt; his copper-tinted skin stretched with the same tautness over high cheekbones.

The interview room, the prisoner, the guard were all the same, she realized. *She* was the one who had changed.

The guard with the clipboard nodded to Grant, then walked out of the room, securing the door behind him.

"Whitebear," Grant said as the second guard escorted his charge to the small table in the center of the room. "You remember Ms. Milano?" While he spoke, Grant casually positioned himself between Sky and the prisoner.

Whitebear flicked a dismissive look at Sky as he settled his big, broad-shouldered body into a chair. "You ain't gettin' no more blood."

"That's not why we're here," Grant stated, then waited while the guard moved away and took position just inside the door. "Ms. Milano and I want to ask you a couple of questions."

Whitebear's hooded gaze swept the small room. "Where's my lawyer?"

"She couldn't make it, but we have her permission to talk to you. Tell us the truth, Ellis, and things might change for you."

"That so?" he sneered. "I did that two years ago, but it didn't make no difference. The both of you put me in this place for slicin' that bitch apartment manager's throat. I didn't do it. Why the hell should I bother wastin' breath about it now?"

Although Grant's expression remained impassive, Sky saw the tic of a muscle in his jaw. He knew, as did she, that the man sitting in shackles might have spent the last two years on death row for a crime he didn't commit.

With smooth grace, Grant settled a hip onto the edge of the table. "You should bother with us now because our minds are open where you're concerned, Ellis. If you are innocent like you say, it won't hurt you to walk us through the day Mavis Benjamin got murdered. Tell us everything you did.''

''Done that. Couple of times.''

''Do it again,'' Grant urged in a quiet voice.

He was good at this, Sky thought as she watched a sliver of uncertainty slide into Whitebear's dark eyes. The cop was offering a ray of hope to a man whose hopes had vanished when a jury pronounced him guilty of murder.

''Can't hurt none, I guess.''

With only a few intermittent questions from Grant, Whitebear recounted the day Mavis Benjamin had been found with her throat slit in the communal laundry room of the apartment complex where he had worked on the maintenance staff. As always, he admitted he'd hated the brassy, loudmouthed woman, that they'd argued often in front of other employees and she'd threatened to fire him only hours before she was found murdered. ''Hatin' her don't mean I killed her,'' he stated, then grew silent.

''True,'' Grant agreed, flicking a look at Sky. ''The problem is, Ellis, Ms. Milano found your blood on Mavis Benjamin's dress. I'm having a hard time figuring how it got there if you aren't the one who killed her.''

The silver cuffs surrounding Whitebear's meaty wrists clacked against the tabletop when he shook his head. ''That's a lie. I didn't kill that bitch, so my blood wasn't on her. Couldn't have been.''

''I didn't lie, Mr. Whitebear,'' Sky countered in a level voice, then paused until his dark, impenetrable eyes met hers. ''The blood I found on the sleeve of Mrs. Benjamin's dress matched what I drew from your arm two years ago.'' She took a step closer to the table. ''There's something different about your blood now. I'm here to try to find out what that something is.''

The man's upper lip curled in derision. ''You think that

means a damn thing to me now that I'm locked up? Maybe whatever's wrong'll kill me before the state has a chance to.''

Sky blinked. ''I'm not saying you're sick. All I'm saying is that I have questions about your medical history.''

When Whitebear said nothing, Grant leaned in. ''There's some questions I'd like to get answered, too, Ellis. Like why, after Ms. Milano and I left here three days ago, did somebody mess with my car, making sure we got stranded here for the night? And why did that somebody burn down a motel room, almost destroying your blood sample, not to mention nearly burning Ms. Milano alive?''

A look of pure bafflement settled in the man's eyes as he stared at Grant. Moments later, Whitebear lowered his gaze to his shackled wrists. ''How the hell would I know anything about all that?''

''Have you had a blood transfusion lately, Ellis?'' Grant persisted. ''Have you been sick since you came here and got some new blood pumped into your veins?''

Whitebear sat in silence, his dark eyes slitted, while his powerful hands slowly clenched. Sky could almost see the white of his bones beneath his copper-colored skin.

''No,'' he stated finally. ''I ain't had no blood pumped into me.'' After a moment, his mouth tightened and he muttered low, indiscernible words.

''Didn't catch that,'' Grant countered. ''Did you maybe mention the name of someone who might have a reason to destroy your blood sample? You're not a stupid man, Ellis. You have to know there's not a thing in the world I can do to make your situation worse—''

''I don't know nothin','' he groused, then jerked his head toward the guard. ''I wanna go back to my cell.''

The stone-faced guard moved to the table. ''Guess you're done here, Sergeant,'' he stated.

"Looks that way." Grant locked his gaze with White-bear's as he rose. "Whether you tell me or not, Ellis, I'm going to find out what's going on—"

"Ain't nothin' going on. I'm just tired of you people botherin' me."

"You're looking at maybe eight more years of rotting in a cell," Grant pointed out. "Then they'll slide a needle into your vein. You claim you're innocent. Fine. Give me something to help prove that, and I'll go to bat for you."

Whitebear jerked his head toward the guard. "Get me outta here."

After the guard led Whitebear through the door back to the cell block, Grant turned to Sky. His eyes were hard, the lines at the corners of his mouth intense. "The guard I talked to earlier checked the prison's records. Jason, aka Spider, didn't sign in to visit his father after we ran into him in the parking lot three days ago."

"That means he must have waited inside the front door here until we drove off," Sky said. "Then he followed us to the café."

"Where he dumped sugar in the cruiser's carburetor, then tailed us until we checked into Delbert's motel. He sabotaged the air-conditioning unit while we ate dinner, then got out of there so he'd have an alibi for the time of the fire."

"Too bad we can't prove any of that," Sky said quietly.

"A damn shame." Grant stared at the doorway through which the prisoner had disappeared. "Sky, is there any way a father and son can have the same DNA?"

"No. They'd have to be identical twins, which, of course, they aren't."

Grant uttered a quiet oath. "I knew you were going to say that."

"We're back to why," Sky said. "If Spider did do what

we suspect of him, why did he want to destroy his father's blood sample? How could he have possibly known the DNA would be different?''

Grant gave her a humorless smile. ''I'll just add those to our growing list of questions.''

Sky acknowledged the same sense of frustration churning inside her that she heard in his voice. ''That list is getting longer by the minute.''

''Tell me about it.''

''Grant, we need to talk to the prison's doctor. He can at least tell us if Ellis has had a blood transfusion while he's been in Department of Corrections' custody. If he has, there's no way that could change his DNA, but at least it would be a place for us to start looking for answers.''

''You're reading my mind, Milano.'' Grant leaned a hip against the table, crossing his arms over his chest as he gave her an assessing look. ''You know, Lieutenant Ryan hasn't filled Sam's position yet. Maybe you ought to apply to be my new partner.''

''Maybe I will.''

He grinned. ''You think so?''

They had a job to do and they would do whatever it took to get at the truth. Still, Sky's sense of professionalism couldn't stop her from picturing again how temptingly disheveled this man had looked standing half-naked in her kitchen. The heated desire she'd felt since that moment stirred deep inside her. To experience such raw-edged need after so many years of repressing her every emotion sent a zip of heady daring through her.

The unease that had plagued her since she'd told him about the rape now slid into oblivion.

Slowly she moistened her lips. She knew her next words would send the controlled, regimented life she'd lived for years veering in a very different direction.

"The partner deal is a good idea, Pierce." On legs that weren't quite steady, she took a step forward until only a mere inch separated them. The prison smells faded beneath his distinctive masculine scent. "I think it ought to happen," she said softly. "Tonight."

He went absolutely still, his gaze sharpening on hers like gray lasers. "Are we talking about the same thing?"

"I'm talking about us becoming partners. You're talking about me taking Sam's job." She shook her head. "Totally different subjects, Pierce."

Grant wasn't sure whether he should throttle Sky or kiss her senseless.

He wasn't dense; it had taken only a split second for the meaning behind her words to sink in. She was ready for their relationship to slide into intimacy, ready to give herself to him. Just thinking about it had heat streaking through his veins. And that was all the reaction he'd allowed himself, because immediately after Sky dropped her bombshell a guard stepped into the interview room and escorted them to the office of the prison doctor.

Grant slid a hooded look sideways. Considering the decision she'd made, how the hell could Sky sit in the chair beside his, looking so calm? So cool. Her hair was swept back flawlessly into a twist that his fingers itched to pull loose. Her blue eyes remained utterly expressionless while need whipped quietly, painfully through him.

Throttle or kiss?

His scowl deepened. The question was irrelevant. He couldn't do either since they were sitting across the desk from the prison's dour-looking doctor.

"There's been no blood transfusion since he's been incarcerated," Dr. David Brace advised while he peered through thick glasses at Ellis Whitebear's medical file. The man was a good hundred pounds overweight and had to be pushing seventy. What hair he had left was gray and sprang from his head in feathery tufts.

Forcing his thoughts to business, Grant leaned forward in his chair. "Look, Doctor, I'm going to level with you. Ms. Milano took a blood sample from Whitebear three days ago. It doesn't match the blood she drew from him two years ago. You got any idea why that might be?"

"Doesn't match in what way?"

"The DNA profile is different," Sky stated.

Brace blinked. "Never heard of something like that happening." He shut the file, then pulled off his glasses and polished the lenses with the end of his polka-dot tie. "Not to cast doubt on your abilities, Ms. Milano, but are you positive?"

"Yes. Another chemist verified my findings."

"Interesting." Brace pursed his lips. "I suppose this anomaly could have something to do with the aplastic anemia Mr. Whitebear suffered. That was before he entered the prison system, though. The man's healthy as a horse now."

Although he wasn't touching her, Grant could almost feel Sky's spine stiffen. "What treatment did Whitebear receive for the aplastic anemia?"

"Allogeneic marrow transplantation."

Grant held up a hand. "You're going to have to translate, doc."

"Of course. Aplastic anemia is a condition where a person's bone marrow no longer produces anything. It's as if all blood cells have been wiped out."

"I'm following you so far," Grant stated.

"Mr. Whitebear had a bone-marrow transplant several years ago," Brace continued. "He was fully recovered when he wound up on death row. The nurse here takes a blood sample from him every six months and sends it to the hospital where the transplant was done. There has been no reoccurrence of the disease. As I stated, he's healthy.''

Sky looked at Grant. ''Remember when I told Whitebear there was something different about his blood now? He asked me if that meant a thing to him now that he was locked up.''

Grant nodded. ''Ellis must have thought you'd come to tell him that his bone-marrow problem had come back.''

Sky angled her head as if analyzing the data. ''Doctor, does the file list who donated bone-marrow to Mr. Whitebear?''

''No. You'd have to ask the inmate.''

She shook her head. ''He's not forthcoming about things right now.''

''Try contacting the hospital where the transplant was performed. That might be a dead end, though. Names of donors are usually kept confidential.''

''It's worth a shot to ask,'' Grant said. ''What hospital?''

''University Hospital in Oklahoma City.''

''I'll call on our way back to the city,'' Grant said as he and Sky both rose.

She hesitated. ''Doctor Brace, have you ever heard of an occurrence where a marrow transplant altered the recipient's blood DNA?''

The man gave her a look that was pure skepticism. ''No.'' He stared down at the file folder on his desk. ''However, I don't keep up with all the studies that come out. I guess anything's possible.''

''This bone-marrow transplant,'' Grant began as he walked beside Sky along the sidewalk toward the lot where he'd parked his red Porsche, ''do you think it could have changed Whitebear's DNA?''

''I don't know. I wasn't aware that anything could change a person's DNA, but something changed his.''

''So maybe one of the samples you took from him is his own DNA, and one contains the DNA of whomever donated bone marrow to him?''

''Maybe.'' She furrowed her forehead. ''I wish I had the answers we need, but I don't know a lot of specifics about bone-marrow transplants.'' She hiked the strap of her purse higher on her shoulder. ''I know you're thinking that Spider is the most logical person to have donated bone marrow to his father. That's not necessarily true. The person whose marrow matched Ellis's could have been an unrelated donor. That's why there are so many nationwide donor registries, because so often blood relatives don't match the person in need of a tissue or organ transplant.''

''Yeah,'' he said, pulling in a deep drag of the hot summer air. His sixth sense told him that something about the investigation had shifted, that he and Sky were closer to finding answers to the questions that plagued them. ''My first thought was Spider.''

''When I got my masters, I studied under a man named Marcus Linley, a professor of hematology. He always kept up-to-date on the studies going on in the field, even the obscure ones. I'll make an appointment to see him. Tonight, if possible.''

''Speaking of tonight.'' As he spoke, Grant moved in front of her, halting her steps on the sidewalk. He hooked a knuckle under her chin and lifted her face. The afternoon heat was tempered by a brisk wind that tugged wispy strands of her dark hair from its twist.

''Let me get something straight, Milano. You're telling me you're ready for us to be together, right?''

''Yes.''

Hearing a ripple of unsteadiness in that one word, he

narrowed his eyes and gazed down into her face. For the first time in his life he felt himself hesitating when it came to the thought of having sex. He'd never had a problem getting women to come willingly to his bed. But sex wasn't his need right now, he realized. His need was for *this* woman. This one woman who had been hurt so terribly by another man's cruelty.

The thought put a tightness in his throat. It also put the fear of God in him to think that he might not give her what she needed.

With the slightest pressure, he inched her toward him. "You're sure? Absolutely sure?"

Her eyebrows rose. "Are you trying to talk me out of this?"

"Not on your life. I just want to make sure I get it right."

Her mouth curved. "Don't look at me to give you pointers, Pierce. I've logged some lean years when it comes to dating, much less sex." Although her words were light, he saw the nerves swimming in her eyes.

"I won't hurt you, Sky. You have my word."

Her smile fading, she placed a palm against his cheek. "I know that."

With light fingertips, he skimmed a windblown curl off her right temple. "I don't suppose you'd want to spend another night at Delbert's motel? It's only about a mile from here, you know." The anticipation twisting his insides into a hot knot had him realizing he was only half kidding.

A glint of amusement joined the nerves in her eyes. "Not on your life, Slick."

"I had to try."

When they reached the car, he used the remote on his key chain to disable the Porsche's alarm while they walked to the passenger side. When Sky slid into the seat, Grant caught a glint of sunlight off a piece of metal on the parking lot's surface.

"What is it?" she asked, leaning out of the open door as he used the toe of his loafer to nudge the flattened metal.

"I'll be damned," he said after a moment, and shoved back one of the flaps of his suit coat. "Remember when Spider showed up here the other day?" he asked, resting a hand on his waist beside his holstered Glock. "He crumpled a soda can, *this can,* in his hand then tossed it aside. I threatened to add littering to the charges I wanted to haul him in on."

"I remember." Sky raised an eyebrow. "You're sure it was *that* can?"

"I remember this neon purple label." Grant crouched to get a closer look. "Spider wasn't drinking a regular soda. This is one of those megabrands that has ten times the usual amount of sugar. It's advertised to give you superenergy to get you through the day and night."

"I've seen the ads." Sky gave him a thoughtful look. "So, are you thinking Spider had another can of that stuff in his pickup truck? That instead of buying a bag of sugar when he followed us to the café, he just popped the cruiser's hood and poured a can of high-test soda in the carburetor?"

"There you go, reading my thoughts again." Grant slid a plastic evidence envelope out of his inside coat pocket and prodded the can inside. "Maybe Spider even had a six-pack of this stuff in his pickup. If this was the only can he'd drank, he could have conceivably poured five cans of this stuff into the carburetor."

"We'll never be able to prove that."

"Maybe, maybe not. If this was the can Spider tossed away—and I'm pretty sure it is—his prints may be on the part of the metal that's protected from the elements."

Sky nodded. "I can check the can's rim for saliva. I might be able to get the DNA of the person who drank from the can."

Grant stowed the evidence envelope in the trunk, then slid into the driver's seat. The Porsche's engine roared to life when he twisted the key in the ignition. "We'll swing by Wade's garage and ask him if that brand of soda has enough sugar in it to disable the cruiser."

"If his answer's yes, have him cut a length out of the fuel line so I can take it back to the lab." As she spoke, Sky adjusted a vent that blasted cool air. "I'll see if I can find traces of the same soda."

Grinning, Grant lightly snagged her arm and leaned toward her. He caught the darkening of her eyes before his lips settled on hers, softly, slowly.

"Partners, Milano," he murmured against her mouth while his thumb ran up and down the vein in her wrist where her pulse skittered then began to race. "Did I mention how anxious I am to get you back to the city?"

"I'm looking forward to getting there myself." He heard the mix of nerves and desire in her soft-as-smoke voice.

Though he wanted her mindlessly, Grant knew he would take more care with her than he had with any other woman.

"Just wait and see, Milano." He turned her hand over in his, then placed a soft kiss against her wrist. The quick jerk and scramble of her pulse had his own pulse skipping a beat. "Ours is going to be a great partnership."

An hour later, with a section of the cruiser's fuel line stowed in the trunk, the red Porsche slashed along the interstate like a bolt of fire. From the passenger seat, Sky listened to Grant's conversation with the Superintendent of Records at Oklahoma City's University Hospital.

"Sergeant…Pierce, is it?" the superintendent asked, his voice sounding thready over the car's speaker phone.

"That's right."

"Sergeant Pierce, I'm sure you're aware I can't discuss a patient file on the basis of a phone call. Without court authorization, that would be a breach of confidentiality."

Sky found herself wondering if the superintendent looked as prissy as he sounded.

"I know the law, Mr. Hakel." As if he were facing the man, Grant narrowed his eyes at the small speaker installed in the leather dash. "You'll get that authorization, but I've got a critical situation here. Two women are dead—"

"I don't mean to sound unsympathetic, Sergeant. If I were to reveal information from Mr. Whitebear's file, the hospital could be held liable."

"Not to mention yourself," Grant grated.

"True." Hakel paused. "I need a warrant in order to release information."

"Right. I'll get back to you on that." Uttering a mild curse, Grant stabbed a button on the cell phone.

Sky shifted sideways in her seat. "I guess we expected him to say that."

"Doesn't make it any easier to swallow," Grant muttered, flicking her a look of total irritation. "Our big problem is at this point we don't have enough to take to a judge to get a warrant. First, we've got no documented proof that a bone-marrow transplant can change a person's DNA. Second, it's just a guess that Spider might have been the one who donated bone marrow to his father, and Ellis isn't in the mood to clue us in." Grant shoved a hand through his hair. "Hell, all I'm sure about is that Mavis Benjamin and Carmen Peña are both dead, and whoever killed them has a certain DNA, which no longer matches the man who's in jail for one of those murders. Where I'm standing on these cases, I have to look up to see the bottom."

Sky blew out a breath. "It doesn't help that Professor Linley is out of town until tomorrow afternoon," she added, thinking about the appointment she'd made with the professor's secretary when she called the university from Wade's garage. "If he can't come up with some scientific data to back up our assumptions that the bone-marrow transplant is the thing that changed Ellis's DNA, we're back at square one."

"I'm not waiting around, hoping something will fall into my lap. We'll swing by the station when we get back to town. The run I requested on Spider's background should be finished by now. I can at least start trying to get a lead on his whereabouts when both homicides occurred."

"Maybe you'll find something." Sky raised a shoulder. "There's nothing more I can do in the lab on these cases. From a scientific standpoint, Ellis's blood has told us everything it's going to."

Grant clicked on the blinker and swung into the passing lane to get around a slow-moving truck pulling a trailer filled with cattle. "If that's the case, it sounds like you've got the night free."

The sudden low timbre of his voice sent a sensual awareness feathering up Sky's spine. "I thought you just said you're spending the evening going through paperwork on Spider."

The smile that curved Grant's mouth was slow and lazy, and she decided it was the sexiest thing she'd ever seen. "I've always found that work goes faster when I have a partner to help me engage in deductive reasoning." As he spoke, he hit a button on the dash; seconds later, a bluesy tune poured out of the speakers.

Sky lifted an eyebrow. "Deductive reasoning?"

He reached for her hand, his fingers linking with hers. She felt the warmth of his palm against hers and thought about how comfortable a sensation his touch had become.

''Your place or mine tonight, partner?'' he asked, his voice a soft slide on the cool air.

She closed her eyes for the space of a heartbeat while her mind scrolled back six months to the moment when they stood in his bedroom and she'd stepped into his arms. She suppressed a shiver at the thought of the panic that had engulfed her. That night seemed like a lifetime ago. She had healed, she reminded herself. Faced her demons and won.

''Your place,'' she answered quietly.

''You got it. I'll follow you home from the station so you can pick up a change of clothes for tomorrow.''

The music faded away, to be replaced by a female singer crooning a love song in a smoky voice. Anticipation heated Sky's blood while she stared unseeingly out the windshield, her nerves humming. They were good nerves, she thought. Strong and sturdy nerves, not cowardly ones. She wasn't afraid of taking that last step into intimacy, not with Grant. She stared down at his long, tanned fingers entwined with hers. For her, to whom a man's touch hadn't always been gentle, hadn't always been kind, a touch like Grant's took away her fear.

Did she love him? Surprised by the direction her thoughts had veered, she slid him a look beneath the dark fringe of her lashes. In the deepening afternoon sunlight, his face was an alluring arrangement of planes and shadows. So much was happening inside her. So much, so fast. Lowering her gaze, she chewed her bottom lip. Maybe she had already stepped off the cliff and fallen in love. She didn't know.

The sudden clench of Grant's hand jerked her gaze back

to his face. His jaw had gone tight, his eyes hard and un-yielding. Wordlessly she followed his gaze out the wind-shield to the highway sign that marked the exit for Ventress, Oklahoma.

"Did you have a bad experience in Ventress?" she asked.

His chin came up. "No. Why?"

"Because you're glaring at the town's exit sign and about to cut off the circulation in my fingers."

His hand instantly slid from hers and settled on the steering wheel. "Sorry."

"It's okay." The white-knuckle grip he had on the wheel sent a ripple of unease down her spine. "Grant, is something wrong?"

"I've got things on my mind, that's all." His voice was light and even, but that didn't prevent her stomach from clutching with the same unsettled feeling that had plagued her after she told him about the rape.

The soft ring of the cell phone had them both shifting their attention.

"Pierce," Grant said after pushing a button on the dash.

"So, you're still alive," a deep, masculine voice boomed out of the phone's speaker.

Grant grinned. "Hi, bro. How are things?"

"Pierce Oil stock is up five points. I'm making you a ton of money, you slacker."

"Somebody's got to keep the world safe for oil moguls," Grant countered, giving Sky a wink.

Grant interrupted the good-natured expletive that came across the line. "Watch your language. There's a lady present. Sky Milano, meet Nathan Pierce."

"Hello, Nathan."

"Nice to meet you, Sky. If my little brother doesn't behave himself, just let me know. I'll hammer him into dust."

"Thanks."

Grant chuckled. "What's up?"

"Just wanted to remind you about tonight."

From the corner of her eye, Sky saw the instant tensing of Grant's fingers on the steering wheel. *"Tonight?"* he asked through his teeth.

"It's Oliver's birthday, *Uncle Grant.* Don't tell me you forgot."

Sky heard the low, frustrated groan that rumbled up Grant's throat. "I didn't forget. His present is bought and wrapped."

"Good. Oliver's requested hamburgers cooked out on the grill for his birthday dinner. Amelia said to tell you we'll eat at seven. Sky, you're invited."

She shook her head as if Nathan could see her. "Thanks, but—"

"We'll be there," Grant piped in before saying goodbye and disconnecting the call.

"Grant—"

"Save your breath, Milano. You're coming with me."

"It's a family dinner. I don't want to intrude."

"You and I have plans, lady, and I'm not letting you out of my sight tonight." His gaze lowered to her mouth, then came back to rest on her eyes. "Not for the whole night. Not for one second."

When he reached again for her hand, she felt the twin impact of the power of contact and the surge of need. "That okay with you?" he asked softly.

A flash of seductive anticipation had her throat going as dry as dust. "More than okay."

Chapter 10

"Pow! Pow! Die, you slimy galactic traitor!"

"I'm gut shot," Grant moaned. Clutching his middle, he staggered backward across the dimly lit flagstone terrace. "You win, Clingor," he groaned, then coughed twice for effect. "I relinquish control of Planet Earth."

Oliver Pierce let out a high-pitched whoop. Holding his new death-ray gun high above his head, he sprang up and down in victory, untied laces flopping around his scuffed tennis shoes.

"Death to aliens!" The smile he beamed at his uncle was minus the front tooth that a baseball had knocked out the week before. "Trent gets his next." With that, Oliver raced off across the expansive manicured lawn to massacre his younger brother.

Chuckling, Nathan Pierce handed Grant a can of soda he'd retrieved from inside the house. "How many times has he nuked you since he opened your gift?"

"I think that makes an even dozen," Grant said, rubbing at imaginary wounds on his stomach.

Nathan settled into an inviting wrought-iron lounger and stretched out his long, jeans-clad legs. "You deserve death for giving Oliver a galactic death-ray gun with the android-annihilation sound feature," Nathan said dryly. "He'll wipe out anything that moves for the next couple of weeks, and Amelia and I will get to hear *every* blast."

Grant grinned. "I'll rest easier knowing the universe is safe." As he took a seat in the chair beside his brother, thunder rumbled in the distance.

"We can use the rain," Nathan observed.

"Yeah." Grant sent an idle glance upward. A full moon skimmed in and out of fat gray clouds, illuminating the pristine lawn beyond the terrace in subdued shades of gray and black, with occasional patches of white. He and Nathan had grown up on the sprawling, oak-lined estate with cobblestone walks. After their parents died in a plane crash, the sons inherited the land and oil company in a fifty-fifty split. Grant had insisted Nathan move his family into the big house that edged the terrace where they now sat. Grant had settled into the guest house on the opposite side of the swimming pool where submerged lights turned the water a shimmering turquoise.

"I like your chemist," Nathan said.

Grant followed his brother's gaze to the far end of the terrace bordered by flowers and shrubs. Amelia and Sky stood beneath the soft spill of a gas lamp, examining a flower box blooming with miniature white roses. The easy smile on Sky's face told him she was enjoying his sister-in-law's good-natured company. Sky's easy interaction with his two lively nephews had earned her the honor of getting nuked several times by Oliver's galactic death-ray gun.

"I like her, too." Grant took a sip of the ice-cold soda while studying Sky over the can's rim. She had changed into a coral knit top and matching gauzy skirt that flared around her ankles in the warm night breeze that had turned heavy with the scent of rain. Her loose hair flowed down her back like a shaft of black velvet. He knew from experience that it felt just as soft.

"A lot," he added.

"She's different from any woman you've brought around before. In fact, she's the first you've actually invited to a family dinner."

"She's the first one I ever wanted to bring."

Falling silent, Grant watched while Sky examined the roses. Her smile was genuine, her profile delicate and clear-cut, completely feminine.

As if sensing his observation, she glanced across her shoulder, her smile widening when she met his gaze. She looked relaxed and at ease, but he could almost feel the nervous tension behind that smile.

The thought of all they would share later that night tightened his chest. He wanted to touch her, so much that he fought the urge to walk across the terrace and pull her into his arms. Closing his eyes for a brief instant, he realized his feelings for her had intensified from even what they had been a few days ago. How deep those feelings went, he didn't yet know. All he knew was how natural it felt to have her here with his family. How natural to have her at his side. How natural it was for him to want to right the injustice she'd suffered when her rapist walked.

His fingers clenched against the unbidden thought that blasted like sniper fire from the dark recesses of his subconscious.

"Want to tell me the reason you've been so quiet all evening?"

Grant slid his brother a look. Nathan had inherited their mother's dark hair, olive skin and talent for quietly observing things most other people missed.

"I've got a couple of cases giving me fits."

"I've been around you when you've had cases giving you fits, bro. This is different. What's up?"

Grant set his jaw. He had always been able to talk to Nathan. Always shared his thoughts, his deepest secrets. He wasn't sure how wise it was to reveal his thoughts now.

Scowling, he stared off into the darkness beyond the swimming pool. If talking to Nathan would somehow help him get a grip on the control that seemed to edge farther from his grasp each second, it was worth a shot.

"When Sky was in college, some slime drugged her, kidnapped her and raped her." Although he kept his voice quiet, Grant couldn't keep the anger that bubbled inside him from lacing his words. "She knew who it was but couldn't prove it, so he walked. He didn't pay for what he did."

Beneath the terrace lights, wariness slid into Nathan's eyes. "In college," he stated. "That was what, six, seven years ago?"

"Nine. The bastard victimized her in the worst possible way, crippled her emotionally. She's just now getting her life back together." Losing his taste for the soda, Grant set the can on a nearby glass-topped table. "She never got justice."

Nathan leaned forward slowly, propping a foot on either side of the lounger. "You sound like you think you're the man to deliver that justice."

"Why the hell not? I know the bastard's name," Grant grated. "He lives in Ventress. I drove within five miles of the town twice today. If Sky hadn't been with me, I probably would have taken a side trip."

"And done what?" The cautious tone in Nathan's voice matched the look in his dark eyes.

"I don't know." Rising, Grant walked a few steps and propped his forearms on top of the wooden railing that framed the terrace. Thunder rumbled again; the wind picked up, stirring the dark shapes of the oaks that dotted the grounds. "Just knowing the slime is out there walking around eats at me. I've tried to let it go, tried to push it out of my head. The cop inside me can't get free of it."

"Not just the cop," Nathan said, joining him at the railing. "If another man laid a finger on Amelia, I'd want to go after him, just like you. I'd want to kill him." Nathan paused. "I'd want to, but I wouldn't."

"Because two wrongs don't make a right," Grant shot back. He'd lost count of the number of times he'd told himself that since the night Sky had told him about her ordeal. Where Kirk Adams was concerned, no words of wisdom seemed to matter.

"True, they don't," Nathan agreed. "More important, I couldn't do something like that, then face Oliver and Trent."

Grant felt a fist tighten in his stomach. "I don't have sons."

"You've got two nephews who think you walk on water. And if you go after this guy, you may not get the chance to have kids of your own. *He's* the one who deserves to have his life ruined. Not you. I know you, bro. You're not the type of man who could take the law into his own hands and just walk away from it."

"In my own hands." Staring down at his clenched fists, Grant pulled in a deep breath, thick with the scent of the advancing storm. "That bastard makes me want to forget I wear a badge. I want to kill him for hurting her like that, Nathan. Destroy him with my bare hands." He raised his chin and met his brother's gaze. "I know how to do it. I know how to do it and not leave a trace."

"Yeah. That's what scares me."

The soft drift of female laughter had both men glancing toward the far end of the terrace. Sky and Amelia had settled into chairs around a low glass table with red geraniums spilling out of a pot in its center.

Nathan looked back at Grant, his eyes grim. "Does Sky have any idea about these feelings you're dealing with?"

"No, and I don't intend to tell her."

"Because you know you'll lose her if she finds out?"

"Because she's been through enough, dammit," Grant countered through his teeth.

"I agree. You just told me she's finally getting her life back together. Do you think she'd welcome your turning into a vigilante on her behalf?" Nathan asked, his voice as hard as the clap of thunder that split the air. "Do you think she'd want anything to do with you after that?"

Muttering a crude oath, Grant swung around, his fists clenched at his sides. "Could you really walk away, Nathan? Could you turn your back if some gutter-slime drugged Amelia, raped her, then dumped her in the street when he was done with her? Could you just forget it, knowing he got away without so much as a slap on the hand?"

Nathan rubbed a hand across his jaw. "I guess I can't say for sure what I would do unless I was faced with it," he said finally.

"Damn right you can't."

"What I do know is that if I did go after the guy, it would be because he hurt someone I love," Nathan pointed out. "Makes me think it's a hell of a lot harder for you to accept what happened to Sky because you're in love with her."

"I don't know...." Furrowing his brow, Grant let his

voice trail off. She was the only woman he wanted to be
with. The only woman he'd brought home to his family,
the only woman he'd considered a future with. He wanted
to make her his, protect her, keep her safe for the rest of
her life.

He let out a slow breath. "Damn," he said quietly.

Nathan settled a hand on his shoulder. "My advice, bro,
is concentrate on those feelings. You've got a hell of a lot
to gain, and even more to lose."

"I like your family," Sky said as she walked at Grant's
side along the lighted cobblestone path leading to his house.
Overhead, the wind swirled, rustling the leaves of the tall
oaks that lined the path.

"You were a hit with them, too."

"Amelia is really nice. Nathan's a lot like you. Well,
this is the first time I've met him, but that's the impression
I got." She was babbling. She knew it, yet the way every
nerve in her body had knotted made it impossible for her
to keep quiet. "And your nephews. They're real charmers.
Both of them."

"Hmm." Grant slid her a look before stepping into the
driveway and pausing beside the Porsche. He opened the
driver's door and retrieved the file folder containing the
background information on Jason Whitebear, and the overnight bag Sky had packed.

"Oliver likes the gun you bought him," she continued
when he shut the door. Folding her arms over her breasts,
she leaned against the side of the Porsche. "I think he shot
everybody about ten times."

"At least." A bolt of lightning split the dark sky, followed by a crack of thunder. Grant glanced up, then gave
her a mild look. "It's okay with me if we stand out here

all night and chat, but if we do, we're going to get wet. And maybe fried by lightning.''

''You're right.'' She pushed away from the car and turned toward the house. She had the sudden vision of how crazed she must have looked six months ago when she'd dashed, sobbing, out the front door and down the porch steps. Running away because Grant had taken her into his arms.

Her fingers clenched over her damp palms. She had been so sure she was doing the right thing by opting to spend the night here. So sure she was ready to give herself to Grant. To let him take what she so desperately wanted to offer. Why then, if she was ready, did just walking beside him up the brick steps and onto his front porch put a cold feeling in the pit of her stomach?

The clay pots holding neatly trimmed shrubs on either side of the front door looked the same as they had on that disastrous night six months ago. The brass door knocker had lost none of its brilliant polish, the wood none of its sheen.

Nerve-aching frustration had her grinding her teeth. She was tired of being afraid of something that should be wonderful. Tired of living a sterile existence with only test tubes, scientific instruments and co-workers she never let herself get close to. She wanted more. She wanted the life that had been stolen from her. Yet, as she stood in the amber pool of light from the porch lamp, she could feel herself drawing back, felt the stirrings of uncertainty begin again.

Grant must have sensed it, too, because before she could draw in the breath to tell him she'd changed her mind, he put a finger under her chin and nudged it up. His mouth lowered, pausing a whisper from hers. ''Nothing's going to happen that you don't want to happen,'' he murmured, his voice a warm sweep against her mouth. "You have my word."

She watched him through her lashes while her breath quickened. Slowly he shifted his head to nibble along her jawline.

She closed her eyes on a moan while his mouth feasted on her chin, then slowly worked its magic down the side of her throat. Her legs began to shake; heat slid into her stomach to melt the cold knot that had settled there.

When he raised his head, the dim light from the porch lamp deepened the hollows in his cheeks, shadowed his gray eyes. Slowly his mouth curved. "You've flipped me onto my butt and given me a good kick in the chest. Trust me, Milano, I won't get out of line tonight."

The lightness in his voice had her forcing back the rawness in her nerves long enough for her to return his smile. "If you do, I'll try not to break too many bones."

"Ouch." He arched a sandy eyebrow. "Maybe we should just play a few games of backgammon and call it a night."

"Maybe." Blowing out a breath, she watched him slide his key into the lock, then push open the front door.

He reached in, flipped on a switch. "After you."

As far as she could tell, nothing about the marble-floored foyer with its subdued lighting had changed, but then the last time she'd crossed it she'd been sobbing. The memory of how badly she'd bungled everything on her first and only other visit to Grant's home edged a sick feeling into the pit of her stomach. A heartbeat later, she straightened her shoulders. *She* had changed, she reminded herself. Healed. She had come here tonight to expel the ghosts of her past, not to let them consume her.

Grant shut the door behind him. The snap of the dead bolt sliding into place hitched her heartbeat up a notch. He set her overnight bag on the floor, then turned and took her hand. "How about a glass of wine?" he asked as he led the way into the living room.

"Sounds good." She harbored the vague hope that the wine would settle her nerves.

The furniture in the spacious room was the same—expensive yet comfortable looking with matching pillows that added inviting splashes of color. A leather recliner with a thick paperback in its seat sat next to a wood side table that held a brass lamp and the TV remote control.

Grant dropped a light kiss against her hair, then walked across the room and laid the file folder on the huge antique desk with a large window behind it. Outside the window lightning flashed, illuminating the swirling oaks in a ghostly white hue.

He turned and nodded toward the sofa. "Make yourself comfortable. I'll get the wine. Maybe put on some music."

Sky nodded, remembering how much she had liked this room. The paneling was dark and gleaming, the bookcases full, the ceiling high, the rug beneath her feet thick and luxurious. She remembered watching Grant build a fire in the hunter-green marble fireplace. She had not stayed long enough to enjoy it.

Too edgy to sit, she walked to the mantel lined with framed pictures. She recognized photos of Nathan and Amelia and their sons. Another frame held a picture of a distinguished man and woman sitting on the sunbaked deck of a yacht. Grant's eyes had the same shape as the woman's.

While Sky examined the photo, the moan of a sax drifted on the air. She turned, realizing he'd switched on the stereo system.

With her hands stuffed in the pockets of her long skirt,

she moved restlessly around the room, examining oil paintings she suspected were originals.

"I opened a bottle of red," Grant said as he came through the door. "I hope it's okay." He had pulled the tail of his gray dress shirt out of his slacks and it was wrinkled from having been tucked into his waistband. His sleeves were rolled up on his forearms, and he'd ditched his Italian leather loafers somewhere. He had opened a couple of shirt buttons, revealing tanned skin and a swirl of gold hair at the vee. He looked calm and relaxed.

How could he look calm and relaxed when she was about to climb out of her skin?

"Red's fine." When she accepted the stemmed glass, his fingers slid against hers, making her stomach somersault. With dryness creeping up her throat, she took a quick sip of wine, barely noticing that it was as smooth as chilled silk on her tongue.

A crash of thunder splintered the air; in the next instant, rain hammered the roof, slashed against the windows. The saxophone ached out its tune, then began another, the pure notes reaching to Sky's soul, putting an answering ache inside her.

She wanted this man. Wanted him desperately, yet she wasn't sure she could give herself to him.

Slipping a hand beneath her hair, she rubbed at the tension at the back of her neck. "I don't…"

Sipping his wine, Grant examined her with intense gray eyes over the rim of his glass. "You don't what, Sky?"

She looked away. "I thought I could do this." She shook her head, then brought her gaze back to his. "I don't know how to do this. Don't know if I can."

Slowly he took her glass, sat it beside his own on a nearby table. He gazed down at her for the length of a heartbeat, then held out his hand. "Dance with me."

When she hesitated, he took her hand, linking his fingers with hers. "We've danced before." Bringing her hand to his mouth, he grazed his lips across her knuckles. "At the department's Christmas party."

We danced before, and I didn't come unglued. Calmed by the thought, she stepped silently into his arms.

There was no choice now but to feel. His touch nudged her emotions to the surface. The war between need and doubt she'd waged for so long battered her, made her heart tremble, her muscles go weak. A quick flash of panic had her turning her head. He murmured her name, placed a soft, soothing kiss against her temple.

Swallowing past the lump in her throat, she closed her eyes, rested her cheek against his chest and inhaled the musky scent of him. His shoulder felt hard beneath her hand. His fingers, linked with hers, were warm and strong. She could feel the firm possession of his other hand at her waist. As they had so long ago when they'd first danced, she had the sense that their bodies fit together like two pieces of a puzzle.

The thought quickened her pulse as the soft music drifted on the air. The feel of Grant's body against hers was so warm, she wanted to sink into him for comfort. But when she found herself doing so, she started to pull back.

"It's okay." His hand slid to the small of her back, easing her closer. "Just relax," he said, his words barely a murmur.

As they swayed to the hypnotic weep of the sax, her body's awareness of his increased. She sensed the hard strength in the arms that held her, the power in the muscular chest against her breasts, the masculine firmness in the thighs that moved against hers.

His hand journeyed up her spine, slid beneath her hair

and closed lightly over the back of her neck. He tilted her head back until her gaze met his. "Still okay?"

She moved her hand from his shoulder and brushed her fingertips along the side of his neck. His pulse jerked beneath her touch. "Yes."

His lips hovered just above hers, his intent gaze locked on her face. She sensed he was focused on her vulnerabilities as if she were a piece of crystal to be handled with care. Her heart rose to her throat. She hadn't felt valued or treasured in so long that she'd completely forgotten what it was like. Here, then, was a man who made her remember.

When he used his tongue to trace a lazy line over her lips, her heart dropped from her throat to her toes.

He captured her bottom lip between his teeth; she closed her eyes and would have sworn the floor tilted beneath her feet. He nibbled, subtly drawing her lip into his mouth to softly suckle. She felt the answering tug deep inside her, felt the soft, wet pulse between her legs come to life. The fingers on the back of her neck stroked her flesh while heat spread throughout her entire body.

His mouth took hers now, soft and warm, and Sky felt herself getting lost in the light, brushing kisses. Her breasts were tight, achy against the hardness of his chest. Suddenly she wanted the taste of him to be more than a memory, wanted it so much that she rose on tiptoe and deepened the kiss herself, tentatively probing his mouth with her tongue as her fingers slid up into his hair.

A low groan rose in his throat. She tasted the tang of wine on his lips as his mouth coaxed and enticed. She made a whimpering sound in the back of her throat. Not a sound of protest. Not of pain, but a cry of need, desire. A dizzy desire that took hold of her, wiping away any lingering fear.

Dozens of nerves jumped to tangle over each other; her

knees turned to water, and she murmured his name against
his mouth.

"A bed," he said, his voice low and husky while he
skimmed kisses across her cheek, her jaw. "This first time,
we need a bed."

Thunder crashed as he swept her up into his arms. He
continued to kiss her, deep and drugging, as he carried her
down the dark hallway into his bedroom.

Her brain vaguely acknowledged that she'd been in this
room before with its sturdy sleigh bed covered in quilted,
masculine plaids. Then she'd been afraid. Of herself, of
Grant. Now all she felt was thrumming desire and hot need.
The knowledge that she could feel again, really feel, made
her head spin.

When he lowered her feet to the floor, she gazed up at
him in the rain-washed dimness of the room, his face lit by
the watery light seeping through the window. She wanted
to tell him how she felt, but she couldn't get the words past
the tightness in her throat. Instead she rose on tiptoe and
placed a soft kiss against his throat.

"Slow," he groaned softly. "We're going to take this
slow."

He eased her down on the bed, his hands firm and sure.
He slid off her sandals, then lowered beside her, his mouth
seeking hers again, not only to reassure, but to seduce.

His hand slid beneath her knit top, his fingers skimming
up her rib cage, upward to the swell of one breast. Her
body shuddered.

Need, deep and dark, heated her blood. She moved
against him, her hands sliding into his hair, her fingers
clutching, while she drowned in his kiss.

When he raised his head, she moaned in protest.

"Let me look at you, Sky. I've thought about having

you here with me. Imagined it countless times. I need to look at you.''

Her lips parted as his fingers brushed through her long hair, letting it feather onto the pillow. His eyes stayed on hers as he slowly unbuttoned her top, spread it open. With deft fingers he unhooked the front clasp on her bra, then nudged it aside. Cool air swept across her breasts, tightening her nipples.

When she raised a hand to cover herself, he linked his fingers with hers, pressed a kiss against her wrist where her pulse hammered. With her hand still in his, he lowered his mouth to her breast. His tongue circled her nipple, teasing it into a hard, hot peak. Then his lips settled, suckled. A moan rose in her throat. Maybe minutes…or hours later, his mouth trailed a slow, maddening path across her flesh. Her hand flexed desperately under his as he shifted to her other breast.

He drew her into his mouth, flooding her skin with a delicious warmth; her body arched willingly as he peeled away her blouse and bra.

His lips grazed the curve and hollow of her shoulder, moved torturously down across her breast, down her rib cage. His fingers slid beneath her waistband; he drew down her skirt and panties together. Inch by slow inch the gauzy fabric whispered down her legs, his lips following its path.

''You're beautiful.'' In the dim light his face was all she could see, and in his eyes she saw herself.

Her body was on fire, burning from the inside out. She had not known she could want like this. Had never thought she would again welcome a man's touch. Now she wanted nothing more than for him to take her where she'd been so afraid to go. Fighting to draw air into her lungs, she no longer heard the storm outside, the poignant moan of the wind. Her body writhing with need, she reached up, fumbled with his shirt buttons, her hands urgent as she shoved the starched fabric down his arms. The weak, rain-washed light seeping through the window played along his shifting, fluid muscles.

He moved away, long enough to rid himself of the rest of his clothing, then he was beside her again. She savored the feel of his hardness against her thigh as his hand flowed over her like silk, moving between her legs to cup her. Slowly, softly, his fingers slid into her wet folds, moving with intimate strokes to arouse, to madden.

She turned her head restlessly on the pillow as the flood of sensation began to rise. The air was too thick to breathe. Time spun to a standstill while his fingers moved, caressed. A roaring filled her brain, then pleasure slammed into her, a velvet fist which had her arching up, gasping his name.

He brought his mouth back to hers, her shuddering breaths mixing with his own as he drove her up again. The ragged explosions of pleasure left her wanting to plead, to beg as wave after wave of sensations battered her. All she could do was float, weightless, while she whispered his name against his damp flesh. And somewhere in the dim recesses of her mind she knew she had left fear far behind.

He shifted, moving on top of her, resting his weight on his forearms on either side of her head. Vaguely she understood that he was careful not to trap her, that she could free herself from his hold. She didn't want freedom. Or control. She wanted to give not only her body to this man, this one man, but her soul, as well.

He slipped into her with one long, slow thrust while his mouth skimmed her bare shoulder. He whispered soothingly to her, words of reassurance she couldn't quite grasp, but the smooth timbre of his voice was more effective than any words. She felt him tremble as she did. His hands sought hers, fingers locking. Against her breasts, she could feel his heart thudding in his chest.

Her nails dug into his hands as he increased the rhythm. Their bodies moved as one, their breath tangled, then caught as pleasure heightened, finally sweeping them together into the heart of the storm.

Grant lay unmoving when Sky's hands slid limply from his back to the tangled sheets. He didn't speak—he couldn't, not while their bodies were still linked so intimately and his heart hammered violently against his ribs.

She was his. In every way she was his, and he was in love with her. He had not known the depth of his feelings until the moment when he'd felt her go pliant with pleasure beneath his touch. Until he'd tasted hot need on her mouth. Until he'd heard that soft, yielding sound she made deep in her throat as she lost herself in him.

More than he'd ever wanted anything in his life, he wanted her.

Gently he feathered a sweat-slicked curl away from her temple, placed a soft kiss there.

"Grant…" Her voice hitched with emotion, her dark eyes were wide, still filled with a cloudy haze of desire. "I…"

"Shh," he murmured, dropping a kiss against her flushed cheek. "You don't have to say anything right now, Sky." He traced her swollen lips with a fingertip. "Just let me hold you."

"Yes, hold me."

Shifting onto his back, he wrapped his arms around her and drew her close. Rain drummed against the roof as she pressed her face into the hollow between his shoulder and neck and murmured his name. The fingers she rested against his chest drew soft swirls against his still-heated flesh.

He loved her and she was his and he was going to make sure nothing bad ever happened to her again. The need to protect, to revenge the hurt she'd suffered welled inside him with a raging force. The cop in him recognized that his need was edging on obsession. A dangerous obsession.

The man inside him didn't care.

He lay in silence, listening to the slashing rain, the tor-menting wind as he traced a fingertip up and down the length of her spine. The storm outside wasn't much differ-ent from the one brewing inside him, he decided. In time, the rain would let up, the clouds would drift away.

Closing his eyes, he hoped to God that, with time, the fury inside him would calm, as well.

Chapter 11

Sky woke to the soft thrum of rain against the window. It wasn't the small pane in her own bedroom that the first watery rays of dawn crept through. Her mouth curved in sleepy contentment at the realization. It was Grant's window. In Grant's bedroom.

The man who immediately consumed her thoughts lay sprawled facedown beside her, one arm draped across her waist. His head was angled toward the window so that in the thready light she could make out the high slash of one cheekbone, the stubble that shadowed the firm line of his jaw, the hair that fell carelessly over his forehead.

A deep sense of yearning had her reaching out. With a fingertip, she nudged back a wayward sandy strand. The small movement brought the awareness of an ache, dull and sweet, through her entire body to remind her of their long night of lovemaking. Lying beside him, with the sound of his steady breathing mixed with the patter of rain, she was filled with a swirling mix of emotion.

On that one terrifying night in her past, it had taken only seconds to drastically change the course of her life. The same was true of the time she had spent in Grant's arms. She'd left the darkness behind and now all she wanted to think about was the future.

She had given all of herself to Grant, but he had given her much more than just himself. He had made her remember how it felt to be feminine, banished her fear of intimacy and shattered the emotional wall she'd built around herself so long ago.

She yearned to tell him how she felt, to relay her emotions in simple, exquisite words. She couldn't, she realized. Not while everything spiraled inside her, making it impossible to know where one emotion ended and another began. This newfound sense of elation had turned her thoughts to spun sugar, airy and light. And it wasn't just emotion that made her feel as if she were floating. Physically her body had awakened. The knowledge that she wanted Grant more now than she had during the night seemed almost overwhelming after years of celibacy.

Raising on one elbow, she shoved her tumbled hair out of her eyes. She needed time to process her thoughts. Time to analyze her feelings. She was used to the logic of her lab where she made decisions using the controlled, precise mechanisms of scientific tests. There, in her lab, emotion played no part in those decisions.

Blowing out a slow breath, she concluded that since she was now fully awake, she could use some caffeine to help get her thoughts aligned.

Slowly she slipped from beneath Grant's arm. His response was to turn his head and bury his face in the pillow.

The rain had put a chill in the air, sending goose bumps prickling over her skin. Her overnight bag that Grant had carried in from the Porsche still sat near the front door, so she plucked his shirt off the floor where he'd tossed it and slid it on. The tang of the expensive, spicy cologne that brought him so clearly to mind had her pulse throbbing hard and quick.

Closing the bedroom door behind her, she padded down the dark hallway, making a quick stop at the bathroom before heading for the kitchen. She found coffee and filters in one of the oak cabinets over a stovetop that looked as if it could do duty in a gourmet restaurant. While she waited for her brew, she checked the school pictures of Oliver and Trent affixed by magnets to the refrigerator door. With a lift of one eyebrow, she suspected she looked depraved standing there, wearing only their uncle's wrinkled shirt and a smile. She didn't care, she thought as she poured steaming coffee into a mug. This newfound freedom felt so good. So right.

Sipping the hot, heady brew, she wandered into the living room, thinking she might check the title on the paperback lying in the leather recliner. She changed direction when the file folder on top of the antique desk caught her eye. Grant had mentioned that the folder contained background information on Jason Whitebear. Sky eyed the folder over the rim of her mug as she dragged a hand through her tousled hair. Since she was the reason Grant hadn't gone through the file last night, she could at least take a look to see if the latest check had revealed any interesting information on Jason, aka Spider.

Setting the mug on a brass coaster shaped like a badge, Sky slid into the leather desk chair and flipped open the file's cover. While rain drizzled steadily against the wide window at her back, she read what she guessed were Sam Rogers's handwritten notes made two years ago after Mavis Benjamin's death. Sam had found nothing to suggest that

Spider had been in Oklahoma City the day the apartment manager was murdered.

Laying the notes facedown, Sky opened two pieces of paper that had been folded together.

A coldness more gray than the dawn seeped into her body, into her very bones, and she heard herself make an anguished little sound. Years dissolved in an instant as she stared into the face of the man who had raped her.

Barely awake, Grant leaned in the doorway of his living room and studied Sky. She looked almost ghostlike, standing before the wide window behind his desk, staring out into the rain-soaked grayness. The stab of panic when he'd woken and found her gone made him wonder if he'd imagined last night. Though the scent of her lingered on his pillow, the feeling of unease had been strong enough for him to pull on a faded pair of cutoffs and go in search of her.

A tightness settled in his chest when he realized how right it felt to find her in his living room in the early hours of the morning. His gaze took in the dark hair that cascaded in a gorgeous mess around her shoulders, then lowered to the hem of his shirt that skimmed her long bare legs midthigh. Like a bewitching phantom, the memory of the soft, silky feel of those legs against his flesh started the blood swimming in his veins.

Over the years he had dated often, seldom seeing any woman more than a few times. Until last night, he had not known, really known, the difference between sex and making love. Had no idea that the mere act could mean so much. That holding just one woman—*the* woman—could be both elating and frightening. With Sky, all the smooth moves he'd always taken for granted seemed rusty. No other woman had made him want so badly. No other woman had made him willing to beg for her touch. If he hadn't been ready to admit the depth of his feelings before, he was more than ready now. She was the one, and she was his. Amazingly his.

He intended to make sure she knew that.

Sky had no idea how long it had been since her legs had stopped trembling enough so that she could rise from the chair behind the desk. No clear concept of when she'd moved to the window. It could have been minutes—maybe hours—since the cold numbness settled inside her.

It wasn't numbness she felt when Grant reached from behind her, swept back her hair and pressed his heated mouth to her throat.

"No!"

He grinned as she whirled around. "Didn't mean to scare—"

She knew by the way his grin instantly faded that her eyes mirrored the despair clawing inside her.

"What's wrong?" He took her by the shoulders. When she tried to draw away, his eyes narrowed. "Did I hurt you last night? Good God, Sky, I never meant to hurt you."

"You didn't hurt me." The jittering of her stomach echoed in her voice.

His hands tightened their hold. "Tell me what's wrong."

She closed her eyes for a brief instant. "I need to show you something," she said, then stepped from his touch and walked the few steps to the desk. She saw his gaze flick to the open file folder, saw realization flash in his eyes.

With an unsteady hand she picked up the two pieces of paper that had been folded inside the file, and held them toward him. "Why did you check on Kirk Adams?"

Grant stood unmoving, the hazy light from the window

slanting across his face while his gray eyes stayed locked on hers. "To find the bastard," he said after a moment.

"Why?"

"To make him pay. I want him to pay for what he did to you."

She felt the blood drain from her face. She had known the reason—of course she'd known—when she found the copy of Kirk Adams's yearbook photo and driver's license information that showed he lived in Ventress, Oklahoma. It had been the exit sign for Ventress that had turned Grant's eyes to steel when they'd driven past it yesterday. Yes, she'd known, yet hearing him confirm it put a knot in the pit of her stomach that went beyond dread into fear.

She returned the papers to the desk. "Have you already done something to make him pay?"

"Not yet."

She took a careful breath to counteract the twisting in her stomach. "Adams isn't going to pay," she managed in a calm voice. Turning, she faced him, her hands gripping the edge of the desk behind her. With the ground shifting beneath her feet, she needed something solid to hold on to. "I accepted that a long time ago, Grant. Kirk Adams will never pay for what he did to me."

"You deserve justice." The same hardness that shone in his eyes sounded in his voice.

"Justice, not revenge. That's the first thing I worked through." Her fingers clenched on the desk's hard wood. "I didn't see his face that night, so I couldn't identify him. That was just another part of the rape I couldn't control. But I could control how I dealt with it. I got my own justice."

"You changed your major," Grant shot back, repeating what she'd told him the night in McAlester. "You get revenge in the lab, using evidence to nail other rapists and killers."

"I get *justice* in the lab."

"That's all well and good, Sky, but it sure as hell doesn't take care of your own unfinished business."

"You and I did that last night."

He narrowed his eyes and took a step toward her. "You're telling me last night wiped away all the memories? You're telling me you didn't think about the rape this morning? That for even a second you didn't think about it? That you won't think about how he walked away from what he did to you, every morning for the rest of your life?"

"I won't ever forget," she said carefully. "But now I can put it in the past. This morning, for the first time, I felt free. Finally the rape no longer has control over everything I do. Every move I make." She flicked a look back at the papers on the desk. The thought of what Grant might do made the coldness inside her turn to ice. "Maybe I was wrong."

Saying nothing, he turned his head, stared out the window. The angry tic of muscle in his jaw tightened her throat. She thought about Dr. Mirren's comment that he needed time to accept what had happened to her. That he had to work through it, just as she had. She was achingly aware that *she* had taken nine years to deal with the anger, the desperate fear. The banked fury in Grant's eyes told her no amount of time would ease his anger. That knowledge sent a bright flash of panic up her spine.

"I lived through hell and I survived. *I survived—*" Her voice broke off as though it had been cut by something sharp. "It's over. I've turned away from my past. That's what you have to do."

"I'm not sure I can," he said softly, keeping his gaze locked on the window.

The honesty in his quiet words heightened the panic clawing through her. "I can't—*won't*—be a part of your life unless you do."

He jerked his head around, his mouth set in a tight line, his eyes shooting gray fire. "If you think I'm going to settle for just one night with you, Milano, think again."

She raised her chin. "It's *my* life, Pierce. You'll settle for what I decide is right for me."

"I didn't mean..." Regret slid into his eyes as he dragged a hand through his hair. "I'm in love with you, Sky. That's a first for me. I don't want to lose you. I want to spend every night with you."

She turned toward the desk before he could see the tears welling in her eyes. She had dreamed of this. Even when she thought she could never have the kind of relationship most people took for granted, she had dreamed of having a man love her. For so long, a dream was all it had been. And now, though she had healed and wanted desperately to accept Grant's love, the rape stood between them.

"I always made it a point to avoid strings in a relationship." His cool, lethal voice, coming just inches behind her, had her jolting. "Despite that, I sometimes imagined I might eventually tell a woman I loved her. What I never imagined was she would turn her back on me when I did."

Dragging in a ragged breath, Sky stared down at the picture of Kirk Adams through a haze of tears. "I'm not turning my back on you," she said after a moment.

"You might come off more convincing if you face me when you say that."

Fighting to gain composure, she turned. She longed to reach out, step into his arms and tell him everything would be all right. Problem was, she had little faith in those words right now.

Her lips trembled before she pressed them together.

"What I'm turning my back on is my past," she said finally, her voice thin and desperate. "I've lived through it, Grant. I can't do it again. I won't. If you can't put this aside, I can't be with you."

"Adams drugged you. Kidnapped you. *Raped* you. I'm a cop—do you imagine I can turn a blind eye to that?" he asked furiously. "Do you expect me to let that bastard walk around free and clear when I know what he did to you?"

"You don't solve every homicide you work." Frustration had her balling her hands against her thighs. "Sometimes you know who did it and you just can't prove it. You walk away easy enough—"

"This is personal."

"For *me,* Grant. It happened to *me*. Not you."

"Do you know what it did to me the night you told me about the rape?" His hands gripped her upper arms. "Seeing the panic in your eyes, hearing the fear in your voice? You were afraid for your life. Terrified. I *felt* that terror, Sky."

Her throat was so dry, she wasn't sure she could speak. He was right—she had relived every horrifying moment of the rape that night. Felt Adams's hands groping her flesh, had cried out when the sharp tip of the blade sliced against her throat. Because the nightmare had been so real, she'd had no defenses left when Grant dragged her out of its torturous grip. She realized now she'd been wrong to tell him so much when she'd had no control over her emotions.

She raised a hand and cupped his cheek. Beneath her palm, she felt the morning stubble that covered his jaw. "When I told you what happened to me, it wasn't a cop I was talking to." She stared up into his eyes, wanting desperately to erase the hardness she saw there. "It was the man who would become my lover. Even then, I knew if I could ever get close to a man, it would be you. Only you, Grant.''

"I can't forget what he did to you," he said through his teeth, his fingers digging into her arms.

"You have to—"

"Don't you think I've tried?" he countered. "If I could take a knife and cut it out of me, I would. I wear a badge, for God's sake. I'm not supposed to have these thoughts. But I do."

"The thoughts are fine." She pulled away, grabbed the two pieces of paper off the desk. "It's when you do something about them that you cross the line."

His gaze flicked to her hand, then resettled on her face. "You want me to play fair and honest, separate things into black and white. Good and bad, right and wrong. From where I'm standing, there are too many gray areas to do that."

"At first, I wanted revenge, too." Squaring her shoulders, she wadded the pages into a hard, tight ball. "I spent hours, days, months contemplating how to make Adams pay. I used my knowledge of poisons to plot an agonizing death for him. I even mixed up a vial." Feeling suddenly cold, she wrapped her arms around her waist. "In the end I couldn't do it."

Grant cocked his head. "What changed your mind? Why didn't you go through with it?"

"Because I knew deep down if I did, it would make me no better than him. Worse than him."

"Yeah." Grant rubbed his palms over his face, a gesture of such misery that she longed to go to him, hold him close. Instead, she remained where she was, the pages wadded in one fist.

"It took me a long time to learn I was giving Adams power by letting what he did to me control my life," she said. "The answer is not to get even, Grant, but not to be a victim. Not to let the past control the future."

He came to her, settled his hands on her waist and stared down into her face with haunted eyes. "I'm not used to walking away from a bad guy."

"I know." Sky's lungs were burning, and the sensation was rapidly moving toward her heart. This man, for whom she cared so deeply, was standing before her with turmoil in his eyes because of *her*. Because of a deep-seated need to make things right for her. Desperation rose inside her like a flood. "Do you think I could handle it if anything happened to you? Do you think I could just go on if you threw your life away because of me?"

"Sky—"

She gripped his arms, her nails digging in. "You have to walk away from this. Give me your word you'll walk away."

He grazed his knuckles down the length of her cheek, and shook his head. "I don't know if I can."

Squeezing her eyes shut, she slid her arms around his waist and rested her head against his shoulder. After so long, after so much pain and suffering, she had the man she wanted in the circle of her arms.

And she was terribly afraid she was about to lose him.

"Just how many jobs can one man hold in two years?" Julia Remington asked Grant hours later.

"And how many apartments can he rent in that same time period?" he asked, looking over the top of the latest printout he'd received from Communications. He'd accepted Julia's offer to spend the afternoon helping him track Jason Whitebear's activities over the past two years. To make it easier to compare notes, she'd taken up residence at Sam's empty desk that butted the front of Grant's.

Lieutenant Ryan didn't seem in any more of a hurry to fill Sam's slot than Grant was to get a new partner.

"The count's up to eleven jobs, six apartments," he stated after checking the list he'd compiled on a yellow legal pad. "People working in construction move around."

"Tell me," Julia commented, flipping her long, auburn hair over one shoulder, "what is this Spider guy, a jack-of-all-trades?"

"Laborer," Grant replied. "All of the construction foremen I've talked to say Spider's tried his hand at a lot of jobs, and he's good at them, but he doesn't have the drive to stick with any one thing for the long run. What he does is hire on as a helper." Grant checked another list. "He's mixed mud for bricklayers. Been a gopher for a plumber. A framing carpenter's helper. Construction's one of those professions where job tenure doesn't much matter—you can usually hire on with any company that needs the labor."

Julia tilted her head. "When Sloan and I had our kitchen remodeled, the contractor had a heck of a time getting some crew members to just show up from one day to the next. I got the impression that was standard practice."

"It is. That's probably one reason Spider has worked in so many jobs—somebody doesn't show up one day, he gets shifted somewhere to take up the slack." Grant laid the printout aside and stretched his neck to try to get rid of the kinks that always set in after he'd spent long hours at his desk. "Sam couldn't find anyone who saw Spider here the day Mavis Benjamin got killed. Our backtracking hasn't changed that."

"Might as well file that under 'dead end.'"

"Yeah." Grant tapped his fingertips against the desktop. "At least we now know what company Spider worked for when Carmen Peña—the convenience store clerk—was murdered.'' Grant checked his watch, was mildly surprised to find it was after four. "When that company's foreman returns my call, I'll know if Spider was working around here the night of the murder."

"He sure would be easier to track if he had a fist full of priors. The guy's squeaky clean, or he's sly enough not to get caught. Either way, there's not much to go on." Julia paused for a moment, her lips curving. "You know, Sam used to say that clues are like ingredients in a recipe with no instructions. Put them together the right way, you have dinner."

"If you don't," Grant chimed in, "you'll be in the kitchen a long time, confused and hungry. Right now I'm puzzled as hell and starving."

Julia's eyes softened as she stroked a palm over the top of Sam's desk. "I guess we both learned a lot from your partner."

"Yeah." Grant rubbed his burning eyes, kept his fingers pressed there for a moment. He wished to hell Sam was around to give him some advice now.

Julia checked the clock hanging over the Homicide assignment board, then closed the cover on a file and tossed it on top of Grant's overflowing in-basket. "Sorry to desert you, Pierce, but I'm out of here."

Grant arched an eyebrow. "You suddenly get a hot lead?"

"Hot date. I've arranged with Ryan to duck out early. Sloan and I have a black-tie dinner tonight." She cocked her head. "I need time to get dolled up so I can sweep my husband off his feet." She slid her gaze around the almost deserted squad room, then leaned forward as if to share a secret. "I happen to be crazy about the guy."

"No kidding?" Grant asked dryly. Julia was a tough,

no-nonsense cop, but when the subject veered to Sloan Remington, she turned to goo.

"Yep, I'm in love."

So am I, Grant thought as Julia rose and headed across the room to her own desk. The fist that clenched in his chest had him setting his jaw. The minute he'd walked in the office that morning, he'd dived into work, had purposely kept his thoughts from turning to Sky. He hadn't wanted to picture the fear he'd seen in her eyes when she'd asked his intentions about Kirk Adams. Hadn't wanted to acknowledge how it had shredded him to pieces to know *he'd* put that fear there.

Leaning back in his chair, Grant blew out a breath. He could close his eyes and hear again the scream that ripped from her throat during the nightmare. Could feel the sick terror that had reduced her to a sobbing, quivering mass in his arms.

He wanted to forget. Wanted to let go of the memory, of the burning need for revenge that raged inside him. A need that had already wedged a sliver of fear and wariness between him and Sky.

Dammit, he loved her. With her, he wanted the now. The future. All he could seem to do was dwell on her past.

His gaze flicked to a row of battered cabinets that lined one wall of the squad room. The cabinets all contained file after file of homicides. It was his job to solve that particular type of crime, to seek justice for each victim. He was well aware it wasn't in his job description to sit at his desk and contemplate murder himself.

Groaning inwardly, he scrubbed his hands over his face. It haunted him that he wanted to hunt down a man and hurt him. That he could be driven by pure and simple unadulterated vengeance. So driven that thoughts of his career, of the code of honor he'd sworn, of the life he'd built paled against the need to take action.

The control he'd maintained since he'd walked into the office that morning suddenly shifted. Emotion coiled inside him like a tightly wound clock, ready to spring.

Muttering an oath, he rose, grabbed his suit coat and stalked toward the door. He had two cases in the toilet and his personal life was teetering on the brink of hell. He had to do something about both issues. He wasn't quite sure what that something was, but, by God, he was going to do it.

Chapter 12

A slate-blue twilight had settled over the city by the time Sky nosed her Blazer into her assigned parking space outside her apartment. Shoving the transmission into Park, she remained motionless, her gaze riveted on the rearview mirror, searching the parking lot for movement. Her already ragged nerves sizzled from waiting for headlights to stab around the corner she'd just turned.

Minutes passed without the appearance of the dark vehicle that had seemed to mirror her every lane change and turn during the hour's drive home from the meeting with her former hematology professor.

Blowing out a weighty breath, she forced her fingers to unclench from the steering wheel while she told herself she'd imagined being followed. She hadn't, after all, glimpsed more than the hood of a dark car...or cars in the heavy traffic and snarling construction zone that had made the drive home seem interminable. It was more a sensation of unease that *someone* had been following her. Watching.

"Get a grip, Milano," she muttered, pinching the bridge of her nose. She knew it wasn't just what she'd learned from Professor Linley that had her senses jittery. It was the fact that, when she'd called Homicide to talk to Grant, no one seemed to know where he was. And he hadn't returned the messages she'd left for him.

The memory of the tense grimness she'd seen in his eyes that morning sent fingers of cold creeping up along her spine. For all she knew, he was in Ventress, Oklahoma, giving Kirk Adams a taste of revenge.

She shrank away from the thought that put an instant curl of nausea in the pit of her stomach. She couldn't think about the man she cared so deeply for that way, she told herself as she switched off the Blazer's idling engine. Couldn't let her dark imaginings take over. Grant was a good, decent man; she had to trust that he could find a way to let go of his anger and accept that Adams would never pay for what he'd done to her.

She was well aware that it had taken her years to do that very thing.

"Please, Grant," she murmured, her voice prayer-soft on the still air. "Please let it go."

A spear of headlights in the rearview mirror had her jolting. When she realized the dark car that swept into the spot beside hers belonged to her petite, red-haired neighbor, Sky forced herself to take a firm grip on composure. The last thing she needed was to indulge in a raging case of paranoia.

Minutes later, she waved goodbye to her neighbor, then swung open the door of her fourth-floor apartment. The security system filled the air with its quiet, reassuring beep. After punching in her code, she settled her briefcase on the kitchen counter beside the answering machine. Its message light was dark. Damn, why hadn't Grant tried to reach her?

Nibbling her bottom lip, she put in another call to OCPD Homicide. The detective on the evening shift told her Grant hadn't checked in since she'd left her last message. Thanking the detective, Sky hung up and called Grant's house. After the tone, she left a message on his machine.

Unable to stand still, she paced her living room with the restless, prowling stride of a caged cat.

"Where are you?" She flung the question in the direction of the phone when her pacing took her on a second pass by the kitchen counter.

It wouldn't do her any good to go back to the lab tonight. She had done all she could where Ellis Whitebear's DNA was concerned. She was far from an expert on warrants— it was her guess the data in her briefcase, courtesy of Professor Linley, was enough to persuade a judge to force the hospital to turn over the name of the person who had donated bone marrow to Whitebear. Grant would know if the data she had was enough. Dammit, she needed to talk to him.

She needed him.

He loved her. The knowledge had her blinking furiously to hold back a rush of tears as she roamed past the dark fireplace. If she allowed herself to examine her feelings for him, she would probably find they mirrored his. But she couldn't—*wouldn't*—let herself indulge in that type of introspection. Not now, not while her past stood in the way of their future. Grant Pierce wasn't a man whom a woman could disentangle herself from easily; she knew that. Yet, that was what she would do if he couldn't turn his back on the past it had taken her torturous years to claw her way out of.

Just the thought of doing that made her feel lost, shaky.

Her head pounding, she jerked the pins out of her loose topknot and headed down the hallway toward her bedroom.

She would go crazy if she stayed there, waiting for the phone to ring. Every muscle in her body was strung tight; a workout downstairs in the complex's exercise gym would at least take care of that one problem. She knew if Grant called and couldn't get her in the lab or in her apartment, he would dial her pager.

Please, God, let him call. And don't let him be in Ventress, Oklahoma.

Nearly an hour later, Grant swung open the frosted glass door and strolled into the small gym where the faint, musty smell of sweat hung in the air. To his right, a potbellied, red-faced man walked on a treadmill to nowhere. Beyond the treadmill, a couple of Arnold Schwarzenegger lookalikes worked with free weights, their muscles bulging.

Grant moved farther into the gym, hesitating when he caught a glimpse of Sky's reflection in the mirrored wall on the opposite side of the room. He knew with intimate sureness she didn't have an ounce of superfluous fat on her body, yet she pumped away on a StairMaster with the speed of someone in need of a strenuous workout.

Her long, dark hair was pulled back into a glossy ponytail that swung across the center of her back with each movement; a pair of loose shorts and a T-shirt concealed her spectacular figure. His gaze tracked the thin rivulet of perspiration that trailed down her right cheek, reminding him of the sweat that had pooled against their joined bodies only hours ago.

Until this moment, he had not known he could want her even more fiercely than he had last night.

With need licking at his veins, he closed the distance between them.

Her gaze met his in the mirrored wall the instant before

his hands gripped her waist. In that slash of time, he saw the mix of relief, need and hesitation in her eyes.

She turned easily enough toward him as he lifted her off the machine's foot pads, her hands locking onto his shoulders as he slowly lowered her to the ground. Still, he sensed her withdrawal. She didn't have to say the words for him to know she'd pulled back emotionally during the hours they'd spent apart. Logically he could accept why. She had fought too hard to escape the black hell that was her past for her to allow him to drag her back into the pit. Yes, when cool, rational thought was involved, he could accept her reason for drawing away. But where she was concerned, he wasn't thinking cooly. Or rationally. All he knew was she was his, and he had no intention of letting her go.

Damning himself to hell and back for his raging need to right the wrong she'd suffered, he wrapped her ponytail around his hand, then tugged her head back. When her mouth, untouched by lipstick and faintly moist, was fully exposed, he took. And plundered.

He devoured her lips until her mouth opened to his, hot and hungry, returning his kiss with equal measure. Despite layers of clothing, he felt her flesh heat, smelled the light scent of her perfume and the salty tang of her skin. When her fingers dug into his shoulders, a murmur of pleasure rose in his throat; he changed the angle of the kiss and dived deeper, his arms tightening around her.

He feasted on her, his tongue inside her mouth, until his own flesh was damp with sweat and he shook with need. Only the knowledge that they were in a public place had him backing off, lightening the kiss.

He pulled his mouth from hers, but kept her locked firmly against him, her hair still wrapped around one hand. Her cheeks were flushed, her eyes glittering like blue gems as she gazed up at him. He chose to believe it was the kiss, not her workout on the StairMaster, that had her breath ragged and her lungs heaving.

"Grant...we..."

He placed a soft kiss against her temple. "We what, Sky?"

"Shouldn't." She ran the tip of her tongue across her flushed, swollen lips. "I can't..."

The thread of anguish in her voice was one of the hardest things he'd ever faced. He rested his forehead against hers, closed his eyes for a brief moment. "Yeah, I know." He ran his hands up and down her arms before he stepped away.

She turned, grabbed a white hand towel off the Stair-Master, then blotted her face, her throat. After a moment, she met his gaze. "How did you know I was down here?"

"Your redheaded neighbor heard me knock on your door. She peeked out into the hall, said you'd walked in together, that if your car was still in the lot for me to check the gym."

When she hooked the towel around her neck, Sky's gaze flicked to his right hand. At the sight of his battered knuckles, her flushed cheeks drained of color as she snagged his fingers. "Where have you been?" Her gaze jolted up to his. "Grant, what did you do?"

The fear in her eyes touched an already-frayed nerve as he focused on his bruised, throbbing knuckles. Dammit, the last thing he wanted was to make her afraid.

"I wasn't out beating Adams to a pulp, if that's what you're asking," he said, tamping down on regret that she'd even had to ask the question. "I spent time at the police gym this afternoon, hammering my fists against a punching bag." He kept to himself that the workout had done little to relieve the frustration festering inside him.

"I'm sorry." She ran a light fingertip over his injured

knuckles, then looked up, her eyes bleak. "I'm sorry you're having to deal with this."

"It isn't your fault." Not wanting to break the contact, he slid his hand around hers and decided they'd be better off talking about work.

"While I was at the gym, I got a call to meet a construction foreman whom Spider used to work for. I spent a couple of hours at a construction site ten miles north of the city—learned some interesting stuff about our boy. The location happened to be a dead zone for my pager. I didn't know that until I called the office on the drive back and got your messages." He paused, glanced around the gym. "I want to brief you on what the foreman said, but this isn't a good place to talk."

"You need to hear about my meeting with Professor Linley, too." With her free hand, she snagged a plastic water bottle off the floor. "We can talk in my apartment," she added as they walked toward the frosted glass door. "Grant, I think what he gave me is enough to get a warrant to serve the hospital."

For the first time in hours, a smile curved his lips. "The plot thickens."

"There's more than just what I learned from the professor. Before I left for my meeting, I finished the tests on the section of fuel line you had cut from the cruiser. The line's gummed up with sugar, and has traces of the same brand of soda as in the can you found in the prison parking lot."

Grant's eyes narrowed. "Maybe we're on our way to catching a spider in our web."

"Maybe."

In less than five minutes, they reached Sky's apartment. Grant stood back while she slid her key into the lock and punched her code into the alarm panel inside the door.

"Want some lemonade?" she asked, crossing the living room toward the kitchen.

"Thanks, I'll pass." Grant closed the door behind him, set the dead bolt and shrugged out of his suit coat.

"So, what did the construction foreman tell you about Spider?" Sky pulled a pitcher out of the refrigerator, then retrieved a glass from a cabinet.

"That he worked for a couple of months as an electrician's helper." He discarded his coat across the back of the couch on his way to the kitchen. "Got pretty good at it."

Sky flicked him a look while she poured pink lemonade into the glass. "Good enough to hot-wire an air-conditioning unit?"

"I'd bet on it." Grant leaned a hip against the opposite side of the counter from her. "Spider also runs with a guy who's a locksmith by trade. Our boy probably has learned a little about the fine art of breaking and entering. Lock picks don't leave any trace."

"Still, all that doesn't prove he broke into my motel room and tried to burn me alive along with his father's blood sample," Sky said as she walked around the counter.

"True. So maybe what we need to talk about is what your professor had to say."

"I've got the file from our meeting in my briefcase. Hold this for a minute," she said, handing him her glass. "I brought back tons of scientific data."

"Great," he said dryly. "I've been wanting something totally incomprehensible to read."

She sent a smirk across her shoulder. "Relax, Pierce. While I was in the professor's office, I wrote up notes in layman's language. I figured that would help explain things to a judge when we ask for a warrant."

Grant raised an eyebrow. "Not to mention certain thick-headed cops?"

"You said that, not me." The locks on the briefcase snicked open beneath her hands. "I couldn't believe Professor Linley had..."

Grant frowned when her voice drifted off. "Something wrong?"

"I'm not sure." She lifted a file folder from the briefcase and met his gaze. "This is the file on Whitebear, but I know I filed it alphabetically."

He angled his chin. "You keep the files you carry around in your briefcase alphabetized?"

"Of course. Don't you?"

He ran his palm down the length of her ponytail. "Get real, Milano."

"Being unorganized makes me crazy." Reaching into the briefcase, she shuffled through a pile of folders. "Every file is in order, except Whitebear's." A frown marred her expression, narrowing her blue eyes. "I could have sworn I put it back in its right spot before I left the professor's office."

"You *know* you put the file back in order, or you *think* you did?"

"I think." She shook her head while reclaiming her glass. "I must be getting paranoid. On the drive home I imagined a car was following me."

Gripping her upper arm, Grant turned her to face him. "What car?"

"A black sedan. It stayed a few car lengths behind me, changed lanes each time I did, then took the same exit off the interstate. I didn't see it after that. I know for sure it didn't follow me into the parking lot here, so it was nothing."

"I don't like the sound of that." Scowling, Grant rested

a hand on his waist beside his holstered Glock. He shot a look across his shoulder at the alarm panel beside the front door before shifting his gaze back to Sky's. "Is anything missing from the file?"

She flipped through the pages. "Nothing." She looked up. "Everything's just like I left it. I was in a hurry to leave the professor's office so I could get back and tell you about the study. I must have just thought I slid the file into its right place."

Grant nodded. "We'll go with that for now. Tell me what the professor had to say."

"I told him about the changes in Ellis Whitebear's DNA and the aplastic anemia he contracted before he was arrested," she began as they walked into the living room.

"Okay, let's see if I have this right." Settling on the sofa beside her, Grant narrowed his eyes, repeating the information the doctor at the prison had related. "Aplastic anemia means Ellis's bone marrow stopped producing blood cells."

"You're a quick study, Pierce." Leaning forward, Sky set her glass on a coaster on the wooden coffee table in front of the couch, then opened the file folder, fanning out papers. "During the marrow transplant, Ellis received blood cells from a donor."

"Which, going with our assumption, could have changed Ellis's DNA."

"Not could have. Did. This is no longer just a theory, Grant. We now have evidence it can happen." As she spoke, Sky retrieved a slick-covered magazine from the file folder. "Professor Linley once wrote a research paper on aplastic anemia, so he has an interest in the subject. That's why he remembered an article in this scientific journal. It details an obscure study conducted on a group of people—a control group—who suffered from the disease. The doctor who did the study contends that, for a short window of eight, maybe ten weeks, a person who receives a bone marrow transplant will produce blood DNA identical to his donor's.''

Letting out a low whistle, Grant rubbed a hand over his jaw while he analyzed the information. ''At least two months,'' he said finally. ''For at least two months, Ellis's body could have manufactured the same DNA as the guy who donated bone marrow to him.''

''That's right. And it's strictly Ellis's blood DNA that the transplant would have affected. If they'd been tested during that same period, his brain, spleen and sperm cells would have carried his own unique DNA.''

''But it was Ellis's blood you drew after Mavis Benjamin's murder. And when you got an identical match to the blood stain on her dress, Sam and I stopped looking for the killer, because we figured we had him. Problem is, we didn't. And two years down the road, the bastard who killed Mavis Benjamin slit Carmen Peña's throat.'' He lifted a palm, let it drop back to his thigh. ''We'd have never known he killed both women if he hadn't left that small bandage underneath the Peña woman's body.''

Sky nodded. ''I'm still having a hard time believing I drew a killer's DNA out of an innocent man's arm two years ago. Probably by the time Ellis went on trial, his body had recovered from the disease and began functioning normally. It still is. That's why what I drew out of his vein a week ago was his own unique DNA.'' She settled back against the earth-tone throw pillows nested in one corner of the sofa. ''It makes sense, Grant. It's the only logical way Ellis's blood DNA could have changed.''

''I'll be damned.'' Leaning forward, Grant shoved a hand through his hair. ''I don't exactly like knowing that Sam and I put an innocent man on death row.''

"And I don't like knowing I helped, but we presented the evidence we had and it all fit. Everything made sense at the time."

"I'll call Lieutenant Ryan and run this down to him," Grant said. "Then you and I will head to my office and dig through the case files. We need to draw up a time line that shows the date of Ellis's transplant, the window when his body produced the donor's DNA, the Benjamin murder and when you first drew Ellis's blood. That, along with the study you got from the professor, is enough for a judge to give us a warrant."

"I was hoping you'd say that," Sky said, then paused. "Grant, think about it. If Spider *is* the donor, we've got a case where a son donated bone marrow to save his father's life, then later watched while his father was sent to death row for a crime the son committed."

"Spider *has* to be the donor. Ellis isn't the sharpest knife in the drawer, but he knew enough to clam up when we started telling him his blood had changed and asking him about transfusions. He knows *he* didn't kill Mavis Benjamin, so it must have clicked in Ellis's brain that the person who gave him bone marrow—Junior—slit her throat and let him take the fall."

"A father sacrifices his life for his child's," Sky said softly. "Ellis would rather die than see Spider pay the price."

"Some types of love are hard to understand."

"In this case, that's one of them."

"Yeah." In his mind, Grant went over the steps they needed to take. "Why don't you get cleaned up while I call Ryan and lay things out to him? If we get the time line on Whitebear's transplant and the Benjamin homicide done fast, we can track down whatever judge is on call this month for warrants and get him to issue one tonight. By this time tomorrow, we might have our killer in jail.''

''And be on the way to getting an innocent man off death row,'' she added, her mouth curving in an easy smile that made his heart clench.

He wanted her smiles. For the rest of his life, he wanted the warmth he saw there.

Watching her shuffle papers back into the folder, he realized his body was as tense as an unshot arrow. He wasn't going to try to kid himself that the unsteadiness he felt had anything to do with the investigation.

Sky—everything centered around Sky. She had told him about the most terrorizing moments of her life, trusted him with her feelings. She hadn't asked for some vigilante cop, obsessed with dealing direct punishment to the scum who'd put his filthy hands on her. But that was what she'd gotten.

It wasn't right, this need for revenge that burned inside him. Grant knew that. Knew if he didn't find a way to douse the fire, he would lose her.

Frustration, vicious and pulsing, pushed him to his feet. ''Before I call Ryan, there's something you and I need to settle.''

Her fingers stilled on the papers as her gaze rose slowly to meet his. ''What?''

The instant wariness in her eyes had him balling his hands into fists as he moved across the room to the fireplace. He ignored the pain that slashed through his swollen knuckles.

''What happened this morning between us didn't change some things. Like the fact someone tried to burn you alive. I'm not leaving you alone at night—''

''It's not a good idea—''

''Making sure you're safe is an extremely good idea, Milano. I can do that by sleeping on your couch.'' He leaned his shoulder against the mantel and took a deep breath. "You've made your feelings clear. If I touch a hair on Adams's head, you and I have no future."

She swallowed hard. "That's right."

The determined edge in her voice started fingers of dread clawing at his gut. "I won't lie to you, Sky. I'm trying to get a handle on this. So far, no amount of cognitive reasoning has made me back off from wanting to rip out the bastard's lungs with my bare hands."

"He's not worth it." Shifting on the couch, she pulled one of the throw pillows against her stomach as if a pain had settled there, then wrapped her arms around it. "He's not worth anything."

"Yeah, I hear what you're saying." He closed his eyes for a brief instant. "I respect you, Sky. And what we could have together. I won't ask to share your bed until I can look you in the eye and tell you how I'm going to handle things where Adams is concerned."

"Let it go, Grant." She hugged the pillow closer. "You have to let it go."

Her somber eyes and pale cheeks tightened the knots in his stomach. "That's a lot easier said than done," he reminded her quietly.

"I know." She looked away, her hands balling into fists against the pillow. "I'm done with the past, Grant," she said finally, her gaze shifting back to meet his. "I can't go back. No matter how I feel about you, I can't go back."

How the hell did she feel about him? Suddenly he wanted her to admit that she was as hopelessly in love with him as he was with her. His jaw tightened when he felt reason slipping against the need to draw her out, force the truth, even.

He turned, stared into the dark fireplace while he battled control back in place. This war of emotion raging inside him wasn't Sky's problem, it was his. What he needed was time and space to deal with his feelings. Right now, with the demands of the investigation, he had neither. So he would back off, keep things between them strictly business.

And while he was at it, go slowly and quietly out of his mind with the need to touch her.

Chapter 13

At half past seven the following morning, Sky rode an elevator to University Hospital's tenth floor. When the door slid open, she stepped into a dim hallway that smelled of disinfectant and fresh floor wax. Her low-heeled shoes clicked sharply along the empty hallway as she sipped the coffee she'd bought from the lobby vending machine. Wrinkling her nose, she wondered how a hospital could get away with serving such a deadly-tasting brew.

"Must need more patients." She dropped the foam cup into a rolling trash bin sitting outside the door displaying a stenciled Medical Records on its glass insert.

Stifling a yawn, she glanced idly around for the janitor who'd left the trash bin sitting in the middle of the hallway, but he or she was nowhere in sight.

Sky briefly considered taking a seat on one of the plastic visitor's chairs positioned on either side of a low metal table, then decided if she had any hope of staying awake, she'd best remain on her feet. She settled for leaning a shoulder against the wall while she thought back over the blur that was the past ten hours.

Last night, she and Grant had taken up residence in the Homicide squad room where they'd dug through case reports and developed the time line on Ellis Whitebear's bone marrow transplant in relation to the Benjamin homicide. With the time line in hand, they tracked down the chief presiding judge on call for warrants, who was attending a banquet. After cooling their heels while His Honor delivered the keynote address, she and Grant huddled with the judge. She'd answered the justice's technical questions; Grant, the ones concerning the Benjamin/Peña homicides. It was nearly midnight when the judge signed the warrant.

She hadn't had to worry about Grant sleeping on her couch.

Minutes after the judge signed the warrant, both her and Grant's pagers had sounded a strident duet. They'd wound up working through the night at a double homicide crime scene.

With fatigue pressing down on her, Sky rested her head against the wall and closed her eyes.

She'd finished her work at the crime scene before Grant, stopped off at the lab to log in the evidence she'd collected, then driven here to the hospital. Grant had paged her from the scene to let her know he was wrapping things up and would meet her outside the medical records office. Glancing at her watch, Sky estimated he'd get there in less than fifteen minutes.

And then what? she wondered. After they served the warrant, checked the records and knew the name of the donor whose DNA had put Ellis Whitebear on death row, what then? Would she and Grant go their separate ways, just as they'd done six months ago when the repercussions of her rape tore them apart? Just as it was tearing them apart now.

Emotion welled up her throat, settled into a hard knot. All she'd wanted for so long was to reconstruct her life. Now it felt as if everything was slowly crumbling around her.

The light snick of a lock twisting open sounded on the still air, pulling Sky's attention toward the medical records office. Seconds later, the door swung open. A man dressed in jeans and a navy shirt with a janitorial company logo over one breast pocket stepped into the hallway. The handler, Sky thought idly, of the abandoned rolling trash bin.

In the swift, fleeting seconds that followed, her gaze caught on the corner of a file folder sticking from the vee in the man's shirt. Her gaze rose. Awareness crashed through her fatigue when her eyes locked with Spider Whitebear's.

The man suspected of murdering two women and trying to burn her alive regarded Sky with unnerving, naked malice. "Well, well, the lady chemist."

"What...?"

"...am I doing here?" His mouth curved. "I had a nice visit to your apartment last night. While I was there, I read your notes." He tapped an index finger against his chest. "Had to get this file and delete my name from the computer before you and the cop got here, didn't I?"

Icy fear had Sky jolting away from the wall toward the elevator. Her arms flailed when her feet nearly went out from under her on the fresh-waxed tiles.

"We've got business, bitch!" Spider shouted, his vicious voice echoing off the walls.

A heartbeat later, the rolling trash bin plowed into the back of Sky's legs, pitching her sideways. She crashed onto one of the plastic chairs, her forehead slamming against the edge of the metal table.

The pain that screamed through her head had stars bursting before her eyes. Nausea rose in her stomach, swirling like flood water. Robbed of equilibrium, she rolled off the chair, one side of her body taking the brunt of the impact against the hard tile.

Get up! her brain screamed. *Get up!* Whenever she instructed a self-defense class, that was the first rule she taught. You're a goner if you stay down.

Her head spun sickeningly as she fought to rise to her knees. Battling to stay conscious, she barely jolted when Spider's hand locked around her throat and shoved her down.

"*Bitch,*" he growled.

The dim hallway swung around her; a warm haze clouded her eyes, rolled down her cheeks. *Blood,* she thought dully the instant before a second wave of nausea rolled through her.

"We're gonna have us a chat, lady chemist."

Keeping his fingers vised on her throat, he clamped his other hand around her upper arm. Sky knew the direction he dragged her was away from the elevators, away from where Grant would come. *God, Grant, please come.*

She forced her hand into a fist, smashed it into Spider's ankle, causing him to stagger sideways. Pain zinged up her arm when the toe of his heavy boot gouged her elbow.

His hand tightened on her neck with vicious purpose, cutting off air in one swift clench. "Ain't gonna do you no good to fight."

Her vision wavered, then went gray. Sky clawed at his hand, her short, sharp nails tearing into his flesh, collecting what she knew to be indisputable evidence. Whatever else came, she would have his skin, his blood under her nails.

Swearing viciously, he jerked his hand from her throat, then slammed his palm against her cheek, snapping her head back.

While the metallic taste of blood seeped into her mouth, Spider changed direction, dragged her sideways, then through a doorway. Against her legs, Sky felt the tile floor give way to cold, rough concrete. The air closed around her in a sickening mix of pine disinfectant and antiseptic. Weak light coming from one corner of the small room illuminated towering shelves of cleaning supplies.

Dumping her on her back, Spider crouched beside her, pressing his knee hard into her abdomen when her fingers clawed upward for his eyes. One of his hands manacled both of hers, then his mouth curved. "I like it when they struggle," he said, his voice full of soft malice. "Makes it more fun. Just keep fighting, lady chemist."

In the next second, Sky felt her body jerk when he yanked the belt from her skirt's waistband. Seconds later, he had the leather lashed around her wrists.

In the weak light, she caught the glint of metal; a bubble of hysteria surged through her pain when the sharp blade pressed against her throat. *Just like before,* she thought in wild terror while her disoriented brain shot her back in time. Suddenly she was again lying helpless in the black insides of a van with a knife angled against her throat.

Squeezing her eyes shut, she dragged in air and shoved back the panic. This was now, and she wasn't helpless. She knew how to defend herself. She *could* defend herself if she kept her mind free of fear and waited for an opening.

"You and the cop should have left well enough alone."

With her head hammering and blood seeping into her eyes, Sky had the sensation that Spider's voice came from all around the room.

"Can't…get…away with this." She barely forced the

words up her bruised throat, knew there was no way she could scream for help.

"Watch me."

He leaned in, his knee increasing the pressure on her abdomen, his eyes filled with naked hatred. "I read your notes, remember? I know everything that's going on," he added while she struggled to breathe. "All I gotta do is get rid of the hospital's records, and the cops can't prove anything."

Shadows seemed to shift around the small room as Sky struggled to free her wrists. The pain of the leather cutting into her flesh seemed far away.

"Cops...already have...proof," she croaked.

"Wrong. The proof's in my old man's file. I'd have had it sooner, but a couple of computer geeks stayed in the records office overnight. I had to bide my time hiding in this stinking closet, but now my name is gone from the computer and I've got the file." His eyes narrowed. "And you. You're the only one who knows I took it. All I have to do is dump you and the file in a trash bin, wheel you out of here and make you disappear. Easy. The cops can suspect me all they want, but they can't prove a damn thing."

"You're...wrong."

"You're dead."

Knowing he meant it pumped her adrenaline to flash point. Sky knew she had time to make only one move before the blade ripped into her throat.

In a quick flash of movement, she shifted her bound wrists and clamped her hands on Spider's right elbow; using leverage and a quick sideways twist of her body, she shoved him off balance.

His breath coming out in a cursing rush, he sprawled

backward, hitting the nearest shelf. Mops, brooms and cans clattered to the floor.

"You…bitch!" he howled.

Bracing for the assault she knew would come, Sky rolled sideways, her lungs heaving as she fought the sickening dizziness. How could she get up when she didn't even know which way up was?

In the next instant the door to the room swung inward, tossing in a wedge of light as Grant burst in. On the edge of consciousness, she heard his feral snarl when he lunged past her. From somewhere behind her came a deafening crash.

Sky ordered herself to get up, get on her feet. All she could do was lay there while pain tore through her head and jagged lights starred behind her eyes. In the dim recesses of her mind, she heard the cracking sound of bone on bone as fists hit their target.

Then the sound changed, swelled. Closing her eyes, she fell into a roaring, buffeting darkness.

Chapter 14

Feeling more tired than she'd ever felt in her life, Sky walked into her apartment, dumped her briefcase and purse on the kitchen counter, then collapsed onto the couch. The fluid throb in her right temple was a solid reminder that she hadn't fully recovered from the blow to the head she'd suffered five days ago.

Raising a hand to her forehead, she fingered the fine line of stitches, carefully sewn by the cosmetic surgeon Grant had insisted on.

A nurse had told Sky with a sigh of envy that "her cop" had insisted on a lot of things after he'd pummeled Spider into mush. Grant had *ordered* a full trauma team upstairs to that dimly lit closet. Liberally dropped the Pierce Oil name—and its annual endowment to the hospital—all over the place to ensure that no one tried to banish him from the emergency room while they treated her. Insisted on spending the night at her bedside. After the doctor released her the following morning, Grant had driven her home, settling her into her apartment with the same care he might take with a piece of Waterford crystal.

She'd barely seen him since then.

Slipping off her shoes, Sky propped her feet on the coffee table and leaned her throbbing head back against the cushion.

She knew Grant had worked day and night, writing a flood of reports and conducting follow-up interviews on both the Benjamin and Peña homicides, and on Spider's two attempts on her life. Spider, with three cracked ribs, a broken nose and multiple lacerations from his resisting-arrest-encounter with Grant, had so far refused to utter a word. His only reaction had been to turn a sickly pale color beneath his bruises during the arraignment when a judge ordered him to give body samples to the police.

After that, Sky had worked mind-numbing hours in the lab to get the samples analyzed and complete her report for yesterday's hearing where she'd testified that Spider's DNA matched that found at both the Benjamin and Peña crime scenes. Spider, it seemed, was on his way to being the next occupant of his father's cell at the state prison.

Grant had left for McAlester immediately after yesterday's hearing. He'd planned to interview Ellis Whitebear and deal with the red tape required to get the innocent man released from Department of Corrections custody.

Now Grant was on his way home.

An hour ago he'd phoned her in the lab, told her he was driving home from the prison and asked if she would meet him at her apartment. The grim determination in his voice had started her nerves swimming. The passage of time had balled those nerves into agonizing knots in the pit of her stomach.

Too edgy to sit, Sky pushed off the couch, roamed across the living room and switched on the stereo. After a few discrete clicks of the CD player, the Stones pumped out of the speakers.

Driving home from the prison, she thought as she moved restlessly around the room where the late-afternoon sun slanted through the windows. Had Grant passed by the exit for Ventress, the town where the man who raped her lived? Or had Grant taken that exit?

Out of what was now old habit, Sky fell into a slow, measured pace along the length of the coffee table and back. She had accepted that Grant might never step back from his need to make Kirk Adams pay for what he'd done to her. Knew it was entirely possible Grant had already acted on that need sometime during the past twenty-four hours. Acknowledged that the future she desperately wanted for them might have slipped from her grasp.

She loved him. She had fallen in love with him six months ago, she knew that now. She loved him, and might have already lost him.

The buzz of the doorbell jolted her heart into her throat. In two strides she was at the door, swinging it open.

It wasn't the deep lines of fatigue at the corners of Grant's mouth that made the air clog in her lungs. It was the somber look in his gray eyes. With her bare feet rooted to the floor and a lump in her throat, she stared at him, standing there in the hallway, dressed in a black polo shirt and khaki pants, his badge and weapon clipped to his belt.

Finally he raised an eyebrow. "You going to invite me in?"

"Sorry." She swung the door wide, closed it behind him, then turned.

"How you doing, Milano?"

"Fine," she said with a calmness that didn't reveal the hard thudding of her heart. "Okay."

He hooked a finger under her chin, nudged upward and

gave her forehead his narrowed-eyed attention. "When do the stitches come out?"

"Next week." She forced a smile. "Your cosmetic surgeon friend is a cool guy, Pierce. I'm planning on keeping his card in case I need a face-lift in about twenty years."

"Twenty years," Grant repeated softly, then dropped his hand from her chin. "Hard to imagine what we'll be doing in twenty years."

Because we won't be together? Sky set her jaw against the thought. She wanted to ask if he'd done something they would both regret, that would keep them apart, but she couldn't bring herself to say the words.

He glanced toward the living room where the Stones belted out a tune, then looked back at her. "How about a glass of wine?"

"Okay." Wine. He wanted alcohol. Whatever he had to say was going to be bad. Her muscles were so tight, she thought she might shatter at any second. "Fine."

Shoving her hands into the pockets of her slacks, she willed her unsteady legs to take her to the kitchen. Glancing across the counter, she saw that Grant had moved into the living room to examine the CD player.

"You can turn it off if you want," she said, reaching into a cabinet for glasses.

"Hmm." He crouched, began flipping through her selection of CDs nested in a wicker basket. "I got a call from the DA's office while I was driving back to town," he said across his shoulder. "Spider's lawyer says his client wants to plead guilty."

Sky turned from the refrigerator, a bottle of white wine in hand. "To all counts?"

"Yes." Grant continued flipping through the CDs as he spoke. "I figure the minute the judge authorized our taking body samples, Spider knew we had him. We'll get clearance on both the Benjamin and Peña homicides, the arson charge in McAlester and the attempted murder count on you. Spider gets a couple of life sentences with no possibility of parole, and avoids the death penalty. The DA's making noises that sound like he's happy.''

Wine poured, Sky let her gaze drift to the security panel beside the front door before she carried the glasses into the living room. ''I still don't know how he got in here without setting off the alarm the night I went to the gym.''

''I did some checking on the locksmith whom Spider pals around with.'' Grant rose, ejected the Stones CD, then slid in a different one. Seconds later, a smoky-voiced singer began torching her way through a song about the man she'd loved and lost. Sky's throat went dry. It was music to make love to. To plan a lifetime by. To weep over.

''Turns out,'' Grant continued when he shifted to face her, ''the locksmith installs security systems as a sideline. When Spider wasn't working construction, he worked unofficially for his pal. Since Spider knows how to install a security system, he sure as hell knows how to slip by one.''

Blowing out a breath, Sky handed Grant his glass. ''I paid big bucks for that alarm. Here I was, thinking I was safe and secure.''

Sipping his wine, Grant regarded her bruised, stitched forehead over the rim of his glass. ''I thought I could keep you safe,'' he said quietly.

The regret in his voice started an ache deep inside her. ''What happened to me at the hospital wasn't your fault.'' She tasted the wine, knew she could drink the whole bottle and not get anywhere near to dulling that ache. ''I get queasy when I think about what Spider would have done if you hadn't been pacing the hall waiting for me when those cleaning supplies clattered to the floor.''

''You already had him off his feet,'' Grant pointed out.

"You'd have survived, Sky. Just like you have for the past nine years."

The past, she thought, setting her teeth. Her past had come between them six months ago, driven them apart. The jerk of panic beneath her skin told her the same thing might be about to happen again.

Keeping his gaze locked with hers, Grant unclipped his badge off his belt, laid it on a nearby table. His holstered weapon followed.

As she watched him, Sky's breathing shallowed. "What are you doing?"

"There's something I need to tell you. I want you to know that it's the man talking to you, not the cop."

She nodded, swallowing around a lump of dread. "Okay."

"I would have gotten here sooner, but I made a stop on my way home from the prison."

"In Ventress." Her voice shook with the words.

"Yes." The hand against his thigh balled into a fist. "The office where Kirk Adams works is right across the street from a restaurant. I got a table by the front window, ordered coffee and waited. For hours I waited."

"You saw him?"

"Yes."

Sky felt a coldness flow over her until she was numb from it. "What…did you do?"

A hard intensity settled into Grant's eyes, turning them the color of tarnished pewter. "I watched the bastard strut out of the building and climb into his car. The arrogance in just the way Adams carries himself sends the message he thinks he's above everyone. Better than everyone."

"He hasn't changed." Sky felt her palms go damp. "Then what?"

"I went outside and got into my own car."

"You followed him?"

Setting his glass aside, Grant reached for her free hand, unballing the fist she didn't realize she'd made. "No," he said quietly, keeping his gaze locked with hers. "It wasn't until that instant that I knew I could walk away from Adams. Walk away from knowing he won't pay for what he did to you."

Her knees going weak, Sky swallowed. Hard. "You didn't…? You won't…?"

"I still want to rip the bastard's lungs out." As he spoke, Grant slid her glass from her trembling hand, set it beside his. "I just know now I'm not going to do it."

"You're sure?" She pulled in a deep breath, forcing some calmness into her voice. "Really sure?"

"Positive."

Gathering her close, he began swaying to the music's slow, seductive beat. Moving with him, Sky tilted her head back, feeling her nerves begin to soothe beneath his calm, steady gaze. Letting out a long, relieved sigh, she slid a hand up to cup the back of his neck.

"I've been so afraid, Grant. So scared…"

"So have I." He dropped a kiss against her forehead near the line of stitches. "At the hospital, I had a split second when I thought I'd lost you," he said, his eyes mirroring the emotion in his voice. "It scared me to death," he added as they continued moving to the music's silky beat. "So did just knowing that if I had gone after Adams, you would have walked out of my life. I don't think I can live without you, Sky. Don't know that I'd want to try."

Tears burned her throat, thickening her voice. "You don't think you can live without me?"

His mouth curved. "Let's put it this way. I *know* I can't."

Nuzzling her neck, his mouth ignited a pool of fire beneath her flesh.

"I've thought too much about the past," he said when he shifted his head to skim his lips across hers. "That's over. I want the future. I love you, Sky. How do you feel about me hanging around the rest of your life?"

Slowly she pulled back so she could see his face. The fierce, unrelenting love in his eyes made her heart do a slow roll. "Is that a proposal?"

"You bet."

"Grant...I..." A mix of relief and happiness had tears spilling over, trailing slowly down her cheeks.

"You're not supposed to cry when a man asks you to marry him." At some point they had stopped dancing. Now they stood unmoving, their bodies locked together while he thumbed tears off her cheeks. "Makes him think he'd better take off before he hears the bad news."

"Try to leave, Pierce, and I'll knock you on your behind." Rising on tiptoe, she trailed kisses along his jaw, his chin. "I've done it before—remember that."

He brushed her hair back so that his hands could frame her face. "I'm not likely to forget anything about you, Milano."

When he pressed a kiss at the curve of her shoulder and throat, Sky sighed. Love, she thought, had healed them both.

"You just need to remember one more thing," she breathed, her hungry kisses mirroring the need building inside her.

"And that one thing would be?" he asked as he swept her into his arms, turned and headed down the hallway toward her bedroom.

Before they even got there, his mouth was devouring her throat, clouding her senses.

"That I love you," she murmured breathlessly against his cheek. "For the rest of my life, I love you."

* * * * *

INTIMATE MOMENTS®

Silhouette®

SUZANNE BROCKMANN

continues her popular,
heart-stopping miniseries

*They're who you call to get you out of
a tight spot—or into one!*

Coming in November 1999
THE ADMIRAL'S BRIDE, IM #962

Be sure to catch Mitch's story,
IDENTITY: UNKNOWN, IM #974,
in January 2000.

And **Lucky's story** in April 2000.

And in December 1999 be sure to pick up a
copy of Suzanne's powerful installment
in the **Royally Wed** miniseries,
UNDERCOVER PRINCESS, IM #968.

Available at your favorite retail outlet.

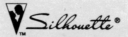

Silhouette®

SIMTDD2

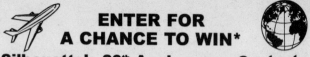

ENTER FOR
A CHANCE TO WIN*

Silhouette's 20th Anniversary Contest

Tell Us Where in the World
You Would Like *Your* Love To Come Alive...
And We'll Send the Lucky Winner There!

Silhouette wants to take you wherever
your happy ending can come true.

Here's how to enter: Tell us, in 100 words or less,
where you want to go to make your love come alive!

In addition to the grand prize, there will be 200
runner-up prizes, collector's-edition book sets
autographed by one of the Silhouette anniversary
authors: **Nora Roberts, Diana Palmer,
Linda Howard** or **Annette Broadrick**.

DON'T MISS YOUR CHANCE TO WIN!
ENTER NOW! No Purchase Necessary

Silhouette®
Where love comes alive™

Name:

Address:

City: State/Province:

Zip/Postal Code:

Mail to Harlequin Books: **In the U.S.**: P.O. Box 9069, Buffalo, NY
14269-9069; **In Canada**: P.O. Box 637, Fort Erie, Ontario, L4A 5X3

*No purchase necessary—for contest details send a self-addressed stamped envelope to:
Silhouette's 20th Anniversary Contest, P.O. Box 9069, Buffalo, NY, 14269-9069 (include
contest name on self-addressed envelope). Residents of Washington and Vermont may
omit postage. Open to Cdn. (excluding Quebec) and U.S. residents who are 18 or over.
Void where prohibited. Contest ends August 31, 2000.

PS20CON_R